PAST PRESENCE

ℰℭ

GAYE NEWTON

Gaye Newton
3-14-03

Galibren
Written Treasures™

GALIBREN WRITTEN TREASURES, LLC

GALIBREN WRITTEN TREASURES, LLC
P. O. Box 7644
Arlington, VA 22207
www.galibren.com

First Printing 2000
Printed in the United States of America

1   3   5   7   9   10   8   6   4   2

Publisher's Cataloging-in-Publication
(Provided by Quality Books, Inc.)

Newton, Gaye.
    Past presence / Gaye Newton. -- 1st ed.
    p. cm.
    LCCN: 00-103790
    ISBN: 0-9700849-0-0

    I. Title.

PS3564.E9866P37 2000   813.6
                    QBI00-500037

For my grandmother,

Harriet McLean

Acknowledgements

Special thanks go to Paige Leverett, Gary and Sharon Newton, and Elena Shirley for helping me turn writer's blocks into building blocks, for their sturdy shoulders, and for believing in me; my fellow writers: Marcia Davis, Winston and Gwen Eldridge, Brenda Jones, David Ruffin, and Jackie Walker, for their honest critique and heartfelt support; D. Kamili Anderson and Kitty Garber for their sharp eyes; my parents, James and Jeanne Newton for the creativity gene and for assuming I could put it to use; Lucy, David, and Sean McLean for their sincere encouragement; Joey Pearson for drawing on his talents; Debbie Newton for the '70's tips; Dale Allen for his many helpful comments; Denise Barnes and Jill Foster for their expertise and for putting up with the strangest questions I could throw at them; Dawn Alexander, Debra and Doyle Logan, Thomas View, Dan Redmond, and Suzanne Samuels for their contagious creativity and excitement; Cecelia and Julie Lee for a delicate helping hand; and all the family members, friends, and colleagues who wished me well.

To Joey, Shannon, Andrew, Evan, and Christian: build that dream and bring it to life!

❧PROLOGUE☙

I
t was the music that bothered him most. Not his sisters and younger brother wiping their tears and sobbing. Not his mother, sitting and staring at nothing, nor his father and older brother, bent forward, with their heads in their hands. Not all those pitying, staring eyes nor the minister's words. Not the excessive cold that the unseasonable November of 1927 had shoved into the room. He could handle all of that. It was the music. It wafted around the rafters, bounced off the walls, and collapsed heavily on his shoulders.

He tried to concentrate on the puttering cars outside, the math test he had taken at school two weeks ago, his plans to improve his batting skills next spring. He thought back to a week ago when everything was fine. He had been playing with friends, laughing, building weapons from the little bit of snow that the early winter had shed. He could still see her, racing across the street with her best friend, leading the spectators in a round of cheers for his side.

But the music invaded the solace of his thoughts and

dragged him back to this terrible place. It forced him to look at her. She was beautiful. Soft, dark curls gently framed her face, and she wore the white dress that their mother had chosen. She would have preferred her favorite dress, but his mother had refused to allow her child to be buried in red.

Cradled in her arm was a small doll that their sister wanted her to have to keep away the loneliness. She's sleeping, he prayed. She's just sleeping, and she'll wake up, and this nightmare will be over. But as he stared at her face, he knew their thirteenth birthday, less than two months away, would now be his alone.

"Hey. It's time to go."

He wasn't sure if he had actually heard the whisper or just felt the hand on his shoulder, but he looked up at his older brother through the blur in his eyes.

"Oh...yes," he said.

He stood with his family and waited to leave the church. He stole a quick glance at his sister's best friend wrapped in her mother's arms. He knew she'd crumble to the ground if her mother let her go, and her tired eyes pleaded with him to make things right again. He quickly turned away. He had controlled himself all day, and he was not going to lose that battle now.

Folding his arms across his chest, he made fists and squeezed as hard as he could until what was left of his gnawed fingernails left indentations in his palms. With eyes half closed, he studied every detail of the wood floor as he followed his family out of the church.

෨෨෬

He was the first to be up and dressed the next morning. Quietly he moved through the house, wanting to get out without waking anyone. He had made it through the nightmarish week of the service, the stares, the suspicions, the house clogged with people, and the anguish burning in his family's eyes. He needed some thinking time. In the kitchen, he tore a ragged piece of flavorless cake from a neighbor's sympathy offering and crowded it into his mouth. After washing it down with a quick palmful of water, he put on his coat and cap and slipped out the back door.

The air was crisp and breezy, and he took it in with one deep breath. As he walked down Fisher Street and around the corner, he drew comfort from the Saturday morning quiet that graced the streets of Louiston, New Jersey. Only Mr. Parker's beat-up Model T trundling by and the faint clatter of the train to New York City broke the silence of a new day.

"Please be there," he whispered as he walked the last two blocks.

Closing his eyes, he pictured his friend. When he opened them, he saw her waiting near the Grant Park sign. Relief rushed through him. Although she, too, was grieving, she wasn't a part of the sorrow that still choked his house. No one understood like she did.

"Are you all right?" he asked, noticing a slight tremble in her bottom lip.

She nodded. "I'm fine."

But he still worried about her. "You don't have to do this. I can do it myself. I don't mind."

"No, I want to help. I have to," she said. "I'm fine."

She wasn't. But he knew better than to argue with her when her mind was so desperately made up. And the truth was, he really didn't want to go alone.

They looked at each other, then without a word, ran into the park to the same wooded area where they had been not long ago. It seemed like it had been years. They began on the west side of the park and separated as their search spread deep into the woods. They moved slowly, whisking away brittle twigs, brown leaves, and the thin veil of snow on the ground.

Looking back at her, he admired her courage. What other twelve-year-old girl would be willing to do this? Most girls would never set foot in these woods, especially now, but she had insisted on helping him. She made this day almost bearable.

He dragged along, poking the ground with a stick, finding nothing. He stopped for a moment. How long had it been since he last heard the crunch under her feet? How far had she gone?

"Over here!" she shouted. Or did she scream?

For a moment he couldn't move. She'd found it. Oh, God, she'd found it. His cake breakfast soured, and his stomach lurched. Resting his hands on his knees, he bent over and waited for bitter sickness to claim him, but nothing happened. He closed his eyes and clamped his jaw to stop its chattering.

She was too good at this. In all these woods, she had found it. He never thought they would find something so small in here. He had almost counted on it.

Forcing himself upright, he ran to her and looked in the direction of her mitten-covered hand pointing to the ground.

"Here," she said as he reached her.

They stared at a small object laying on the ground under a tree, surrounded by dried, rotting leaves. They looked at each other, then down at a palm-sized box wrapped in badly warped and weathered paper. It had small tooth marks on it; some animal must have carried it there. Funny, but in that one little spot where it lay, there were no dead, shredded leaves. No leftover snow.

The knot in his stomach tightened. He knelt in front of the box, careful, for some reason, not to disturb its tiny clearing. He scooped it up with both hands as if it were a baby bird fallen from its nest. She gripped his shoulder. Looking up at her, he watched her stand there with her hand covering her mouth, her eyes dreading. He turned the box over and over in his hands, studying it. Wishing she hadn't found it. Grateful that she had.

They walked out of the woods, sat on a nearby bench, and quietly stared at the box.

"I think..." she said, "I think you should tell them."

"No!" he said, louder than he had intended. Why would she want to betray him now? What was wrong with her?

"They need to know. Maybe they can help," she said, shivering.

"Help what? Help bring her back? They can't!"

His gloved fingers pressed into the small box, and he felt the strain all the way up to his shoulder. He had relied on her to understand, but she wasn't helping. Instead, she was acting like everyone else, and now she was starting to cry. He didn't need this. Not now! He put his arm around her like he used to do for his sister. It had always helped before, and he hoped it would help now.

"You have to tell somebody," she pleaded through her tears.

"No," he said, calmly staring deep into the woods where they found the box. "I'll figure out what to do, and I'm not going to tell anyone. They won't understand. They'll never understand."

"You can make them understand."

He knew she didn't believe that. "You're the only one who knows except me, and we have to keep it that way!"

She stared sweetly into his eyes forever. Then, reluctantly, she nodded. ·

"I'll take care of things. I promise." He wanted to chase the fear from her eyes. "I promise," he repeated, gently squeezing her shoulder.

She smiled weakly and nodded again. "Let's go. It's scary here," she said.

Wrapped in their own thoughts, they walked back to Fisher Street and stopped in front of her house. As she reached her front door, she looked back at him.

"I promise!" he said.

He smiled at her and waved goodbye. After she went inside, he took the box out of his coat pocket and looked it over again. A single tear fought its way out of his eye and tumbled down his face. He wiped it away and ran down Fisher Street to his home.

෨1ඎ

Bright red lights pulsed in the rearview mirror as Anitra fumbled through her purse for her license and registration. Everyone on the Garden State Parkway blurred by to make up for lost time at crowded toll booths, and the trooper had chosen her. What a privilege. Just one more thing to add to a disastrous week. Damn.

"Do you know how fast you were going, ma'am?" the officer asked as he reached her window.

Why did they always ask that? And why did they always have to call her "ma'am?" She wasn't sixty. She was thirty-five and looked even younger. She gave him her registration, then after a minor struggle with her wallet, handed over her license with the smiling picture of Anitra L. Cole.

Anitra stared at the officer with as much woe in her deep-brown eyes as she could stuff into them.

"Not really," she answered. "I guess I wasn't paying attention. Just keeping up with everyone else." She felt a faint tremble in her voice.

"Mm hmm. Eighty-two, ma'am. You were going eighty-two in a fifty-five. I'm going to issue you a ticket for speeding..."

She nodded and let his sermon fade into the background. So why the hell wasn't she watching her speed when every trooper in New Jersey was prowling the Parkway this morning?

It was the dream. The vague dream that had returned every night this week. The one she couldn't remember when she woke up in a shivery sweat. Coarsely shredded nerves pressed on her right foot, sent her car flying, and compelled the trooper to race after her.

She looked back at the driver's side window expecting him to still be there, staring at her, waiting for a better explanation. But he had returned to his car to prepare the ticket.

She settled in for a long wait and flipped through her overstuffed burgundy planner. She made a note to call the cranky client who couldn't handle the fact that she was taking a rare few days off. He needed serious reassurance that she would be back to work in plenty of time to restructure his organization. Such was life at her management consulting firm.

She made another note to call those so-called contractors remodeling her kitchen. If she didn't grab them firmly by their ears and drag them around pointing at sloppiness every other day, they'd get the greatly mistaken impression that she was satisfied with their work. One more note to have her assistant find a good restaurant for that meeting with a prospective client she'd been after for months, and...she'd run out of things to jot down.

Anitra zipped up her planner and tossed it onto the passenger seat. She reached for it again, then changed her mind, pulling her hand back sharply as if the book were wrapped in barbed wire. Sighing, she wished for another problem to solve. Nothing came to mind, so last weekend invaded her head. She hadn't meant to leave any room for that, but suddenly it was Saturday night again.

"…soooo…will you marry me?" John had asked. For a minute Anitra couldn't recall the words that had come before that. "Will you marry me?" he wanted to know.

෩෨

"You like it?" John asked for the ninety-ninth time as he nervously watched her finish her last chocolate-covered strawberry.

"It's wonderful. Stupendous! Magnificent!" Anitra said, smiling. She was running out of adjectives.

She knew what he was up to. Had known ever since the other day when he'd insisted on cooking for her that night, when he'd bit his bottom lip and told her it would be special and warned her not to be late. Earlier, she'd had to work around a permanent grin just to put on her makeup.

An hour ago he'd served her favorite salmon with capers, wild rice, asparagus tips, strawberries, and white wine. And then there were the red roses, the idly melting candles, the yellow-orange glow in the fireplace, the Will Downing CD gently brushing the air. All perfect.

"Honey?" he said.

She tried hard to keep her ridiculous grin at bay. "Mm hmm?" She was going for matter-of-fact, but it came out too rushed and a little shrill.

"Honey," he repeated, lightly touching her cheek. "Anitra, I love you. More than I've ever loved anyone else, and I want to spend the rest of my life with you…" He pulled his hand out from behind his back and dropped to one knee.

Anitra's heart sped up as she practiced the word "yes" in

her head and struggled to keep three of them from tumbling out of her mouth too soon.

"...soooo..." He opened his hand to reveal a small, black velvet box.

Anitra's eyes locked onto it. Then the whole living room froze. And so did she.

"...will you marry me?" he asked, shakily opening the box. It made a soft, creaky click.

The sound of it smacked her face and shoved her upright on the sofa hard enough to leave her dazed.

John grinned and beamed at her.

That box. She couldn't tear her eyes away from that box. She never saw the shimmery diamond nestled inside. Just the bitter black of the box and its icy, gaping mouth.

"Anitra?" John said, his smile dying. "You okay, baby?" His voice sounded like it came from a dank basement.

That thing crouched in his palm, the sound it made, forced all the air out of her body. Pain pinched the back of her neck. Suddenly she was a lost, quivering child.

"Anitra?" John's voice journeyed further away.

Say something! Her jaw dangled uselessly as she tried to form at least one word. Say something! Say yes! Tell him yes!! But it was all she could do just to stay conscious.

"Anitra!" He grabbed her shoulder and shook.

"Nnnnnooo," she heard herself moan.

"What?" John frowned. "What...what did you say?"

She shook her head. "No," she said, a little louder.

"No?!"

His voice tore through her head and crashed against the back of her skull as her lips formed one "I don't know" after another.

Red tinted the brown of John's face, and his eyes darkened. "What...what's going on here?!"

"I'm sorry, John, I'm sorry, I'm sorry," she said. "I can't…I can't…I can't marry you!"

"You can't…!" He slowly stood as hurt fell on his face in layers.

Anitra jumped off the sofa, sending throw pillows to the floor. She ran to the powder room, slammed the door, and squeezed her eyes shut to ward off the pallid face in the mirror.

∞∞

"Ma'am?" The officer knocked on the car door. "Ma'am?"

Anitra jumped, and a short scream popped out.

"Sorry to startle you, ma'am."

She nodded, putting her hand on her chest to check for a heartbeat.

The officer returned her license and registration, gave her the ticket, and insisted that she slow down. Anitra mechanically thanked him, silently cursed him, and watched him in her side view mirror as he walked back to his car. She stuffed the ticket into the glove compartment and sat a minute to allow her heart to stop pounding and her hands to stop shaking. Self-consciously, she put her car in gear and slowly pulled out onto the road.

She left the window open to take in the early spring air. The radio blared on about the Unabomber, mad cow disease, AIDS treatments, and the '96 Olympic games in Atlanta that were just a few months away. Enough of all that. She pushed a button to start a Luther Vandross CD. It didn't matter which one. Luther understood.

Anitra pulled down the sun visor and inspected herself in the mirror. The breeze had sent her wavy, shoulder-length hair into a rage, and she had walked right out of her house without even thinking about makeup. Well, she wasn't about to stumble into her parents' house looking like death's poster child, so she closed the window and scrunched her hair back into place. She pulled her purse onto her lap and, glancing between it and the road, fished around for her lipstick. With her caramel complexion still bronzed from the quick trip to the islands that she and John had taken back in January, she needed only a bit of her favorite shade to look human again.

She reached her exit, threw thirty-five cents into the basket at the toll booth, and headed east toward her hometown of Hammond. Eventually, the cars, stores, and traffic lights all melted into a hilly suburban neighborhood where Anitra pulled into the driveway of a large brick house.

A week of vacation would help. Yes, some family time would help her get everything sorted out, get herself back in order, maybe even figure out why these days she couldn't seem to manage her personal life in the same orderly, sane manner in which she ran A. L. Cole & Associates. She would spend time with her parents, then maybe, if she could, just maybe she would drive to Louiston to see her grandfather. Even after her grandmother's death last fall, he still chose to stay in the gently aging family house on Fisher Street that gave Anitra chills.

She rummaged through her purse for a set of keys and prepared for explanations. As she walked through the back door, she immediately relaxed. She was home.

"Anitra, honey!" her mother said as she entered the kitchen. "I thought I heard you come in."

"Hey, Mom," Anitra said as she dropped her bag on the floor.

Her voice trembled at the sight of her mother. She couldn't hold it in any longer; she burst into tears in her mother's arms. Barbara Cole was several inches taller than her daugh-

ter, and Anitra always felt as though her mother could sur-
round her completely and shield her from anything. Here
Anitra didn't have to be the boss with all the answers.

She let her mother lead her to the kitchen table where
two glasses of iced tea, their favorite apple turnovers from
the best bakery in town, and a box of tissues waited. The table was set for another one of their open-heart chats.

"Your dad's teaching a couple of Saturday classes. He'll
be on campus all day," Barbara said. "It's just you and me.
Now you tell me why in the world you turned down John's
proposal."

Anitra stared at her mother for a moment and sighed.
"You just get right to the point, don't you, Mom?"

"Well, that is why you're here, isn't it, honey? Don't we
do this every time? When you broke up with Michael, and
Steven, and..."

"Okay, Mom, okay! I get the picture!"

Why did her mother have to be so right all the time? It
would've been nice just to get a little sympathy for a change.

"Anitra, what happened? What's wrong with John?"

So her mother wanted to know what was wrong with
John? Nothing. Not a damned thing. He was educated, managed a successful banking career, and listened when she had
something to say. He massaged her shoulders when she was
tired and loved the way she massaged his. He cooked like a
chef. He picked all the right music, sent her flowers on her
birthday, and made her feel loved.

On a cold, rainy day, as they sat cuddled on the sofa, he
compared her beauty to Lena Horne as they watched her
sing "Stormy Weather" in black and white. He had learned
from the mistakes of his first marriage. He knew how to
love. On top of all that, he was fine!

So what if he lost his mind during football games? Who

cared if he left a trail of clothes on the floor as he headed for the shower? What did it matter that the beginnings of a spare tire appeared on his basketball-player-type body shortly after his thirty-ninth birthday? He loved her, he wanted to marry her, and now he was deeply hurt through no fault of his own.

"I don't know, Mom. Nothing. Nothing's wrong with John. I just...I'm just not ready." Her memory latched onto the ring box, sitting upside down, abandoned, on John's coffee table.

"Ready for what?" Barbara asked.

"To get married." Anitra picked at a turnover and watched her mother's face twist.

Barbara shook her head. "Honey, I just don't understand what you're waiting for. First you said you hadn't met the right man. This one was too stuck up, that one worked so much you never saw him, another one wasn't treating you right. Those I could understand."

"Yes, but..."

"You said you wanted to finish school first. Get your career off the ground. You did that. Then you wanted to buy your first house on your own. Get promoted to management. Travel. Go out and start a business. You did all that."

"Well, yeah, but..."

"Then you wanted to make sure your firm was successful, and you had to devote all your time to that. Done. You've done everything you've wanted. Everything but this, Anitra."

"Well, I can't be perfect at everything," Anitra said. It was the best she could come up with.

"Mm hmm," Barbara said in that tone Anitra hated. "There was always something wrong. Now, I have to say that a couple of times I agreed with you, honey. But what about Michael? What was wrong with him?"

"We just weren't getting along..."

"And what about Steven?"

"I told you before. We just couldn't agree on anything..."

"And now John. Anitra, I just knew he was the one. He fits in so well with the family, and everyone can see how he treats you like you're the best thing that ever happened to him. Everybody just loves him! Now has he done something to you?"

"No..."

"Nothing but ask you to marry him."

Anitra put her head in her hands and cried. "Mom, I don't know! I just can't do it!"

Barbara put her hand on Anitra's arm. "Anitra, do you love John?"

Anitra nodded and blew her nose.

"Then what's the problem, honey?"

Anitra just shrugged and put her hands in the air. She bit into her turnover and tried to hide her thoughts behind the freshness of the apple filling.

Barbara sighed and wiped a pastry flake from the corner of Anitra's mouth. "I'll tell you what. We have all week to talk about this. Why don't you go upstairs, clean yourself up, and unpack. Don't worry, honey, we'll get it all straightened out."

"Okay," Anitra said, hauling herself out of her chair.

Barbara's face suddenly brightened. "Oh, they had some sweaters on sale at that petite store you like. I picked up a couple for you. They're in the dresser. And I found something of yours when I was boxing up some old things. I thought you might enjoy seeing it, so I left it on your bed." She offered a warm smile.

"Thanks, Mom," Anitra said as she hugged her mother and headed for the stairs.

Her mother may have told her not to worry, but Anitra knew better. Her brothers and sister were married and had kids. Anitra was the youngest, the only single one left, and she was feeling the pressure. Her parents had met in college and married before graduation, her grandparents had married before the age of twenty, and they all had had their first child within a year of marriage. She was going against the grain of family history. Worse yet, Anitra had no good reason for turning John down.

It had all been perfect. Until that box.

৵2৲

Anitra walked into the sunny bedroom she once shared with her sister, turned on the clock radio, and twisted the dial until she found a song she liked. Toni Braxton told everyone to "Let It Flow." Anitra wished she could. She put her bag on the bed and noticed a manila envelope lying on the floral pillowcase.

She shook the envelope and pressed it between her hands. Something small, not too bulky, some kind of paper. It was probably some old school assignment that had tickled her parents, like the second grade parents' night project for which she had written, "My two grandmothers are old" in large, red, shaky letters for the whole town to see. It had taken years to live that one down.

She opened the envelope and let the contents drop out. Suddenly chills scraped her skin, and her heart bumped out of sync. Her legs buckled, forcing her to sit down on the blue comforter. She stared at the thing on the bed, afraid to touch it. Cold sweat dampened her T-shirt and gathered in a beady gang on her forehead. A piercing tightness seized the back of her neck.

But she didn't know why.

The envelope had been white that day in 1974 when she had sealed the letter inside, addressed it, and pasted a ten-cent stamp on it. It had been white when she'd ridden her bicycle to the mailbox, hesitated, then decided not to mail it. Instead, she had hidden it inside an old book and forgotten it. Those memories were buried, sealed like the envelope that now threatened to free them.

But why?

Somewhere deep inside, Anitra knew what was in that yellowed, dirty envelope. The memories stalked her. Several times she started to reach for the envelope, and each time she pulled back. Finally she ran her fingers cautiously across the name on the envelope, the writing a bit faded now. Large, loopy letters penned by a thirteen-year-old. Why couldn't she remember what was inside?

The envelope was addressed to Carrie A. Morgan, her best friend since the age of five. Carrie had lived down the street from Anitra's grandparents in Louiston, and for years they had shared everything: games, friends, dating stories, and secrets. Secrets.

Anitra gathered her courage, grabbed the envelope and ripped it open. Her stomach tightened as she pulled out a single, folded stationery page and listened to the quiet crackle as she unfolded it. At the top of the first page was the date: August 1, 1974.

Dear Carrie,

I keep thinking about all the things that hap-pened. I can't talk to anyone here because they will think I'm crazy and send me away someplace. I wish you lived here so I could talk to you. I keep dreaming about everything and it's scary. I don't know what to do. I stay in my room a lot now. My mom thinks it's just me being 13. I heard her tell my dad about it and he said I was "at that age." Whatever that means. She doesn't know what it really is and I can't tell her. Maybe we can ask our mothers to let you come stay over one weekend. The hardest part is I don't think I can stay over my grandparents house ever again. And I hate that. I wish you were here.

Your best friend,
Anitra

Was that all it said? The tremors in her fingers made the words jump around on the old piece of paper, and she wondered if she might have shaken some of the words right off the page. Anitra turned the paper over. There was nothing on the back but a small blotch of blue ink. The letter didn't say much, really. Why should it scare her so much? Damn, she needed a vacation more than she realized.

Anitra stared at the letter and tried to relax, but a strange, sharp pain traveled up the back of her neck as her stomach began to churn. She made it to the bathroom just in time to drop in front of the toilet and vomit acrid turnover and the cold, leftover chicken and fistful of chips that had served as her breakfast.

She rinsed her mouth, washed her face, and looked into the mirror, shocked to find the same anguish that had stared back at her last Saturday night. After wobbling back to her room, she folded the letter, quieted her hands enough to put it back in the envelope, and curled up tightly on the bed to wait for the sharp stabs in her head to stop.

ഇൗരു

She awoke tangled in a light blanket. Two hours had passed, and according to a note on the night stand, her mother had gone to the supermarket. Anitra was sure that she had slept, but she didn't feel rested at all. In fact, she felt worse. As she rubbed her eyes, she tried to remember the murky pictures that had hovered in her nightmarish sleep. That same dream again. She didn't remember the details, but this time it was... louder.

Anitra stared at the letter that had fallen to the floor. What was that damned thing all about? Why couldn't she remember? Part of her wanted desperately to keep the secret buried. The rest of her wanted to know, but she couldn't do it alone. On the radio, the DJ played "Count On Me," by Whitney Houston and CeCe Winans. He'd read her mind. Whatever this letter was all about, Carrie knew about it, and Anitra needed her help.

Ignoring her grumbling, angry stomach, Anitra went to her parents' room and dialed Carrie's number. Carrie Ann Morgan was now Carrie Morgan-Brooks: chemical engineer, wife, mother.

"Be home, please be home," Anitra whispered as the phone rang.

"Hello?" said the voice on the other end of the line.

"Hi."

"Hey, girl!" Carrie's voice brightened. "How ya doing? You make it to your parents' house yet?"

"Yeah, I'm, uh..."

"What's wrong?"

Anitra sighed. "Ya busy? I need to see you."

"You mean right now?"

"Yeah."

"Sure, come on... Anitra, what's going on? Is this about John?"

"No. But it's important." Anitra pictured Carrie's eyebrows rising. "My mother found an old letter I wrote to you and never mailed."

Carrie laughed. "Oh, I'd love to see that." She paused for a moment. "But...what's it about? Must've been some letter."

"Yeah, well, it's from back when...that time when..." Anitra shut her eyes. "I wrote it in 1974. That summer."

A long silence darted through the phone line. Carrie knew. "You...you okay?" Her voice was tiny.

"I got sick just reading it." Anitra wadded the curly phone cord in her hand and squeezed. "I need to see you."

Another patch of silence.

"Tell you what. I'll get Alan to take the boys out for the day. You come on over here right now."

"Thanks, Carrie," Anitra said.

Anitra scratched a note for her mother explaining that she'd gone to Carrie's. She grabbed her keys and ran out to her car.

෫෨෬෫

An eerie feeling crept over Anitra as she drove to Louiston. She had been there countless times to visit her grandparents and Carrie, but this time was different. The closer she got to the town, the stronger her anxiety grew. She tried to think positive thoughts and smiled as she remembered her surprise five years ago when Carrie told her she was moving back to Louiston.

At Princeton, they had both sworn never to return to their boring hometowns, but Carrie had broken the vow. She had returned to Louiston after landing a job in New York.

The train would make for an easy commute to the city, she had told Anitra, defending her actions.

Now Carrie and Alan and their two boys lived only two miles away from Fisher Street. They had found a beautiful old home to restore to good health, and Anitra remembered endless trips with Carrie to furniture stores and out-of-the-way spots to find just the right decorations.

Anitra finished her trip in a daze, and now she found herself standing in Carrie's living room looking at the sofa that she and Carrie had picked out during one of their shopping adventures. The remainder of the forty-five minute drive, the doorbell ring, the greetings were already a blur to Anitra as she paced and waited for Carrie to bring two mugs of soothing herbal tea from the kitchen.

Quickly skimming the bookshelf, Anitra's eyes fell on two paranormal psychology books just long enough to scan titles that hinted at exploring the unknown. She looked away; the subject repulsed her for some reason. Strange little hobby for an engineer, especially this one, but Carrie'd been into it off and on since becoming obsessed with it in the eighth grade. Moving to the fireplace, Anitra looked at the family pictures on the mantel. She admired the little boys sitting securely with their parents. Even after two babies, Carrie still kept the same slim figure that flattered her tall, brown frame.

"Here we go. This'll help," Carrie said as she placed a tray with the two mugs of tea and a plate of dry wheat toast on the coffee table. As always, Carrie was prepared for the stress that attacked Anitra's stomach.

"Thanks," Anitra said.

"C'mon. Let's sit down. How ya holding up?" Carrie asked with a twinge of worry in her voice. She rubbed Anitra's shoulder and gently led her to the sofa.

"I've been better," Anitra said, trying to talk and cope

with the toast's dryness all at once.

Carrie half-smiled. "Yeah. Right about now I'm looking forward to Monday's dental appointment. So, that letter. You bring it?"

Anitra took the letter out of her purse and held it up for Carrie to see.

"Let...me...see it." Carrie's words struggled out as she reached for the letter, unfolded it with unsteady hands, and stared at it for a few horribly long seconds. Her smile faded, and her eyes darted back and forth between the letter and Anitra.

"Go ahead and read it," Anitra said.

Carrie jumped a little as if she'd been shaken out of a trance. She read the letter aloud, and her eyes filled with sympathy. And fear.

"Oh, Anitra!"

Anitra's heart raced out of control. At that moment the lid blew off the pressure cooker that kept old, unwanted memories imprisoned, and they all exploded into view. She covered her mouth with her hands and leaned forward.

"Oh no!" she said as she burst into tears.

Carrie reached for Anitra.

"Carrie, do you remember?" she sobbed. "Do you remember what happened that summer, all those things I told you, all those things we said we'd never talk about?"

Carrie nodded and fought away tears. "I couldn't forget it if I tried."

"Well I did. I forgot so much of this for so long. Now it's coming back, and, oh God, it's terrible!"

Carrie put her hands on Anitra's shoulders and looked directly into her eyes. "How much do you remember?" Carrie asked, afraid of what the answer might be.

Anitra shook her head. "I'm not sure. I remember that

day, that first day, how hot it was, and..."

She felt the trembling begin again, and the sick feeling rolled through her stomach. She shuddered and looked up at Carrie with wide, red eyes.

"I remember it all," she whispered...

Anitra stood motionless at the edge of the Grant Park pool, plotting her strategy in the seconds before the whistle. The summer sun, fueling the heat wave of 1974, beat down on her shoulders and seared her back. Crouched and ready to dive, she knew that she would win the race, even if her opponent was a boy. She would settle this once and for all. She didn't live in this town, and Eddie didn't know her very well. But a dare to Anitra Leigh Cole was like a bet to a gambler. Carrie and her friends knew that. Too bad for Eddie. He couldn't know that she had been taking swimming lessons since before she had memories.

As the whistle blew, the swimmers plunged into the water. Eddie pulled ahead of Anitra and stayed there until they reached the opposite side of the pool. As she turned for the second lap, Anitra saw his blond head bobbing away from her and, spurred on by the girls' shouts at the edge of the pool, found the extra energy she needed to catch up with him. Her hand touched the pool wall just ahead of his.

Cheers surrounded her as she pulled herself out of the pool, and the girls greeted her with hugs and slapped each other fives.

"So what were you saying about girls?" Anitra shouted.

The boys roaming around on the other side of the pool distanced themselves from Eddie, who slunk off to the side railing and tried to make himself disappear.

The girls laughed at the disgusted looks the boys threw at them.

"You almost didn't win, ya know! You were just lucky!" Eddie yelled back.

Anitra turned in his direction, put her hands on her little hips, and said, "But I *did* win, which means *you* lost. To a *girl!*" She raised her nose into the air. "Take it like a man!"

The girls roared.

"Just be glad she doesn't go to our school!" one girl said, her vengeful grin pushing her freckles together.

"Don't worry," another shouted across the pool. "We won't tell anybody when we get back to school!"

"Yeah, right," Carrie said. "Maybe now he'll stop teasing every girl in our whole class."

"That's the one?" Anitra asked.

"Yup," Carrie said. "He's been calling me 'metal mouth' and 'household appliance' ever since my parents got all this crap put in my mouth." She smiled, letting little sun rays bounce off the hated braces.

Angie, Carrie's friend, tugged at her bikini top for the millionth time because she didn't have enough up there to keep it in place.

"That's nothing," Angie said. "He calls me 'flatso'! In front of everybody!"

The girls folded their arms, rolled their eyes, and shook their heads. Well, he wouldn't be calling anybody anything for a long time!

On the other side of the pool, the boys pushed Eddie back and forth between them, and one threw a wet towel at his head. His face turned pink, almost purple. Roger, the boy Carrie had a crush on last year, stared at the pool as if it had let him down, and his droopy, wet Afro bobbed as he shook his head. The rest of the boys huddled together to plot revenge. Then the biggest one suddenly ran to the edge of the pool and cannon-balled into the water, splashing as many of the girls as he could.

"HEY!" the girls yelled.

"Forget it," Carrie laughed. "They just can't handle it."

The girls settled into the lounge chairs, happy to have their constant battle of the sexes won for the moment. Refreshed from all the excitement, they were oblivious to the relentless heat wave that had been choking Louiston all week. For the past five days, the temperature had hit 100 degrees, and there hadn't been any rain in two weeks. The pool was definitely the place to be on a scorched Tuesday morning.

Anitra looked at her watch on the table and jumped up. Her grandmother would be expecting her.

"Hey, Carrie, I gotta go. It's time for lunch," she said.

"I'll walk with you," Carrie said.

Anitra put on her Jackson Five T-shirt, denim cutoff shorts that used to be her favorite bell-bottom jeans, and pink flip-flops.

"You coming back this afternoon?" Angie asked.

"No," Carrie said, pulling her clothes on over her blue and white checked swimsuit. "We're gonna pick some blackberries. Anybody wanna come?"

The girls nodded and said they might.

Anitra stuffed her towel into an old, beat-up Girl Scout backpack that she and her sister had taken on tons of camping trips. As she and Carrie gathered their things, they said goodbye to the girls.

Then they turned to the boys and sang together, "Bye!"

The boys glared at them and said nothing.

"That was soooo much fun!" Anitra said as she and Carrie walked the four blocks to Fisher Street.

"You should've seen his face when you won," Carrie said. "You know everybody's gonna find out when school starts!"

Laughing, she threw her head back and flung the last bit of water out of her short Afro.

"I'm really sorry I put him through that," Anitra said, shaking her head.

"Psych!" She and Carrie both yelled, laughing hysterically.

Anitra looked up at Carrie and grinned. Another triumphant moment to add to their eight-year friendship.

Anitra dug into her backpack and pulled out a little yellow, ball-shaped radio. Twisting the tuning dial, she stopped at the station playing "Rock the Boat," the song the girls had chosen as their favorite of all time. Or at least for the summer.

Carrie stretched a long, brown arm up to a low-hanging oak tree branch and grabbed a leaf. Throwing their voices into the leaf-stem microphone, the girls sang along with the Hues Corporation and pranced cha-cha style all the way to Fisher Street.

"So, what time do you wanna meet?" Carrie asked when they reached her house.

"How 'bout 1:30?"

" 'kay. Let's take the bikes this time. See ya later," Carrie said as she ran up the stairs to her front door.

"Bye," Anitra said.

Anitra looked forward to the afternoon. Picking blackberries had become a tradition several years ago. They would pick as many as they could from Grant Park's blackberry bushes, then bring them home for Carrie's father to make mouth-watering, homemade ice cream with an old, hand-cranked ice cream machine.

Anitra strolled the last two blocks to her grandparents' house, stopping to pop a tar bubble or two on the side of the road. She pulled the pony tail holder out of her hair and shook it loose. In all the heat, her thick, wet hair felt good on her neck and shoulders. She took a deep breath, and the lingering chlorine smell made her feel cooler.

Although she should have been in a hurry, she stopped to look at a house that stood on land that had once belonged to her grandmother's family. The original house was long gone, but she pictured the old house, standing there in place of the present one, as she had seen it in her grandparents' photo albums. She brought to life vivid pictures of Grandma Charlotte playing in the yard as a child, Grandpa Jeff knocking nervously at the front door years later to date her for the first time, and bits and pieces of her grandparents' other stories. She couldn't get enough of those stories during her two-week summer visits.

A loud VW Beetle rattled by and snapped Anitra back to the present. She looked at her watch. Late again! She ran the rest of the way to the family house as fast as her flip-flops would allow.

The house was older than any other house on Fisher Street, and one of the oldest in town. Big and spacious, it stood out from its neighbors, a generous coat of yellow-beige paint making it look like an old photograph. It almost glowed when the sun set. This was the house where all the stories lived, the heart of the Cole family for four generations.

Grandpa Jeff's father, Russell, had built the house with his three brothers. Papa Russell's wife, Sarah, had drafted his two sisters to help her decorate until the one everyone called "fragile" became too upset with the whole process.

The house became home for Papa Russell's growing family as the brothers founded their furniture business. Years later, after Papa Russell died, Grandpa Jeff and Grandma Charlotte had insisted on returning from New York to care for Mama Sarah. The move became permanent. After Mama Sarah died, they stayed on to raise their children there.

Anitra flew into the kitchen, apologizing for her lateness. The scent of freshly squeezed lemons made her mouth water.

"You're doing better than yesterday," Grandma Charlotte said, looking at the clock and smiling. She pulled a loaf of bread from the pantry. "Did you have fun at the pool?"

"Sure did!" Anitra said as she poured herself a cold glass of water. "This kid kept going on and on about how girls can't swim as fast as boys. I told him he was wrong, and I could prove it. We had a race, and I beat him! You shoulda seen all the boys. They were soooo mad!"

Grandma Charlotte laughed as she adjusted the white sleeveless shirt tucked into the elastic waist of her powder blue polyester shorts.

"Good for you! Those boys will think twice next time, won't they?"

"Yup!"

Grandma Charlotte took Anitra's chin between her fingers and bent down to kiss her forehead. "That's my grandbaby!"

Anitra grinned.

"Oh, honey, your hair's flinging water on the floor. Go get into something dry. It's too hot to cook today, so we're just going to have some sandwiches for lunch as soon as your grandfather gets home."

It was hot enough for Grandma to fan herself with her

long, slender fingers. "Hoo! I'll be glad when all this heat breaks!"

She stood in front of the electric fan to soothe her cinnamon brown skin creased by only a few modest wrinkles. She plucked a tissue from a nearby box and dabbed it on her roundish cheeks, underneath her plastic-rimmed glasses, and along her round-button nose.

"Me too!" Anitra said. She gulped down the rest of her water and bounced out of the kitchen.

⊱⊰

Anitra showered and put on her red cutoff shorts with the patch pockets in the back and a sleeveless cotton shirt with red and yellow flowers. She rifled through the top drawer of the dresser and found her leather bracelet with her name on it. Snapping it into place, she remembered how hard it was to find one small enough to fit her tiny wrist. As she slipped her feet into her wooden Dr. Scholl's sandals with blue straps, she sat on the bed she always slept in when visiting and dried her hair.

"Anitra, Grandpa's home, honey," her grandmother called from the kitchen.

"Be right there."

"And remember to hang your swimsuit and towel on the shower curtain rod."

"I will."

Anitra pulled her hair back and braided it, then she took her swimsuit and towel into the bathroom. She stopped to look in the mirror and inspect her face for any sign of the pain-in-the-butt acne that had started attacking in random spots. As always, she stood ready to pounce with an army of creams and ointments. But today she found nothing but the whitish edges of sunburned skin peeling from her little Cole-shaped nose. All that suntan lotion stuff did nothing to keep her from broiling like one of her father's favorite steaks. Grandma Charlotte had once told her that a wet tea bag was good for sunburn. Maybe she would try that later, but for now, a little lotion would do just fine.

As she turned to go downstairs, she stepped into the room her grandparents used as a library and office. Behind the door on the right wall was a staircase leading to a large attic where the family's history slept in old trunks and boxes. To her cousins, the attic was just some dusty old place with a lot of junk. What did they know? She could dig around up there for hours, holding in her hands the very things that were a part of people's lives generations ago. She could even pretend to be those people.

She skipped downstairs, reminding herself to ask permission to go to the attic this afternoon. That wouldn't be easy today; the attic had to be an oven.

Anitra and her grandparents enjoyed a lunch of chicken sandwiches, Grandma's signature high-octane lemonade, and chocolate pudding topped with syllabub, Grandma's whipped cream with the secret ingredient. Anitra wasn't supposed to know that the secret ingredient was a small dose of port wine, but an older cousin had broken the code at the family reunion down South two years ago.

Anitra waved her arms as she told the great swimming race story and raved about Grandma Charlotte's power lemonade and laughed about the Loco-Motion dance she and her friends did to Grand Funk's song and talked about her plans to pick blackberries with Carrie and marveled at how hot it was and absolutely-positively-definitely-thoroughly made sure her grandparents were up for stories that night. There were plenty of family stories she had yet to hear, and she planned to get her fill during this summer's visit.

"Slow down there, Peanut!" Grandpa Jeff said, patting the slight paunch he had developed from eating too much pie and ice cream over the years. His real name was Jefferson, but he hated it, and his parents had been the only ones to call him that. No one else had the nerve except Grandma Charlotte when she was mad.

"Charlotte," he said, "we'll have to put our heads together and come up with some stories as interesting as these swim races and dances and all. Swimming faster than the boys! Have you ever heard of such a thing? I shouldn't be surprised, though."

He reached over and tugged her braid. Anitra looked proudly into her grandfather's caramel face and soft, brown eyes that were so much like her own. He called her "Peanut" because she had been such a small baby. "No bigger than a peanut," he had said.

"Jeff," Grandma Charlotte said, "I'll be back at the Community Center later this afternoon."

Another one of their millions of volunteer projects. There wasn't a charity within striking distance that didn't have their names on it. They even took in foster kids up until two years ago.

Grandpa Jeff smiled. "Charlotte, I thought those girls were giving you fits. What happened to all that talk about not going back?"

"Well," Grandma Charlotte said, "they're not that bad. They just want somebody to care about them." She paused for a moment. "They need me."

Grandpa Jeff looked into her eyes and ran his hand across the top of his balding head. "That's right," he said. "We can never forget that."

He reached across the table and squeezed her hand.

Grandma Charlotte nodded. And for a moment, their eyes locked in something private.

Anitra scrunched her face. It wasn't that deep, was it?

Grandpa Jeff sighed as he pushed his chair away from the kitchen table. "Charlotte, where is my..."

"In the living room. You left it upstairs this morning. I brought it down," she said.

Anitra smiled as she watched her grandparents leave the kitchen fussing at each other. It always amazed her how fast they moved, especially for people closing in on sixty! Shouldn't they be old by now?

Grandpa Jeff had always said that telling all those family stories kept them young. That sounded really weird to her, but he was the doctor. Her father had once told her that it was because they had loved each other for so long, even longer than their marriage that had begun at age eighteen, that they couldn't remember things any other way. They'd been together so long they even thought the same thoughts, read each other's minds, and shared a secret language.

"I've got to get back," Grandpa Jeff said as he entered the kitchen with his newly recovered pipe in his mouth.

Grandma Charlotte followed, still fussing as usual about that nasty pipe-smoking habit of his, and the way it smelled, and why didn't he know better, being a pediatrician and all? He replied that he just liked to, and he didn't plan on stopping any time soon.

As their perpetual argument trailed off, he picked up the beige cotton hat that he wore to protect the bald part of his head. He kissed his wife, tugged on Anitra's braid again, and walked outside to his cherished blue Ford LTD. Gas crisis or no gas crisis, Grandpa Jeff had repeatedly refused to give up that cruise ship of a car. At least the thing had air conditioning. Someday, her father, uncles, and aunt would talk them into getting air conditioning for the old house, and she would have an easier time getting her hands on the treasure in the attic. But today it would be a challenge.

Anitra placed herself in front of her grandmother. "Um, Grandma, may I please go up to the attic for a few minutes?"

Grandma Charlotte whisked a bright yellow sponge across the counter at top speed. "Now? You want to go up there now in all this heat?" She looked at Anitra like all good sense had popped out of the top of her head.

"Mm hmm," Anitra said in her best no-problem-here tone. "Just for a little while."

"Oh, I don't think so, honey. It's much too hot up there right now. Hotter than it is outside." She kept the sponge in motion.

"It's okay. I mean, I won't be long."

"Now, Anitra, you know that every time you go up there you get to rummaging around so much that you don't come down for hours." Grandma Charlotte smiled. "Some other time, honey. It's not safe for you to go up there right now."

"Not safe?"

"That's right. It's not safe."

Anitra smiled. "Is there a ghost up there or something that'll come after me?"

Grandma Charlotte stood suddenly straight, her eyes fixed on something in mid air. The sponge fell out of her hand and landed on the floor.

⊱4⊰

For a moment, Grandma Charlotte looked paralyzed. Then she shuddered. It took her a few seconds to find her voice again.

"Don't you get smart with me, missy," she said, her voice low and hoarse. It even shook a little.

Her soft eyes sharpened, and her nose flared. Anitra was sure she could see that mysterious pulsing vein that Grandma swore appeared in her forehead whenever her children got a bit too out of pocket.

"I'm sorry," Anitra said, lowering her eyes.

Grandma Charlotte picked up the sponge, rinsed it off, and started wiping the same counter all over again.

"Anitra, I see no sense in you waiting until the hottest day of the year to go poking around in that musty old attic. You've already seen everything up there fifty thousand times. What reason do you have to think anything is different today?" Her words came so quickly, they almost bumped into each other.

"Yes, ma'am, but..."

"Not a thing has changed up there but the temperature. Why can't you find something better to do? Where is Carrie this afternoon?"

Grandma Charlotte had one hand on her hip now, and the other waved the sponge in the air.

"Well, I just like all your stories so much, Grandma. All that stuff in the attic is a part of it. Besides, yesterday I was telling Carrie about your stories, and she wants to see some of the pictures. I would just get a few pictures and come right back down."

"Well, not today." Grandma Charlotte put the sponge on the edge of the sink and dried her hands on a dish towel. "Now you can wait until it gets cooler and spend a whole day up there if you want to. But it's just not healthy to be up there right now. Grandma Charlotte is truly sorry, but you are not to step foot in that attic today. No, ma'am, not today."

She sounded a little calmer, but why was she still drying her hands?

When Grandma Charlotte started calling herself "Grandma Charlotte," it meant her feet were firmly planted wherever she stood. Anitra wished that asking one more time would work. But Grandma Charlotte's final reason would simply be because she said so, and no child of hers, including Anitra's father, thank you, had ever had a problem with that answer. Did she?

So Anitra resorted to her most deadly weapon: silence. But Grandma Charlotte was no pushover. She was a schoolteacher and had no problem handling even dozens of unruly children at a time. She and Grandpa Jeff had raised five children of their own, two boys and three girls. Not to mention all the foster kids. She knew every trick.

Charlotte Thomas Cole looked at her granddaughter, a little sunburned, caramel girl with a pouting lip and wide brown-baby eyes so big for her tiny size. Grandma Charlotte dearly loved all of her ten grandchildren, but Anitra was special, and she was counting on that now.

She was the image of Elizabeth Cole, Grandpa Jeff's twin sister and Grandma Charlotte's closest and dearest childhood friend. According to Grandpa Jeff, Anitra couldn't have been more like Elizabeth if Elizabeth had been her twin instead of his. So much like Elizabeth. She almost always got her way with Grandma.

After a few moments of Anitra's pitiful silence, Grandma Charlotte's mouth began to tighten. She was about to give in.

Anitra seized the opportunity. "Just a few minutes, Grandma. I promise." Then in the tiniest voice she could manage, "Please?"

"Just a few minutes," Grandma Charlotte said. She meant it. "You get the pictures, and you come right back down. Right back down!"

"Thank you, Grandma!" Anitra said as she turned to leave the kitchen.

"Just a few minutes!" Grandma Charlotte repeated.

"Yes, ma'am."

Barely satisfied, Grandma Charlotte dryly waved Anitra out of the kitchen.

಄಄಄

Anitra didn't understand her grandmother. The attic was always too cold or too hot or too something. It never bothered her. But she slowed as she reached the top of the stairs. Grandma was right this time. It was stifling, the air thick with the aroma of rotten paper, mothballs, and old wood. But that wasn't going to stop her now. She stood at the top of the stairs and looked around, plotting. What to plunge her hands into first. What to salvage from its dusty hiding place. Oh, and where to find the pictures she wanted. She almost forgot!

The huge attic held overflowing boxes, gray garment bags filled with generations of colorful clothing, worn brown trunks with rusty hinges, and scratched and beaten furniture. These treasures filled every space and formed the twists and turns and corners of a maze. Finding the photo albums wouldn't be easy. But it sure would be fun!

There were two rooms in the attic, one on either side of the stairs. In both rooms, the floor was wooden and worn, and in the corners were bits of the beige linoleum that once kept splinters away from small feet. For years, this was a bedroom for Grandpa Jeff and his brothers, and a generation later, for Anitra's father and uncle. How could they sleep up here in the summer without bursting into flames?

She looked around the room to the right of the stairs. A faded trunk next to the wall where the roof slanted downward housed her great aunts' seven little brown dolls and their pretty dresses. Papa Russell had made the whole set for his four daughters one Christmas, and Mama Sarah had made the clothes. The best Christmas presents his sisters ever got, Grandpa Jeff had said.

The trunk sat next to a dusty wooden table holding a feeble, rusty sewing machine. It was a black Franklin rotary electric masterpiece that hadn't worked in decades. Grandpa Jeff said his mother had used it almost every day to keep her seven children presentable. There were more boxes containing old toys, books, games, and pictures drawn by generations of Cole children. Anitra wiped her forehead with her arm and fanned her face with her hand. No photo albums here.

Anitra slowly moved to the side of the attic that had been her grandfather's childhood bedroom and opened the top drawer of an old dresser. She found three photo albums and took out the biggest one. Back in the forties, Great Uncle Adam had made the album's cover, a heavy binder made of wood, scraps of leather, and metal hinges. It creaked as she opened it. Smiling, she sat on the floor with it to savor the pictures. She pulled a small piece of corrugated cardboard off a box and fanned herself.

She looked at the first page. Ah, there they were! Every generation of Coles alive during the age of photography, their friends, their lives. Anitra wandered slowly through the pages reciting to herself pieces of the stories that went along with each one while trying to take in big gulps of flat air. She tossed away the useless cardboard fan.

Toward the middle of the album she found one of her favorite pictures: Grandma Charlotte and Elizabeth at age eight, in their play dresses, standing in front of a large tree. Elizabeth and Grandma had been very close, almost inseparable from the time they were four and the Thomas family moved into the house down the street. Anitra noticed how serious they looked; even little girls didn't smile for pictures back then.

On the facing page was Anitra's absolute favorite picture: the family portrait. Papa Russell and Mama Sarah sat together on a bench looking very proud of the seven children surrounding them. Adam, Lillian, Naomi, and Irene stood behind and to the sides of their parents. They were all close in age, from Adam's nineteen to Irene's fourteen.

The younger three, Jeff, Elizabeth, and Jordan, stood in front of their siblings. Jeff and Elizabeth were twelve, and Jordan was six. Anitra could clearly see in all their heart-shaped, caramel faces, wavy hair, and soft, dark eyes the "Cole look" that her grandmother often talked about. Grandpa Jeff, she said, could never deny his brothers and sisters.

This picture had been taken on a special day in October 1927. Planned for weeks, it would be the first portrait taken since the youngest child, Jordan, had been born. It had been a happy time for them with the children thriving in school and the furniture business a success. But one month later, Elizabeth had died. Grandma and Grandpa didn't talk about her very much, and when they did, they kept it short and always looked sad for a while afterwards. Long ago Anitra had learned not to ask much about her.

Anitra looked at Elizabeth. She had seen this picture many times before, but now that she was about the same age Elizabeth had been when she died, Anitra really noticed it now. Grandpa Jeff was right; she and Elizabeth could have been twins. In the picture, Anitra saw herself in another time, standing next to Jeff, waiting for the photographer to snap the picture. Elizabeth wore a beautiful dress and a big bow on the side of her curled hair, and although Anitra couldn't tell from the picture's soft sepia shades, she knew the dress was a deep red. She had even held the dress twice before. She put the album down and rubbed her leg where the heavy album cover left a red crease.

Wiping a drop of sweat out of her left eye, she turned to the back of the room. A whole row of garment bags hung from the long wooden bar that ran the entire width of the room. The whole history of the Cole family could be told in those bags: Great-Great-Grandmother Martha's wedding dress, the first pair of pants worn by a Cole woman, shoes, hats, accessories, christening gowns, party clothes, graduation suits, and a zoot suit worn by crazy cousin Jerry back in the day. The Cole women had kept the clothes with any special meaning. There was enough stuff in the attic to start a Cole family museum!

This was Anitra's favorite spot in the room. She thought of the endless hours she and her sister had spent trying on the clothes, pretending to be their grandmothers and aunts. Of course, this was allowed only after solemn promises to be careful and stern warnings to leave the clothes as they had found them.

She dug into the third garment bag and pulled out the red dress. It was that waistless straight style she'd seen in pictures from the twenties, and cream lace trim graced its collar and full length sleeves. The fabric felt soft, even satiny. In Anitra's imagination the red hadn't been an overly-bright, gaudy color, but a deep, rich tone. It had faded over the years, but to Anitra it was still a beautiful red.

A small pouch on the hanger contained Elizabeth's matching red bow and a small silver locket. The bow, crushed and wrinkled, slowly opened like butterfly wings as Anitra patiently pulled and massaged it back into place. It still didn't look new, but at least it had a chance.

She lifted the locket out of the pouch and let it dangle from its chain. A bit of shine poked through the tarnish and sent little light flecks into Anitra's eyes as the locket twirled. She caught it between her fingers and opened it, hoping to find a picture or two that she hadn't yet seen, but it was empty. She closed it, careful not to press too hard or tangle its squirming chain, then set it aside and rubbed away the cool tingle it left on her fingertips.

Plunging back into the garment bag, Anitra took out Elizabeth's black patent leather shoes and wiped away the dust. Last, she took out the dress, and the smell of mothballs and rose potpourri chased away the heat-induced drowsiness that pressed on her head. She carefully shook the dress and removed the hanger. She hadn't been in the attic long, but in a few more minutes she knew Grandma Charlotte would demand that she come downstairs. She had to hurry, but she probably had just enough time to try on the dress. This year, she was finally big enough for it.

She quickly pulled off her sweat-drenched clothes and pulled the dress over her head. Grinning like she'd won a prize, she pulled and stretched and twisted until the dress was in place. The skirt fell below her knees, and the sleeves were just the right length. It fit perfectly, as if it had been custom-made for her.

Elizabeth's shoes didn't exactly fit, but they were close enough. Anitra untwisted the two blue beads in her ponytail holder and pulled it out. She unbraided her hair, parted it on the side with her fingers, and fastened the large red bow on the side. Elizabeth would have worn curls, but this looked fine. To complete the outfit, Anitra carefully placed the delicate silver locket around her neck.

She stared at herself in the grainy mirror. A huge grin raced across her face as she grabbed the photo album and looked back and forth between Elizabeth and her own image in the mirror. Wow! She looked more like Elizabeth than Elizabeth did. Anitra laughed, thrilled to become a girl who lived so long ago.

The dress was clingy and hot but moved effortlessly with her as she danced in front of the mirror. She was Elizabeth in her red dress, dancing with her three sisters to an old, old song played on an out-of-tune piano.

She twirled once and stopped. She felt dizzy, thirsty, and hot. Sweat poured down her forehead and neck. It was hard to think, and she started to gasp for air. She felt a sharp pain travel up the back of her neck...her legs felt shaky...she reached for the garment bag...and collapsed.

ဆာလ

The thing in her head was kind of a dull ache, or a gentle throb. Maybe the memory of the pain that was there not more than a minute ago. The stifling heat was gone. It still felt warm, but the stuffiness had cleared, and she could breathe easily. But the fog in her mind was a different story; it lingered, waiting for daylight to burn it off or a breeze to shoo it away. It crowded her brain.

Before she opened her eyes, Anitra stretched her arms and rolled onto her side. She felt weak. Slowly, she sat up, running her hand across her brow to brush her hair aside. She rubbed her face and opened her eyes. Her breath caught somewhere in her throat.

The garment bags, the boxes, the trunks, all gone! No stale attic smell. Just a bed, a wooden desk and chair, a dresser, a green upholstered chair, and a bulky wooden wardrobe. A wool cap rested on a hook in the wardrobe door. Several books and a strange-looking lamp sat on the desk. The floor was completely covered with a dull beige linoleum.

Anitra put her hands on the floor to stand up. But they weren't quite touching the floor. She looked at her palms then tried to hit the floor. Her hands stopped as if they had hit something, but they never, never touched the floor, and they never made a sound.

She looked at her feet and legs. She felt normal, like she was sitting on something, but none of her actually touched the floor. She hovered a fraction of an inch above the floor, and no matter how hard she hit and kicked, nothing made a sound.

"Oh, my God! Grandma Charlotte! Grandma Charlotte!" she screamed. No answer. "Grandma Charlotte! Grandpa Jeff! Please!" Still no answer.

Anitra willed herself to stand. Although she knew her feet didn't touch the floor, she felt no different than if they could. Walking to the dresser, her footsteps made no sound. In a small mirror on the dresser, she could see the other side of the room but didn't see herself. She moved closer and put her face directly in front of the mirror. Still no image. She waved her hand. Nothing. She had to be dead!

Anitra stepped back. Panic crawled all over her, and her eyes darted around the room in search of a hiding place. But she had no idea what she'd be hiding from. She jumped up and down a few times to clear her head and looked around the room for an explanation of what was happening. A calendar hung on the wall above the desk across the room. She moved closer.

According to the calendar, it was April. 1928.

"**G**randma Charlotte! Grandpa Jeff! Some-body!" she screamed.

Anitra shuffled across the floor, afraid to pick up her feet and maybe float up, further away from the floor. Kind of like the men on the moon. She didn't feel weightless, but she still wondered if that could happen. She tried out a tiny jump and landed just as she would if things were normal. Good. At least she didn't have that to worry about.

She walked to the other side of the attic. Another bedroom with two beds and furniture like the stuff in the first room. Not a trace of the familiar old trunks and boxes. No rickety sewing machine.

A bag of marbles and a small wooden horse sat on the floor near a rocking chair. Anitra reached out to touch the horse. Her hand was as close to it as possible, and it looked like she touched it, but she didn't. She tried to push it. Her hand stopped as if she had, but the horse didn't fall, didn't even wobble. She tried to hit the rocking chair, but it didn't move either.

With every try, her heart pounded harder and harder until she thought it might burst out of her chest, and she felt dizzy again. Kneeling on the floor, or maybe right above it, Anitra wrapped her arms around her body and rocked herself. Where was Grandma Charlotte? Why didn't she come running upstairs all worried when Anitra screamed? Slowly, she stood and stepped delicately across the room. She sat on the bed, but it didn't move under her weight.

Then she heard the noise. Voices. Downstairs. Faint, but growing louder every second. Anitra jumped up, and her stomach tightened. *Voices*?!

"She told us she'd watch him!" a girl said.

"Maybe so," another said, "but you know she'll only watch him for so long, then she gets bored. We always have to find him and get him cleaned up before Mama and Papa get home."

Someone was at the bottom of the stairwell. Anitra searched for a place to hide as loud, impatient footsteps fell on the bottom stairs. Anitra lunged for the wardrobe door, but she couldn't touch the doorknob. Angry footsteps clopped somewhere in the middle of the staircase. Anitra strained to press her hands against the knob as the footsteps grew closer and closer until someone's head, then shoulders, then arms and body and legs gradually emerged at the top of the staircase. Anitra could no longer move.

This person, wearing a blue plaid, twenties-style dress, faced away from Anitra and looked into the other attic room. Anitra began to shake. Then the person turned and scanned the room where Anitra stood. Anitra jumped and took two steps backwards. But the teenage girl didn't seem to notice as she stepped into the room, still searching for something. She looked in Anitra's direction, but she didn't look *at* her. She looked right *through* her, as though Anitra weren't even there!

The girl's dark brown hair was short, parted on the side, and delicately curled. It had probably been perfect and neat when the day began, but now wavy strands of hair danced wearily against her caramel, heart-shaped face. Anitra knew that face! She knew it! It was Lillian, Grandpa Jeff's oldest sister! But that was impossible!

"Jordan, are you up here?" Lillian yelled.

"Hhhhhi…" Anitra squeaked, her feet riveted to some spot just above the floor.

Lillian put her hands on her hips. "Jordan!"

Anitra waved her hands in tight little circles. "Can't you see me?"

"Jordan!" Lillian yelled louder, stomping her foot.

Anitra felt panic climb back into her head but pushed it back. She took a step closer to Lillian. "HEY! I'm right here! In front of you!"

Lillian tapped her foot.

A tiny giggle came from inside the wardrobe. Anitra turned her head so fast to look, she almost snapped her neck. A small boy of five or six wearing brown knickers and a green sweater burst out of the wardrobe laughing uncontrollably.

Anitra jumped two feet, stumbled backwards, fell against the edge of a bed, and landed on her butt on the floor. Had she been able to touch things, that sure would've hurt. She stared at the little boy and tried to say something, but her mouth wouldn't work.

"Jordan, I should tan your hide!" Lillian said. "Where is Irene?"

Jordan stopped laughing long enough to answer, "Helping Mrs. Barrett next door."

"Hey," Anitra said, finally finding her voice again.

"HEY!" She crawled over to Jordan and tried to poke his leg. She didn't feel it, he didn't budge.

"Mm hmm," Lillian said. "She should be helping me keep an eye on you, and she goes next door. Sometimes I wonder about that girl! Come with me, Jordan Cole. You've caused me and Naomi enough trouble today, and I still need to get supper started for Mama. You can stir the biscuit batter, little boy!"

The boy rolled his eyes and groaned as his sister grabbed his hand in her fist and marched him downstairs, fussing all the way.

Anitra sat with her mouth dangling helplessly open. Years of Grandma's and Grandpa's stories and memories of faded, crinkled pictures flooded her mind. Nothing that she had ever imagined about them, nothing she had ever pretended, could begin to compare with what had just sprung to life all around her.

"Lillian, Jordan, Naomi, Irene!" she said to the lifeless air. "Grandpa Jeff's sisters and brother. They're ghosts! And this is what the attic looked like when they were kids. How'd this house get haunted all the sudden?" She raised one eyebrow. "Hey! They didn't see me! Maybe I'm not dead!"

Anitra jumped up to run downstairs hoping Grandma Charlotte could help. But how would she tell her grandmother about the ghosts in the attic? She had to try.

Anitra bounded down the stairs and made not a sound along the way. The stairwell opened to her grandparents' office, but everything familiar was gone. Instead, the furniture looked like the antiques Grandma Charlotte had shown her in a shop they had visited months ago, and the walls were covered with plain white paint that needed some touching up instead of the peach paint that had been there for as long as she could remember.

The roll-top desk, scratched and nicked, was swamped with piles of papers, a metal lamp, and a large green ledger. Next to the desk sat a monstrous black typewriter that looked like it could mangle the fingers of anyone who tried to tackle it. Dark bookcases lined the walls and held a variety of books, a three-level stationery cabinet, papers, a camera that looked like an accordion, a paint-spattered hammer that she was sure didn't belong there...wait a minute! *None* of this stuff belonged here!

"Oh...no...no!" Anitra ran into the hall and stopped abruptly as she saw that it, too, had changed. The soft, bouncy carpet was gone. Instead, she stood on a dark hard-wood floor with a long, patterned rug covering the center. The built-in storage cabinets were still there, but without the white paint that Anitra remembered. And delicate, dark brass fixtures replaced the ceiling light she knew. At least the bathroom and bedrooms were all in the right places.

She walked into one of the bedrooms. "Wow!" she whispered.

She thought of all those old pictures she'd seen. That's how this room looked. As if someone had peeled the images right out of the photo albums and the tiniest details of her imagination. Then they threw in a million brilliant colors and tossed it all into the air to scatter and float like glitter and settle softly in place all around her. She had so often tried to wrap herself into the pictures in the attic, to live in them even if only for a few seconds at a time. Here it all was. Everywhere she looked!

The two beds, dresser, and desk, older and simpler than the furniture Anitra was used to, lured her into the room to look more closely and find the well-hidden "CF" burned into every piece from Cole Furniture. Then she found four of the hand-made, wooden dolls that she loved so much sitting on a bookcase. Their painted faces were bright and new, and four pairs of little red lips smiled at her as if welcoming her to their eight-inch-tall world. The wavy, brown hair glued to their heads reminded Anitra of the girls who owned them. And the dolls' twenties-style dresses, now brilliant shades of red, yellow, blue, or green, all had white collars, matching cloth belts, and buttons made of tiny white beads.

Seeing them here, now, before their faces flaked off or their beads disappeared or their dresses turned a faded gray was like having two birthdays in one year. She wanted so badly to pick them up. Maybe sit down with Irene and play with them, ask her their names, pretend they lived in some glamorous, far-off place. She reached for one. It remained stubbornly motionless under her fingers.

On the dresser, a string of shimmering blue beads spilled gently over the sides of a wooden jewelry box and came to rest next to the base of an olive green glass lamp painted with red and gold flowers. A rose-colored shade with gold braid and a small, red flower topped the lamp. She ran her fingers over tiny tins of powders and jars of cream, small baskets of pearlish barrettes decorated with diamond-like stones, and hard rubber hair combs stuck into stiff-bristled brushes. So pretty! If only she could feel the soft smoothness of the barrettes. Pick them up. Put them in her hair.

Anitra peered past the half-open closet door. The dresses and skirts that would show not one knee, three sort of bell-shaped hats, and the sailor suit-looking blouses all looked just like some of the clothes she knew were stored in the attic. But these were fresh, new. No mothball-scented, weary cotton remnants drained of the best part of their color. Everything here came to life. Yeah. Even the ghosts.

Voices and some kind of jazzy, dancy music floated up from the first floor. Anitra snuck to the top of the stairwell and listened, but she couldn't hear what anyone said. It sounded like there were more people...ghosts...downstairs than there had been in the attic. She wanted to go down there. Lillian and Jordan hadn't seen her in the attic; maybe the others wouldn't see her, either. Or maybe they would! Maybe they could help her. But there were others downstairs now, and she had no idea who they might be. What would they do if they saw her?

She crept slowly, quietly, down the stairs wondering if she wanted to be seen. She stopped on the last step and took in the sights of the new...old...living room from the pictures she had stared at for years. Golden brown tapestry drapes and lacy white curtains framed each window. A leafy-patterned sofa and two chairs matched the colors of the drapes.

Anitra tried in vain to reach for a corner of one of the drapes. She longed to hold it in her hand, pull the heavy cloth to her face, rub it on her cheek. In her imagination, it felt warm, almost velvety. She grabbed at it twice, then took a mean swipe at it when it ignored her. Why couldn't she touch the tassels and feel the silky cords slide between her fingers? Or open the front cover of the family Bible that hadn't been moved for fifty years and see the empty spaces where pictures of new Coles would be placed years later? Or play a few notes on the piano in time with the metronome on top?

She watched a record spin under a huge needle in the open Silvertone phonograph case. It sure didn't look anything like her record player; she had to tape a penny to her needle to keep it from skipping all over her Jackson Five and Stevie Wonder records. This needle had to weigh a couple of pounds. The Brunswick label on the record spun its fancy letters at an amazing pace, but Anitra could still read the song title, "Soliloquy," as The Washingtonians played shaky-sounding trumpets, clarinets, and something that sounded like a banjo.

She wished she could pull the records out of the cube-shaped case that sat open next to the phonograph, which now looked brand new, not exhausted like it did in the attic. How come she couldn't feel the cool, glossy wood of the cabinet? How could she come all this way, see everything so real in brilliant color instead of the coarse brown-grays in the photo albums, and not be able to feel them, too? Was this some kind of joke? It wasn't funny!

Voices in the kitchen lured her, pulling her out of her brooding. She slipped into the dining room and stood outside the kitchen doorway. Ever so carefully, she peeked in and quietly gasped. In the kitchen, three teenage girls busily prepared a meal. Lillian, Naomi, and Irene looked just as beautiful as they had in the family portrait. Heart-shaped faces, curly brown hair, and all.

Anitra didn't understand. In the movies, the ghost always looked like the person did when he died. Same age, same clothes, everything. So why were these ghosts here as kids? Anitra closed her eyes and thought about Grandpa Jeff's stories. Lillian, the oldest girl, died before Anitra was born, but she lived long enough to be a grandmother. Irene was a college professor who died less than a year ago, and Naomi died only three years ago. At the table, cherub-faced Jordan stirred batter and protested the misery of it all. Anitra remembered that he had joined the Army during World War II and was among the Negro troops sent to Europe. Anitra knew his story well. He was in his twenties when he died in France. Why was his ghost here as a six-year-old?

She had never seen ghosts before and hadn't even thought much about whether she believed in them. But this was the most amazing thing she had ever heard of. Not just one ghost, but four. Not just people, but the whole house! Could that really happen?

"Um, hello?" she said. No one looked her way. "HELLO?" They still didn't notice her.

She sighed and leaned against the wall, crossing her arms as her lips formed the beginnings of a pout.

"...and Mrs. Barrett asked me to help," Irene protested. "Then she said she had some books for me to look at, and I wanted to borrow one. Jordan didn't get hurt or lost, Lill!"

Lillian's eyes narrowed. "Lucky for you!"

"You and Naomi were here the whole time."

"But Mama asked us all to help. And you go running off and don't tell anybody."

"Oh, don't get in such a lather," Irene moaned, rolling her eyes.

"What?" Lillian said.

"Lill, let it go!" Naomi said, sighing loudly.

"But she..."

"Jordan is fine, supper'll be fine, and Irene didn't hurt anybody."

Lillian stopped stirring long enough to place a hand on her hip and point a spoon at her sister. "She needs to be more responsible!"

"Oh, Lill, please..." As she spoke, the pendant around Naomi's neck bounced in rhythm with her waving hands.

"Please nothing! She'll never learn if you keep making excuses for her!"

"Lill! Stop fussing!" Irene said, exasperated.

Anitra chuckled at the argument then quickly looked up at the girls. It didn't matter; they didn't hear her. She slowly slunk into the kitchen and sat in a chair in the corner of the room to watch.

"You wouldn't be whining about me fussing at you if

Mama came home and we had to tell her we lost Jordan!" She waved her spoon as if swatting her sister's last outburst into the back yard.

"All right!" Irene said. "I was wrong! Wrong, wrong, wrong! I'm sorry! I'm very, very, very, very, sorry! Are you happy, now?"

Naomi stifled a laugh. "Careful, Irene, she might attack you with that spoon of hers!"

Naomi and Irene laughed. Anitra just knew smoke would come shooting out of Lillian's ears any minute.

"I just want you to learn to be more responsible," Lillian said.

"I am..."

"No, you're not! Don't you know that every time something goes wrong, I get blamed?" Lillian pointed the spoon at herself, now.

"That's not true!"

"Yes it is! Mama leaves us *all* in charge, but I always end up taking care of everything. And getting blamed when something goes wrong." Dropping the spoon on the table, Lillian tossed both hands in the air and let them flop to her sides.

Naomi smiled. "That's 'cause you're so good at it."

"My name is Lillian, not Sarah," Lillian said, referring to their mother.

Irene softened her defense. "I'm sorry," she said. "I'll do better." She turned to Naomi and scrunched her face into something sour.

Naomi sighed loudly. "Just...let's just finish this, please."

Anitra sat quietly, and as the argument faded, she began to look around the kitchen. Pots on a black, cast-iron range with curved legs. Two twisted wire brushes on the edge of the sink next to a sponge that looked like it was pulled right out of the ocean. No yellow, pink, or green rectangles there. A can of toothpicks. A wire mesh fly swatter hanging on the wall next to ruffled curtains in the window. Some cabinet thingamajig that might have been their version of a refrigerator. Not one bit of plastic anywhere.

Irene rinsed and dried her hands and left the kitchen. Anitra followed her into the living room where the record, long finished, spun tirelessly on the phonograph. Irene stopped the machine and pulled the record off, placing it carefully in its cover. She took a new record out, shook her head, put it back, and picked a different one.

"'L'il Farina?'" she asked herself. "Mmm, no." She flipped the record over and grinned. "'Animal Crackers!'" She put it on the phonograph.

Anitra giggled at the title and looked at the label. "(I'm Just Wild About) Animal Crackers." Duke Ellington and His Washingtonians. As it spun, itchy bassoons and saxophones filled the room. The quick, bouncy music made Anitra want to dance, and when Irene reached the dining room, she skipped the rest of the way back to the kitchen. Anitra skipped behind her.

By now Lillian and Naomi were fuming and muttering to themselves as potato skins flew. But either the music or Irene's grin rubbed off on her sisters, and they managed to smile a little.

"I'm finished!" Jordan said as he stopped stirring. "Can I go now?"

"Thank you, Jordan," Lillian said, inspecting his work. "Yes, you can go play now, but please don't go far. Mama and Papa will be back soon from the train station with Adam. Now don't get dirty, and *do not* make us..."

Before she could finish, Jordan fled to the back yard.

"...come looking for you again!" she called after him.

"Poor little bunny," Naomi said with a giggle as she watched his escape.

Lillian gave up and sighed.

"I can't wait to see Adam," Naomi said, quickly changing the subject.

Lillian smiled and placed a large, heavy pot on the stove. "I miss him, too. But I love when he comes home. He makes college sound like fun! Tennessee is so far away, though, and Mama still hates that."

"Think that's far?" Naomi said. "I'm going to Oberlin. All the way in Ohio!"

"Oh, swell! You know Mama and Papa will never let you go!" Lillian said, laughing.

"But I could be good enough for the conservatory of music. 'Sides, Uncle Marcus sent Jack there. He'll still be there when I'm ready to go. I won't be alone." Naomi smiled slyly. "We already talked all about it."

"And who's 'we'? You 'n' Jack? Ya didn't talk to Mama, I bet!" Lillian gave Naomi a you-poor-thing look. "Jack can't help you with her."

"Well...I'm working on it," Naomi didn't sound so sure.

Irene let out a long, sad sigh. "Everyone's going away."

"Huh?" said Naomi.

"Everyone's going away," Irene repeated. "Adam is at Fisk, Lillian's going to college next year, and you...you want to go all the way to Ohio. It's just not the same anymore. Everyone's going away, and ever since Lizzie died, Jeff just keeps to himself all the time."

Naomi's and Lillian's busy hands stalled. They looked at each other then at Irene. All three fell silent as they stirred the pots on the stove and removed dishes from the cupboard.

Anitra's fabricated comfort with her situation quickly

vanished. If they were all ghosts, how could one of them be... well...dead?

ಬ6ಅ

Anitra raced out of the kitchen and sprinted up the two flights of stairs to the attic. She feverishly paced the floor.

"Okay. Okay...okay, I can figure this out. Don't panic. Don't panic," she said, wringing her hands and squeezing her eyes shut. "There's always an answer. Always an answer." She repeated what Grandpa Jeff had told her long ago.

But the ghost explanation that she had pieced together had failed. There was nothing left to take its place, so she gave in to an overwhelming need to get back to the familiar surroundings of the present.

She sat on the floor where she had awakened earlier and ordered the room to confess. Tell her what was going on. How to get back to her own time. She pulled her knees to her chest and didn't move for a long time. Then she curled up on the floor with her eyes sealed shut and tried to will herself back to the present. But when she opened her eyes, nothing had changed.

A wave of nausea washed over her. There might not be a

way back! What if she was stuck here forever? Small beads of sweat pooled on her forehead as she thought of a life where she could neither be seen nor heard, where she could touch nothing, where she could never see her own world ever again.

Anitra closed her eyes and swallowed hard, desperately beating the horrible thoughts out of her head so she could think through this mess. If those people downstairs weren't ghosts, what were they? Who? She looked at the calendar again. April 1928. Elizabeth died in November 1927, so she kind of understood what Irene had said, but this still didn't make sense.

Anitra trembled but forced herself to keep thinking. Well, if the answer to her problem wasn't here in the attic, maybe it was somewhere within the family's conversations or actions. But maybe it wasn't such a good idea to be seen or try to talk to them. What would they do? They'd never believe her if she told them who she was. She didn't think they'd hurt her; they were family, after all. But she couldn't be sure. She wanted so badly to talk to them, share her stories with them, ask them about their lives. It wasn't fair that she couldn't talk to them. But for now, at least until she could figure out what was happening, she'd just have to be careful.

Her thoughts were interrupted by the muffled clamor of footsteps and more voices coming from downstairs. For a while, she stayed on the attic floor to decide what to do. Then she got up, crept down to the second floor, stood at the top of the stairs, and listened. Several conversations swirled together.

"Yes, Mama, it's almost ready. We're setting the table now..."

"...and Irene, where is Jeff?"

"...school's swell...Jordan, you're getting so big!"

"Adam! Look what I made! It's for you!"

"Papa! You found the book! Thank you..."

"...and then they made me make the biscuits!"

Anitra came halfway down the stairs, sat down, and rested her forehead in the space between the wooden balusters that lined the bottom half of the staircase. She watched in awe as more family members came into view. Adam, tall and handsome, had his mother's cheekbones, dimpled smile, and those little puffs under his eyes. Just like the pictures. A pair of wire-rimmed glasses teetered and threatened to fall off his face, and he pushed them back up the bridge of his nose as he greeted his sisters and brother.

Russell Cole came into the room, and Anitra marveled at her great-grandfather. He had that same, slight bump in the middle of his nose that Grandpa Jeff had, and he was about the same height. Adam was taller. Papa Russell's hair, including his mustache, was a mix of gray and dark brown, and he kept a pipe perched precariously at the edge of his mouth. He looked just like a younger version of Grandpa Jeff!

Tall and graceful, Mama Sarah flowed across the room as she spoke with her daughters. Grandpa Jeff always described her as "stately." She removed her coat and uncovered a blue striped dress that she had probably created herself. After carefully lifting her hat off her head, she patted the short brown curls and wisps of gray framing her face. She instructed her children to wash for supper. Anitra pressed herself against the balusters to make way for a herd of kids then followed Mama Sarah and Lillian to the kitchen.

"It looks like things went well here, Lillian," Mama Sarah said.

She pulled the chicken out of the oven, smelled its aroma, and methodically added her own special touch of salt and pepper here and there.

"Everything was fine, Mama," Lillian said, "except Naomi and I had to chase Jordan all over the house!"

Mama Sarah quietly laughed as she returned the chicken to the oven. "He certainly is a handful."

"Please don't laugh, Mama. We had a time finding him. Irene's so unreliable when it comes to watching him. She went to see Mrs. Barrett again and didn't even tell us!" Lillian said.

"What a snitch," Anitra whispered.

Mama Sarah put her hand on Lillian's shoulder. "Irene will find her way."

"And lose Jordan while she's looking."

They both laughed as they filled serving dishes. Just like Grandpa Jeff had said, Mama Sarah always knew how to get things under control.

"Mama?" Irene walked into the kitchen. "We haven't seen Jeff all day. He left the house right after you and Papa left this morning. He said he was going to play ball with his friends, but Mama, he's just not the same..."

"I know, Irene," Mama Sarah said smiling sweetly at her daughter. "These days, he seems to stay away as much as he possibly can. But he's thirteen years old. He's not a small boy anymore. You can't expect him to stay in the house all day with his sisters."

"But Mama, it's not just that. Even when he's home, he's...well, he's just not like he was...before."

Mama Sarah eyed Irene suspiciously, but the smile remained. "Before what, dear?"

"Well, before..." Irene tried to replace elusive words with vague hand gestures.

Mama Sarah's face suddenly clouded, and a frown hovered over the smile that struggled to stay in place. "Irene, don't worry about your brother. All boys his age go through times like this. Adam certainly did."

"But Mama, he misses Lizzie. It's been five months, but sometimes he still acts like it just happened yesterday!"

Lillian glanced back and forth between her mother and sister.

Mama Sarah's smile barely hung on. "Irene, Jeff is fine." The dishcloth in her hand trembled a bit.

"No he's not!" Irene answered, startling herself.

Lillian gasped and almost dropped a plate.

"Irene!" Mama Sarah's smile was long gone as she stepped closer to Irene and waited for her daughter's eyes to meet hers. "There is *nothing* wrong with Jeff! Do you understand me!" She didn't ask. She insisted.

Irene said nothing, though her eyes continued to plead. Mama Sarah dropped the dishcloth on the table and stared, waiting for an answer.

"Yes, Mama," Irene whispered, her eyes now focused on the floor.

Mama Sarah nodded once then grabbed a bowl and delivered it to the dining room.

Lillian glared at her sister. "What do you mean upsetting Mama like that?" she whispered. "What's wrong with you?!"

"Somebody has to listen!" Irene said. She tried to busy herself with plates and knives and forks, but she still had to swipe at a tear.

"Leave her alone!" Lillian said as their mother reentered the room, composed and smiling.

The back door swung open, and a boy burst into the kitchen. Anitra gasped and smiled as she immediately recognized her grandfather. Thin and awkward, he looked a lot like one of her own brothers. Here was the full head of curly brown hair, the baby-smooth face that had been hidden for years below the laugh lines and sun-cured furrows in his brow, and the quiet smile that would never change.

"Hi, Mama. How was New York?" Jeff asked in a crackly kid voice as he kissed his mother's cheek.

"New York was fine, dear. And where have you been all day?"

"Playing ball with some friends from school."

She inspected the smudges on his face. "Jefferson Cole, did you leave any dirt on the field?"

He smiled.

"And how did you do this time?" she asked.

"We lost. But we played good."

"Well. You played *well*, Jeff, not good," Mama Sarah said.

Jeff smiled and nodded. "We played well."

Naomi now stood in the kitchen doorway wearing a sly smile. "Did you see Charlotte Thomas today?" she asked.

"Oh, uh...she was...she watched our games." A strange smirk popped up on his face.

Anitra grinned.

"Did she...*congratulate* you for playing so *well?*" Naomi asked, enjoying the torture.

Jeff rolled his eyes, and Lillian and Naomi laughed. Irene watched quietly and frowned.

Mama Sarah stepped in to save her son. "Girls, that's enough. Jeff, go wash for supper."

Jeff gratefully slunk out of the kitchen with Anitra right behind him. Hands shoved into his pockets, he dragged himself through the dining and living rooms and pained his way stiffly up the stairs to the second floor. His shoulders drooped so far forward, Anitra thought he might topple over on his way to the attic stairs. There was something picking at him, and he carried it all the way up to his room.

In the attic, Anitra sat on the floor and watched as he sat on his bed, emptied his pockets, and studied the contents: a few coins and a half-eaten piece of candy. Certainly nothing deserving of so much attention. He turned and looked at his dresser for a moment. Slowly, he walked over to it, opened a drawer, reached under a stack of sweaters, and pulled out a small piece of paper that had been crumpled then neatly folded in half. He unfolded it and stared at it.

"You look so sad," Anitra whispered. He didn't look as if he'd spent the day playing baseball.

"Hey, Buddy, you over there?" Adam called from the other side of the attic.

Anitra jumped and looked in the direction of his voice.

Startled, Jeff hurriedly stuffed the paper back in the drawer and closed it. "Um, yeah. Just a minute."

He put his elbows on the dresser and rested his forehead in his palms. He shook his head no, maybe answering some nuisance of a question in his mind. Then, letting his arms drop so that his hands landed on the dresser with a dull slap, he sighed, stepped away, and went to his brother.

"Hi," he said, giving Adam a quick, manly jab on the arm.

Jordan sat on the floor playing with a new toy train that Adam had given him, and Jeff reached down to ruffle his wildly curly hair. Jordan waved him away.

Adam smiled at his brother and continued his unpacking. "It's the baseball star! You win?"

"Nah, not this time. But I hit a double today and made a few big catches!"

"Knew you could, Buddy. But can you put up with my snoring for a few nights?"

"I can live with it. You always keep the whole house awake when you're home, so it doesn't matter what room you sleep in!"

"Thank you so much," Adam said, pretending to punch

Jeff's jaw.

Jeff sat on Jordan's bed. "How's school?" he asked, sounding like he was already thinking of something else.

"Good. The work's getting harder, but I'm keeping up. Hard to believe I'm almost halfway through with college."

"You like it there?" Jeff asked. "I mean, being away from home?"

"I like it. I miss everybody, of course, and I have to do for myself more. But I like it. Why?"

"I don't know," Jeff shrugged. "Just wondering."

"You plan on going somewhere?" Adam asked, pulling a sweater out of his suitcase.

"No! Just asking."

Adam stopped unpacking and squinted at his brother. "What's eating you, Buddy? Tired of big city life in Louiston?"

"Nothing's wrong. I'm just askin' is all." He twisted one of Adam's ties and wrapped it around his fingers.

Adam studied Jeff's face. "Tell ya what. Before I leave, let's talk to Papa about letting you come visit me in Tennessee for a weekend sometime. How 'bout that?"

Jeff smiled and looked relieved. "Ya think we can? Really?"

"We can play some ball and take a look at some of those science labs you like so much. We'll make a doctor out of you yet!" Adam unraveled his tie from around Jeff's fingers.

Jeff finally smiled a little. "Maybe."

"Who knows, you might save some lives."

Jeff's smile disappeared.

"Something sure smells good down there. Let's go eat!" Adam put the last of his clothes in the dresser, then grabbed Jordan and carried him like a football to the stairs.

"Hey!" Jordan laughed.

"You coming?" Adam asked.

"In a minute. I have to wash up first."

Adam nodded and carried Jordan downstairs. Jeff went to his room, grabbed some clean clothes, and went downstairs.

Anitra stayed in the attic and thought everything through two, three, four times. None of it became any clearer.

She thought about what she had just seen. What was Jeff so sad about? Irene had said he was sad about Elizabeth, but even she thought something else bothered him. Anitra went back to Jeff's room and looked at the things Jeff had taken out of his pockets. Three cents and a piece of taffy. No big deal there. Anitra really wanted to see the paper that Jeff had taken out of his dresser drawer. But, of course, she couldn't touch the dresser. She rolled her eyes and tried to kick it. It remained defiantly untouched. Shaking her head, she stomped her foot and went downstairs.

Anitra found the family at the dining room table where grace had just been said and a huge Sunday-looking dinner sat ready. Anitra marveled at the scene. Papa Russell and Mama Sarah sat at either end of the long table, Jeff sat between Adam and Lillian, and the other kids sat on the opposite side. Plates of chicken and biscuits, bowls of potatoes and vegetables, and dishes of butter and gravy flew around the table competing with a string of conversations that constantly changed directions.

Jeff dug into his meal, barely chewing, stopping between bites only long enough to occasionally join the family chatter. He seemed almost happy compared to the way he had looked upstairs. Well, not quite happy. Normal, maybe.

"Adam, it's so good to have you home," Mama Sarah said.

"Couldn't wait to get here, Mama," Adam said, smiling.

"Easter came just in time. Everybody was ready for a break."

"Got you working hard, huh?" Papa Russell said, probably remembering his own days at Fisk.

"They sure do!"

Anitra tip-toed into the room and sat against the wall in a chair that matched those at the table. She wished she could wave her hands and get their attention, even jump into the conversations. She'd already decided not to try, but it was kinda fun to think about anyway.

"There's a lot of talk on campus about the elections," Adam said. "Since Coolidge isn't running for reelection, everyone has their own idea of who'll end up in the White House, like..."

"Papa, I think it should be you!" Jordan chimed in.

"Jordan, I don't think the world's ready for President Russell Cole!" Adam said.

Everyone laughed. Then Anitra laughed, too. But Jeff didn't. He looked up and froze with a forkful of potatoes aimed at his open mouth. Anitra held her breath. She sat still and silent. Had he heard her laugh?

Naomi, sitting directly across from Jeff, tilted her head and looked at him. "Jeff? What are you doing?"

The room fell silent. With the whole family staring at him, Jeff put his fork back to work and shook his head. "Nothing...I just remembered...I...I think I left something on the field."

Anitra felt relieved; it wasn't what she thought. Still, she stared at his face. Although his eyes were now fixed on his plate, he looked shaken. Had he heard her? Seen her? Noticed her as she sat watching him and the rest of the family? No. No, he was okay.

"Papa, thank you for the new book." Irene said.

"What book is it, Irene?" Lillian asked.

"*The Souls of Black Folk*, by W. E. B. DuBois! It's exactly the book I was looking for!"

"Irene!" Adam said. "You've been doing your homework. People have been reading that one for years."

"Mrs. Barrett told me all about him. She has every book anyone ever wrote, and sometimes she lets me borrow them."

As Irene babbled on about the books she loved, Anitra watched Jeff. He just sat there staring at his plate, pushing the potatoes into a blob surrounded by a gravy moat. From the corner of his eye, Adam looked at Jeff, looked at Jeff's plate, looked at Jeff, and smothered a laugh. He nudged his brother and glanced at Mama Sarah. Surely their mother wouldn't like this. Jeff stirred the moat away.

Irene, meanwhile, hadn't slowed down yet. "...and her brother lives in Harlem, and he knows all the best writers! And they all go to these parties at someone's apartment."

Irene waved her fork higher in the air with each word. Naomi caught her arm and gently pulled it down to the table.

"What kind of parties?" Lillian asked.

"Just parties. With writers and artists and people like that. Sometimes she goes to them with her brother, and she says everyone has a swell time." She sighed. "I wish I could go."

"Irene!" Mama Sarah said.

"Oh...but I won't go, Mama," Irene said. "It just seems so exciting to meet people like that. At a party!"

"Irene, has Mrs. Barrett said anything about taking you to one of these...speak-easies?" Mama Sarah asked.

"No, ma'am," Irene quickly replied. "But Adam goes to Harlem all the time to see his friends or go to those fraternity basketball games. Even Jeff goes with him!"

Jeff's head popped up. "What?"

"I wasn't talking to you!" Irene said, throwing a pitiful

look his way.

He shrugged and ducked back into his private world.

Irene turned back to Mama Sarah. "Mama, if they can go, I don't see…"

Mama Sarah shot a look at Irene that stopped her cold. "They do *not* go to parties." Bang. Subject closed.

Papa Russell grinned and waited for his moment to jump in and quiet things down. Just like Grandpa Jeff said.

"So, Naomi, how are the piano lessons coming along?" Adam asked, winking at Irene and rescuing her with a quick subject change.

Naomi's face lit up. "I'm starting…"

Jeff jumped in. "She finally stopped playing all that funeral music over and over and over! We can walk around the house without plugging our ears!" He seemed to force himself to laugh, and Jordan joined him.

Mama Sarah frowned, and they immediately stopped. Slapped with guilt, Jeff turned his attention to something meaningless on the other side of the window.

Naomi ignored her brothers. "My teacher says that I might be ready for Oberlin in two years." She looked at her mother and winced. "Mama, it's a good school," she whined.

Jeff glanced somewhere in Anitra's direction. She felt a chill.

"Yes, it is a good school," Mama Sarah said, "and I know you would be very successful there, Naomi. But it's in Ohio. That's just too far."

Lillian gave her sister a frosty I-told-you-so look.

Goose bumps popped up on Anitra's arms. He did it again! Jeff looked at her or around her or above her. Just for a second. Then he turned back to the nothing in the window.

"Papa!" Naomi turned to Papa Russell.

"It is a very good school, Sarah." Papa Russell said. "Jack

is there now and doing very well."

"He'll be there when I go, Mama."

Jeff went back to picking at his food.

"*If* you go," Mama Sarah said. "Russell, I just don't like the idea of my children being scattered all over the country, especially my girls. Adam in Tennessee, Naomi in Ohio, I just don't like it."

Slowly, Jeff lifted his head.

"Now, Sarah," Papa Russell said, "we can't expect them all to stay in Louiston for the rest of their lives. There's a lot of world out there for them to see."

Slowly, Jeff looked at the window.

"It worries me so," Mama Sarah said, her brow pinched into a tired frown.

Papa Russell smiled. "I know, dear. We'll discuss it later," he said, smiling at Naomi.

Slowly, so slowly, Jeff turned and looked right into Anitra's eyes.

The jolt burned Anitra. She watched Jeff watch her. She watched his mouth begin to move and watched as no words came out. She watched his eyes turn glassy as he looked around the table to find the rest of the family still chatting away.

Every part of her shuddered. She knew it! She knew she couldn't let them see her. He was terrified! Hoping her legs would hold her up, Anitra eased herself out of the chair, and by the time Jeff turned to look at her again, she had backed herself to the wide arch between the living room and dining room. Staring at her empty chair, Jeff's face gradually relaxed, and he let out a silent sigh. He didn't look around to find her.

Anitra kept backing away, backing right into the piano in the living room. If she had been able to touch it, it would have left a huge purple bruise on her back. Steadying herself, she turned and ran all the way up to the attic.

How did he know she was there? How did he know?!

None of the others ever saw her. Why him? Why didn't he see her in the kitchen? Or in the attic? Why just at the din-

ner table? And why didn't he jump up and run away, screaming his head off?

Okay, she really had to get back to her own time, now.
This was way too weird, and all those butterflies in her stomach had turned into vampire bats. And after watching the
family eat, she was starving. No way to eat if she couldn't
touch anything.

That nagging thought crept back, that there might not be
a way home, and she had to fight even harder this time to
keep it away. She sat up and put her face in her hands, listening to the pounding heartbeat invading her ears. She had to
find a way back before she starved to death. Or before Jeff
saw her again.

Jeff ran up the stairs to the attic. Anitra jumped up, tripping over herself trying to find a hiding place. Too late. Jeff
reached the top of the stairs...and plodded right past her! He
didn't see her! He didn't see her at all!

He pounded his fists on the dresser and covered his head
with his hands. For a moment he didn't move, and a frail, on-
erous sigh bubbled up from somewhere deep inside him.
Slowly he opened his eyes, opened the dresser drawer, and
reached in for that same piece of paper he had stared at earlier.

He flopped down on his bed, unfolded the paper, and
ran his finger along each wrinkle, each fold. It looked so
worn in one spot, it must have had that soft, frayed feel paper got when it was about to fall apart. Jeff turned the paper
sideways then upside down, folded it then unfolded it, and
stared at it long enough to burn a hole in it. He crumpled it
into his palm, and, for what seemed like forever, gazed va-
cantly out the window with his head resting on the wall.

"What's on that paper?" Anitra whispered. She wanted to
look over his shoulder, but after what had happened at the

dinner table, she was afraid to get too close to him. Besides, he had it all crumpled in his hand.

Gradually, Jeff got up and put the paper back in the drawer. But then he reached under the sweaters again, and this time, he pulled out a small box covered in tattered wrapping that looked like it used to be pretty. Just like he had done with the paper, he studied the box, rolled it over and over in his hands, then put it back in the drawer. Tears pooled in his eyes. With his back against the dresser, he slid down to the floor. Burying his face in his fists, he let quiet sobs rumble through him.

Across the room, Anitra knelt on the floor. She'd never seen her grandfather cry before. Even at family funerals, he'd looked terribly sad and had teared up a little, but never actually cried. But now she longed to protect this scared kid who was not much bigger than she.

"Oh, Jeff, please don't cry," she whispered so softly, she could barely hear her own words.

She pictured herself taking his hand, resting her head on his shoulder, explaining who she was, telling him he didn't have to be afraid. She hated this! She couldn't do a thing to help him.

Jeff had stopped crying, and now sat with his eyes closed, calming himself. He stood and wiped tear stains from his face with his shirt sleeve. Faint piano music wafted up to the attic. Jeff shoved his hands into his pockets and looked toward the stairs. His face softened a bit. Gradually the music pulled him to the stairs, and he picked up a little speed on the way down.

Anitra wanted desperately to get into that drawer and look at that paper and box. She had to know what they were and what they meant. She kicked at the dresser again and followed Jeff downstairs.

꙰ඌ

She found the family in the living room quietly chatting and enjoying Naomi's piano music. Watching Naomi's hands fly over the keys, Anitra unwrapped her own cherished memories of Aunt Naomi's soft, mildly wrinkled hands making the piano sing. It wasn't just her hands that played, she had told Anitra long ago, it was her heart, her mind, her whole being. It just came out at her fingertips. The hands that played now were the smooth hands of a girl, but Anitra still recognized the dance they performed across the keys.

After Naomi finished, Papa Russell turned to the bulky wooden radio that looked just as Grandpa Jeff had described it. The speaker, a large, curvy, horn-shaped thing, sat next to the radio and reminded Anitra of the tubas kids played in the school band. Papa Russell twisted a knob, and the family listened to one of those old radio shows that Anitra had heard so much about. The man on the radio announced, "the RCA Hour with the New York Symphony Orchestra."

Pretty amazing. Even though there was nothing to look at, the family still gathered around the radio just like she and her family sat around the television. As they listened, Papa Russell and Adam discussed some hot item in the local newspaper, Mama Sarah wrote a letter or something, the girls pored over a Parchesi game, and Jeff seemed to be back to normal as he and Jordan plinked an assortment of glass and clay marbles. Anitra sat on the floor and enjoyed her family's company. She even let herself relax a little.

The radio program ended, and Mama Sarah put her writing aside. "Everyone, time for bed now."

While they said their good nights, Anitra scrambled to reach the second floor before six pairs of feet hit the stairs once again. Even if they couldn't touch her, no need to chance being trampled.

Upstairs, Lillian and Naomi exchanged fashion advice for the next day's Easter service.

"Maybe I should wear this one," Lillian said, pulling a green dress out of the closet.

"That's a nice one," Naomi said, "but I like the blue one better for you."

Anitra agreed. This dress had a blue and cream pattern and a wide collar. The sleeves were a little bit puffy like shirt sleeves.

"Remember," Naomi said, "Tommy Johnson will be there!"

Lillian blushed. "Naomi! This is church! We shouldn't be talking like this!" she said, but she smiled quietly just the same. Then she looked around, worried that someone might be listening. "Do you think he'll like this one?"

Naomi nodded enthusiastically. "I think he'll like anything you wear. I've seen him look at you when he thinks you won't notice."

"You think so? He's just the nicest boy."

Naomi nodded. "Never mind nice! He's the handsomest! And Mrs. Ellis says he's quite a catch. Imagine, Lill! Mrs. Thomas Johnson. Lillian Johnson!"

"Naomi!" Lillian said, embarrassed. "Well...he really is nice looking. But don't marry me off yet!"

"He's the cat's meow," Naomi said in a high-pitched voice. "The bee's knees!"

The girls laughed hysterically, and Naomi fell onto her bed holding Lillian's blue dress. Anitra laughed with them. She'd never heard anything like this.

Lillian held both dresses up. "So, which one?"

Naomi looked back and forth between the two dresses.

"Let's ask the judge. Irene? We need your help!"

Next door, Irene sat on her bed reading in the weak light. "Be right there," she said without looking up from her book.

A delicate pair of thin wire glasses similar to Adam's sat on her nose and annoyed her until she finally pulled them off and tossed them onto the bed. She got up and walked past Anitra to her sisters' room.

With Irene gone, Anitra went into the room she always used when visiting Grandpa Jeff and Grandma Charlotte. There were two beds there. Irene must have shared this room with Elizabeth. But that meant the room Anitra used, this very room, had once been Elizabeth's. Grandma had only told her it had been Irene's room. She never mentioned Elizabeth.

Anitra turned to a bookshelf along the wall and smiled when she found the other three hand-made dolls sitting on top. Like the four in Lillian and Naomi's bedroom, each doll wore a dress of a different color, and these were a bright red, yellow, and green. On the shelves, Irene had a huge collection of books, and some looked familiar.

A book of poetry by Langston Hughes, one of Grandma Charlotte's favorite writers, sat on the top shelf with some school books and today's new addition to Irene's collection. Then Anitra realized that two of these very books were in her father's study. Gifts from Aunt Irene, he had told her, from one English professor to another.

Two children's books on the middle shelf looked out of place. Anitra reached for one, and…she could touch it! She jumped and pulled back her hand. Then she reached again and picked up the thin book of fairy tales with unevenly edged pages and a drawing of fat-cheeked children frolicking on the cover.

The book's spine crackled when Anitra opened to the

first page. Inside the front cover, "Elizabeth S. Cole, 1921" was lavishly hand printed in black-brown ink. Anitra's eyes gaped, and some unintelligible word mumbled out of her mouth. To calm her shaking hands, she sat down on Elizabeth's bed. It moved under her weight.

Startled, Anitra popped right back up, turned around, and gave the bed a suspicious glare as her jaw dropped to the floor. She ran a cautious hand across the bed to smooth the blanket where she had sat and felt the thick, prickly wool under her fingers. Dropping to her knees, she picked up a corner of the blanket with both hands and pressed it against her cheek. To finally touch something, anything, almost made her cry.

"Girls! To bed, now," Mama Sarah called from downstairs.

Anitra jumped to her feet. Irene would be back in seconds. Anitra stood in the middle of the floor clutching the book and staring at the bookshelf. Hastily she replaced the book, but a small, torn piece of bookmark gently slid from the pages and onto the floor. She picked it up and tucked it under the collar of her dress, then realized the book was in the wrong place! But it was too late to move it. Irene was back.

Irene put her glasses on the table and got into bed. As she reached for the lamp, she stared at the bookshelf. Anitra's heart thumped. Hard. Irene got out of the bed, looked more closely at the books on the shelf, then backed away. She sat silently on her bed for a moment, looking back and forth between the bookshelf and her wringing hands. Finally, she got back into bed and turned off the light. Anitra fled the room and escaped to the attic.

The boys were already asleep. Adam snored obnoxiously, and Anitra wondered how Jeff and Jordan could sleep with the blare. But they were both out cold. A thin, faint ribbon of light seeped through the window above Jeff and fell across the back of his head.

In the darkness, Anitra found her way to the green upholstered chair in Jeff's room and sat with her knees pulled to her chest. She tried to think through her fear. She was tired and hungry, and Elizabeth's dress and shoes had grown fiercely uncomfortable. Here she was roaming around in 1928, and she had no idea how she had gotten there, why she was there, or how to get back. She had thought the people were ghosts, but they weren't. She'd thought no one could see her, but Jeff could. She'd thought she couldn't touch anything, but she did. The rules kept changing.

Anitra finally gave in to the tears that had formed in her eyes. She had been strong all day, but this was too much, and she was scared. Through her sniffling, she heard the rustle of sheets as Jeff turned in his bed. She could just barely see the features of his face as it moved into the path of the light from outside.

His eyes opened. He turned his head in her direction and said, "Lizzie?"

ಐ8ಐ

Something pounded on the inside of Anitra's head while tiny spots of light popped in front of her eyes. She found herself lying on the floor among the familiar attic clutter. The choking heat embraced her and welcomed her home. She remembered being very quiet after Jeff had spoken, but she had no idea what had happened after that.

Anitra sat up, dusted herself off, and tried to think. The last thing she remembered was a quick dance in front of the mirror, then relentless heat and tremendous thirst. And the pain that shot straight up her neck. She must've fainted and dreamed the whole thing. What else could it have been?

But she was starving. She had eaten right before racing to the attic, and she hadn't been up there long enough for Grandma Charlotte to come looking for her.

She got up and wobbled to the mirror, gratefully peeling off the red dress, bow, and locket and kicking the black shoes off her feet. After putting on her shorts and shirt, she wiped a spot of dust off the dress then placed it back in the garment bag. She returned the accessories, then stared at the garment bag, running her fingers absently through her hair. She hated to admit it, but Grandma Charlotte was right. Next time, Anitra would pick a cooler day to go roaming around in the attic. Shaking her head, she zipped the bag and dragged herself to the stairs.

But halfway down, Anitra turned and flew back up the stairs. She frowned at the garment bag, almost expecting it to frown back. Seven tottering steps brought her back to the bag, then, tightening her jaw, she yanked the zipper open and grabbed the dress. Turning it from front to back, she ran her fingers under the collar and inside the sleeves, then she gave the dress a harsh shake. She looked down and watched something flutter to the floor. Reaching under the bag, she picked up the bookmark.

₭)Ὁ•

Anitra jumped onto her orange Schwinn ten-speed bike and raced down Fisher Street to Carrie's house. According to Grandma Charlotte, she had only been in the attic for about fifteen minutes, but Anitra knew she had spent hours in the past.

A plastic bag carrying a second lunch swayed from her handlebar. She wished she could tell Carrie what had just happened to her, but only a crazy person would believe it. At least it would help to go bike riding with Carrie. Maybe then her mind would clear up and things would start to make sense.

Carrie waited patiently at a picnic table under the Morgans' shady apple tree. Sipping from a straw in a soda can, she bopped her head to Stevie Wonder's "Don't You Worry 'Bout a Thing" playing on her radio. Wisps of Afro peeked out from beneath the bill of her red baseball cap, and brown sunglasses shielded her eyes. Anitra flopped down across from Carrie and dumped her sandwich and soda onto the table.

"Didn't you just eat lunch?" Carrie asked, looking at Anitra over the top of her sunglasses.

"Sort of," Anitra answered as she dove into the sandwich. "Um, I didn't finish."

Carrie shrugged. "Everyone went back to the pool. It's just you and me for the berry bush side of Grant Park."

" 'kay," Anitra said through huge bites of her sandwich.

Carrie looked at her with a raised eyebrow. "I know your grandmother feeds you!"

"I'm hungry, okay?"

Carrie's other eyebrow flew up. "Ohhhh...kay."

The back door opened, and Carrie's older brother jogged out. For a grateful moment, Anitra forgot her problem and stared. It was...*him*! Zip Morgan, star of the Louiston High track team!

"Dad just called, Carrie," he said. "He wanted to know if you're gonna pick blackberries. I told him you were on your way."

"'kay," Carrie said.

He took a sip of Carrie's soda. "Hey, Anitra," he said with a quick wave and no-big-deal smile.

Anitra felt her face flush as a tiny "Hi" peeped out.

Like Carrie, he was tall and brown. And, as always, his Afro thrived in full bloom, picked to perfection, with just the slightest glint of Afro Sheen spray. Cuter than any boy in her school! He was bad! Anitra watched him head back to the house and admired the black fist on the pick handle jutting out of his back pocket. Whew! He was *bad*.

Carrie laughed. "You can come back to Earth, now. He's

gone."

Anitra blushed, guilty as charged.

"Anyway," Carrie said, still grinning, "let's see if we can get lots of berries. I can taste the ice cream already!"

"Let's get moving," Anitra said, popping the last piece of sandwich into her mouth. She smiled, remembering the last time she'd had dinner with the Morgans.

"I just have to get a couple of those container things. I'll be right back." Carrie disappeared into the house.

Though Anitra felt a little better, all the confusion came screeching back after Zip left. It swirled in her head.

"Ready?" Carrie popped out of the house carrying two containers.

"Yup."

Carrie lifted the kickstand on her metallic green ten-speed. The girls headed for the park, passing younger kids on banana-seated bikes with blue and white streamers flapping from the handlebars, the kind of bikes the girls had outgrown last year. The ride whipped up a hot, soothing breeze, and Anitra tried to concentrate on nothing but avoiding the bumps in the road.

Five minutes later, the girls entered Grant Park. The huge park included a pond, picnic areas, two baseball fields, tennis courts, a wooded area, and plenty of bicycle and walking trails. That morning, Anitra had won her victory in the pool on the other side of the tennis courts.

"Let's go over there," Carrie said, pointing to the woods along the bicycle trail. "There's usually a lot in there."

"And I bet it won't be so hot in there," Anitra said.

Carrie nodded. "Yeah. C'mon."

Anitra was right; the wooded area felt a lot cooler, even refreshing. They rode past old, gnarled trees, unnamed plants, and a startled rabbit. On the other side of a small foot bridge, they parked their bikes near a clearing where the blackberry bushes stood in a row on the edge of the sunlight.

"Remember Mary from the pool?" Carrie asked as she started picking blackberries.

"Yeah."

"Well, you won't believe this, but she used to like Eddie!"

"Eeewww! Gross!"

Anitra shuddered at the horror, and Carrie pretended to gag.

"Some boys are pretty nice, though," Carrie said with a crooked smile.

"You mean like the one who calls you? What's his name again?"

"Curtis!" Carrie said, hurt that Anitra didn't remember. "He's fourteen, and he's soooo cute!" She grinned and pulled at her puka shell necklace. "My mom's going all crazy about him calling, though. Thinks I'm too young."

"Too young? How old are you supposed to be for a phone call, anyway?"

"I don't know. This one time I asked her, and she goes, 'I think sixteen is about right.' Do ya believe that?"

"Sixteen?! Why?"

"I don't know. I think that's how old she was when she started talking to boys. Way back in the stone age!" Carrie laughed.

Anitra thought of the 1928 stone age she had just seen and wondered if Carrie could possibly believe it.

"They're boys, not monsters," Anitra said.

"I know. She just worries about all the things you hear about girls getting into trouble and stuff. But all I want to do is talk on the phone and maybe go to a movie or something."

"Yeah. Like, the worst thing that can happen is you eat too much candy and get real fat!" Anitra puffed her cheeks and laughed.

For nearly an hour, they filled their plastic containers and dodged an occasional bee. While they worked, they plunged into conversation about the boys at their schools, the girl in Anitra's class who'd been wearing a rather large bra since... well...forever, that other girl Anitra couldn't stand who thought she was sooo great (someone should tell her off!), that Funkadelic concert Anitra's brothers saw in New York, the new eight-track tape players they had bought together, their favorite TV shows, boys, boys, and boys.

Anitra gathered her courage. "Carrie?"

"Yeah?"

"Ever read time travel stories?"

"Sometimes. Why?"

"Ever wonder if it can really happen?"

Carrie looked up, smiling and curious. "I don't know, maybe. What do you think?"

"Well, um, I think maybe it can. What if...what if it was so hot right now that you passed out, and when you woke up it was sometime in the future or the past?"

Carrie knew Anitra's insane imagination well, and she always played along.

"Hmm," Carrie said. "Let's see. I pass out and wake up and it's some other time. Well, I hope it's after I graduate, and I don't have to go to school anymore!"

"Nope. You're the same age as you are now. It's just a different time. Like before you were born, and your mom's thirteen."

"Wow! Mom's my age. I'd go hang out with her. That'd be cool!" Carrie laughed.

"Maybe, but would you tell her who you are?"

"No way!"

"Why not?"

"She'd have one of her 'spells' or something! She'd never believe me. Think about it. You go to somebody our age and tell her you're her daughter. From the future. No way! If I said that to my mom, she'd tell *her* mom. And knowing my grandmother, they'd send me to a mental hospital. I bet they had a lot of those back then, ya know. I'd play it safe. I'd tell her I was her long lost cousin or something."

"Yeah, I guess," Anitra said, picturing herself back in 1928 again.

"What would you do?" Carrie asked.

"Oh, I don't know," Anitra said. "I guess I'd do the same thing. If somebody came to me right now and said she was my daughter, I'd want her put away, too."

She laughed...a little. Carrie's mental hospital idea sounded pretty scary.

"Straight jacket and padded cell!" Carrie sang.

"Okay, okay. Now, how would you get back home?"

Carrie thought for a minute. "I don't know, I guess the same way I got there in the first place." She shrugged.

Anitra nodded. She couldn't think of anything better, either. As the girls continued picking blackberries in silence, Anitra replayed her last moments in the past, but she still couldn't remember what had happened after Jeff had spoken his sister's name.

"Dad should be able to do a lot with these," Carrie said, happy with their harvest.

"Should be good," Anitra said, snapping out of her tortured thoughts. "Let's get back so he can get started soon as he gets home."

As her bike bumped along the path in front of Carrie, Anitra felt as if she were floating, almost lifting off the bicycle, moving in slow motion. The rustling breeze, the distant laughter of swimmers, the tartness of the berries she had sampled were all someplace else. The sunlight glared brighter.

As she approached the edge of the woods, a sudden cool breeze swirled around her. No, it was cold. And it passed *through* her. A faint sound tapped her ears. It seemed like voices, or one voice, maybe. No words, just garbled mumbling. Something...someone...was there. But only for the brief seconds that the breeze flew by.

At the edge of the woods, the feeling disappeared. Anitra slammed on her brakes, put her hand on top of her head, and looked in all directions.

"Carrie!"

Carried stopped. "What's wrong?"

"Did you feel that?"

"What?" Carrie looked around.

"It was cold air. It just...went by," Anitra said, still looking for the source.

Carrie lowered her sunglasses. "A *cold* breeze? In July? In the middle of a heat wave?"

"No, really, I'm not joking! It was cold!"

"Yeah, right."

"It was a cold breeze!"

Carrie just kept staring at Anitra, her mouth slightly open.

"Okay, I'm just kidding," Anitra said, laughing slightly.

Gradually the worry melted from Carrie's face, and she rolled her eyes. "I thought you were serious!" she groaned. She picked up a twig and threw it at Anitra.

For the rest of the ride, Anitra's heart beat out of control. The cold breeze was no joke, and what little relief she had gained from her fear and confusion had quickly dissolved. Something was very, very wrong.

ಐ9ಲ

Anitra needed answers. It had been a normal Tuesday until the attic. She had gone up there today just like she had a million times before, but this time she'd ended up in 1928. Then in the park, that eerie, cold breeze had run straight through her. Oh, yeah, she needed answers.

As soon as she reached her grandparents' house, Anitra headed straight for the back yard. Grandpa Jeff would be home by now and would probably be in the garden. She knew he could help, but she'd have to fish for information without revealing the problem. That wouldn't be easy.

Every summer the back yard garden was rich with tomatoes, collard greens, carrots, and cucumbers. It also produced a few assorted things that Anitra couldn't bring herself to eat, like turnips, okra, and, worst of all, beets. The thirsty ground was a light, crumbly brown except the darker spots surrounding the plants in the garden. Anitra followed the green garden hose and found Grandpa Jeff performing delicate surgery on a tomato plant.

"Grandpa Jeff?" she called.

"Hey, Peanut!" he said, interrupting the operation. "I thought you were at the park picking berries with Carrie."

"I was. I'm going back to her house for dinner tonight. What're you doing?"

"Oh...getting these tomato plants to stand up straight," he said, pulling green string out of his pocket, "and pruning a few so they'll stay healthy. See this part? You can pull it off so the tomatoes will grow bigger. Haven't done this like I should because it's been so hot out lately. Should've done this sooner."

He handed her some string and showed her how to tie the plants to the trellises.

"Like this?" she asked, following his instructions.

"That's right, Peanut, not too tight," he said.

"How long have you kept a garden, Grandpa?" she asked.

"Oh, my. Well, let me see now." He stopped and looked upward, searching for an answer in the haze. "This garden has been around for a long, long time. Ever since I was a boy, I can remember something growing here. Sometimes it was much bigger than this, especially during the Depression. We always had some vegetables, sometimes more than our big family needed, even. Mama would cook some of them and can the rest for winter. Remember those jars I showed you in the basement?"

Anitra nodded.

"But sometimes Mama planted flowers, too. Bright colors, they were. Sometimes they ended up as a centerpiece on the table when company came, and sometimes the girls would have some in their rooms. They all liked flowers."

"Did you ever give any to Grandma?" she asked. The conversation was heading in the right direction. She followed him to the next plant, still tying the green string.

"Yes, I did." Grandpa Jeff smiled at the memory. "I did bring your Grandma some flowers. And you know, Peanut, the first time I did that, Adam found out and teased me every chance he got! He thought it was the funniest thing, his little brother giving flowers to a girl. But when Mama found out, she like to tan my hide! You see, I hadn't asked her permission to pick her flowers." He laughed.

"Why did Uncle Adam think it was so funny?" Anitra asked.

"Well, I suppose I was about fourteen at the time. And your grandma and I, well we'd been friends for so long. It was the first time I had shown interest in a girl, or so Adam thought." He stopped to pull a small piece of string out of his pocket and tie another sagging plant. "Truth was that I had my eye on a girl at school named Lois. But your grandma, well, she put an end to that. Yes sir!"

"Grandpa?"

"Mm hmm?" he said, laughing at his thoughts.

"Did all of your sisters like the flowers?"

"Yes, indeed. They all but fought over the prettiest ones."

Anitra bit her tongue. She had to ask. "Even Elizabeth?"

His hands froze. "Why do you ask, Peanut?" The easy flow of his voice gave way to something jagged and chafed.

"Well, I remember you said she was kind of a tomboy. You know, she liked to climb trees and stuff. I didn't think she'd like flowers."

Grandpa Jeff leaned on the trellis. His voice softened. "Oh...she did like to run and play and keep up with me. Yeah, the only girl I knew who liked climbing trees. But she was still a little girl, and she loved the flowers and pretty dresses and things like that."

Anitra watched him stare at the air.

He sighed as an old memory poked at him. "She and your grandma used to carry on so about clothes and jewelry. You couldn't pull them away from a store window with a dress or some shoes in it."

"She had pretty clothes," Anitra said, "like the red dress in the attic. The one she wore in the portrait."

"Her favorite red dress." He paused for a moment then nodded slowly, looking into the haze. It wasn't Anitra he was talking to anymore. "She just loved that red dress. Mama made it and wrapped it up and hid it in a closet. It was supposed to be a Christmas present. But Elizabeth found it one day when she and Charlotte were playing in the house. Unwrapped it and everything. Somehow..."

Anitra waited.

He shook his head and smiled. "Somehow she managed to convince Mama to let her have it right then and there. Didn't want to wait for Christmas. Then she insisted on wearing it for the family portrait. Our Lizzie...she..." His voice trailed off, and Anitra never heard the rest.

"She looked so pretty in the picture," she said softly, hoping he would continue.

He looked at her, startled that she was standing there. "Oh...yes. She did, indeed." He smiled a borrowed, prepackaged smile.

The green string in his hand vibrated, and a foreign look spread across his face way beyond that sad look he always got when anyone mentioned Elizabeth's name. She decided to stop asking questions; she had never seen him like this. She had already learned something important, and that was enough for now. They chatted lightly about the garden as she helped him finish their chore. As he touched each plant, it trembled in his hands.

Anitra tossed Grandpa Jeff's story around in her head as

she worked. The red dress, Elizabeth's favorite, had been planned as a Christmas gift. But Elizabeth died that November. If she hadn't found it, she never would have had it.

ഇരുൽ

Only nervous energy kept Anitra awake. At the Morgans' dinner table, she'd had a hard time keeping her worries at bay; even gawking at Zip hadn't helped. After slurping down the rich ice cream made with the berries she and Carrie had picked, she'd wearily returned to her grandparents' house.

She now sat hoping for answers as Grandma and Grandpa told the stories she loved so much. But their college days littered tonight's stories, and she was too tired to listen to much, anyway. Her day had lasted so long that the morning's swimming race seemed like weeks ago. Grandpa Jeff sent her to bed. No arguments from her tonight; she welcomed the thought of sleep.

Despite the quiet and the weak breeze that brought a hint of relief from the heat, Anitra slept fitfully. As she tossed and turned, her dreams burst with memories of the bizarre events of the day.

In her dream, she watched the 1928 Cole family at the dining room table, but she wasn't sitting in the chair against the wall. Instead, she hovered gently, weightlessly above the table. She circled the room, and the red dress flapped gently at her sides as she sailed through the warm, buoyant air above the family.

As they passed bowls of food around the table, an intense aroma filled the room with memories of all the past holiday dinners she'd had at Grandma's and Grandpa's: juicy turkey roasted to perfection, spicy wild rice stuffing, homemade cranberry sauce that wasn't shaped like a can, sweet potatoes topped with marshmallows, greens and more greens, steamy rolls, Grandpa's hot apple cider with cinnamon sticks, deep-dish apple pie fresh from the oven, and vanilla ice cream. Gradually, faint voices of parents, aunts, uncles, and cousins mingled with those of the family at the table. Anitra felt warm and safe as she floated.

Gently descending from the ceiling, she felt the strange sensation she always got in her stomach when riding the roller coaster. As she landed in the chair against the wall, the family abruptly fell silent. All heads turned. Harsh light cast dusky shadows on their faces and made them look hollow. And they stared. Cold, empty stares.

"Lizzie?" Jeff called. "Lizzie?"

"Eat your supper, Elizabeth," Mama Sarah said.

Anitra suddenly found herself seated at the table before an overflowing plate of food. She tried to speak but couldn't.

"Elizabeth!" Mama Sarah shouted. "Eat your supper!"

Over and over Anitra tried to pick up her fork but couldn't touch it. All eyes glared at her. No one spoke, no one moved. Her breath came in short, panicky gulps as she scrambled to reach the fork with both hands. Anitra squeezed her eyes shut, but she could still see right through her closed eyelids.

"Elizabeth!" Mama Sarah growled as she grabbed Anitra's arm with a hard, icy hand. "Eat...your...*supper!*"

Anitra's arm ached where the cold fingers squeezed, and when she thought she would scream, she found herself standing alone in the dark, barren attic of 1928. It looked much larger than the real attic, maybe the size of her school's gym, and the furniture was gone. Thin strips of bluish-gray light streamed in from a large, window-covered wall, and the light formed a checkerboard pattern on the floor.

A small pair of feet quickly darted from one square of

light to another like a child playing hopscotch. Anitra wanted to follow, but the feet moved too fast.

"Hello?" Anitra whispered. "Hello? Who's there?!"

The only answer was the lithe, scurrying sound of shoes scratching the linoleum floor. Suddenly, Anitra felt something brush against her legs. She gasped and spun around. But it was too late; the feet had scampered away. A child's faint, echoey giggle bounced off the walls and teased Anitra.

"Who's there?!" Anitra screamed.

Now she stood in the middle of the living room of the past, the overly tall walls covered from top to bottom with doors and windows. The radio broadcast a grainy, bouncy tune of soft, muted trumpets and a whiny violin. Anitra pushed and pulled at each locked door, each sealed window. She was trapped. Scared. Panicked.

She heard a voice, distant at first then gradually closer, louder. She couldn't understand what it said, who it was, or where it came from, but she knew it was calling to her. Loud, blaring music gushed from the horn of the old radio, and the voice grew stronger. Anitra spun around trying to find it. She saw no one.

The music on the radio turned into a grating, raspy din, and the voice swelled louder and louder and closer and closer until she felt it screech into her ears. She dropped to her knees and covered her head with her arms, screaming.

Anitra sat straight up in bed, suddenly awake and trembling. Her sheets bound her body like a straight jacket, and a corner of the fitted sheet that had popped loose from the mattress fully enveloped her left foot. Silence buzzed around the room. With unsteady hands, she turned on the light.

Carefully, she untangled herself from the sheets and untwisted her pajama top. To calm down, she ran her hands through her soggy hair and stretched her arms, reminding herself that it was all just a dream. Nothing more. But as she looked toward the door to her room, she suddenly gasped, scrambled to the corner of the bed, and pulled the disheveled sheets to her chin. Her eyes popped, and her jaw dropped open.

In the doorway, surrounded by a dim glow of light, was a young girl in a red dress.

Elizabeth.

ಐ10ಝ

A t first, Anitra thought it was a reflection of herself. Maybe that horrible dream refusing to end. But she was wide awake, and the doorway had no mirror. She stared, too frightened to move. The ghost stared back and looked just as frightened. Still in the doorway, she looked around the room and back at Anitra. This had to be Elizabeth. She wore the same red dress, locket, and shoes, and the red bow on the side of her head sat atop perfect, dangling curls. Just like the girl in the family portrait.

Elizabeth took two timid steps into the room. Anitra managed to close her mouth before she started to drool, but she still couldn't will herself to budge. And Elizabeth looked so distressed that any sudden move might scare her away. Strangely, Anitra didn't want her to leave.

Ghostly brown eyes remained fixed on Anitra and scanned her from the top of her sweaty head to her trembling toes that dangled from her bed and barely touched the floor. The eyes traveled back up to Anitra's face and hypnotized her. So intense, those eyes, so frightening, so frightened, so much like her own. They bore right into Anitra's soul and singed her thoughts so badly, she felt them scream.

The eyes released Anitra and jumped to the night table as two of the clock radio's black tabs with white numbers flipped over to read 1:40. Their soft click disturbed the silence and startled Elizabeth. Amazement filled her face. For a flash of a second, it crossed Anitra's mind to show Elizabeth what it was, but the thought quickly died out. Anitra's mouth was stalled, paralyzed like the rest of her.

A drop of sweat seeped into Anitra's eye, and the sting snapped her out of her trance. She blinked her eye clean and looked up to see Elizabeth at the dresser contemplating the blow dryer. Cautiously, the ghost touched it with her index finger then quickly drew it back. She touched it again, this time a little longer, and seemed to relax a little. But when she pushed the "on" switch, her hands flew up in startled surprise as the dryer whirred into action. She smacked it onto the floor, and the cord pulled Anitra's little yellow ball of a radio flying after it. As the radio rolled in Elizabeth's direction, she scrambled out of the room and stood trembling in the doorway.

On an normal day Anitra would have laughed at this, but there was nothing normal here. She lunged at the dryer and turned it off, hoping that it wouldn't wake her grandparents, that it wouldn't scare Elizabeth away. For a moment the girl and the ghost locked eyes once more: Elizabeth petrified in the doorway, Anitra sprawled on the floor clutching the blow dryer.

Anitra gathered her nerves and lifted herself off the floor. The carpet felt hot and scratchy under her feet, and her clammy pajama top clung to her back. She inched to the dresser and put down the offending blow dryer. Facing Elizabeth, she took a step closer, hoping her mouth would begin to move and something intelligent would miraculously pour out. But she could only stare stupidly at this ghost, this image of herself, standing in front of her. Elizabeth's eyes widened, and she glided into the hall.

After tripping over the radio ball and kicking it out of her way, Anitra slowly crept into the hall, where the only light came from her room and Elizabeth's glow. Elizabeth, too busy to notice Anitra behind her, paced in circles in the middle of the floor. Then she stopped and ran her hands over the wooden doors of the storage cabinets. She looked at the floor and stomped each foot into the plush carpet.

"What is she doing?" Anitra whispered, wondering if all ghosts acted like this.

Anitra slapped her hands over the bottom half of her face. She was shocked to hear actual words come out of her own mouth. And she was sorry to have scared the ghost, who immediately backed away.

Elizabeth looked at the stairwell, then at Anitra, then back at the stairs. Anitra shook her head "no" and held out her hand. But Elizabeth shot, glided, down the stairs, stopping at the bottom. As Elizabeth headed into the living room, Anitra quietly descended the stairs.

While Elizabeth roamed around in the dark, Anitra wondered if the ghost could see past her glow. She flipped the light switch, and Elizabeth jumped. Her eyes once again seized Anitra, warning her to keep her distance. Then turning away, the ghost studied the beige carpet, the slightly worn but cozy sofa, Grandpa Jeff's favorite chair, and the wooden television console with its dark, blank screen. She seemed almost horrified by the recent family pictures on the console: people with colorful polyester shirts, crocheted vests, pointy lapels, Afro puffs, bell bottom pants, and huge smiles. The grandchildren. Elizabeth turned away.

A painting on the wall drew her gaze. It was a portrait of her parents, Russell and Sarah Cole, that a family friend had painted in 1946. Elizabeth moved closer, taking in the two gently wrinkled faces, the hair overcome with gray, the eyes softer than they had been in the twenties. She reached up and gently traced her mother's chin.

"Mama!" she whispered. Stepping backwards, Elizabeth covered her mouth with her hands and shook her head. "Mama, what happened to you? Papa?"

"Don't be scared," Anitra said, her voice barely audible.

Elizabeth shot teary eyes at Anitra. Watching her, Anitra's heart sank as she wondered if anyone else had ever seen a ghost cry.

"It's okay. I won't hurt you," Anitra whispered.

Elizabeth looked past Anitra at the stairs as if pleading with them to come get her and take her safely away.

"Really, I won't hurt you," Anitra said. "I promise."

There had to be something better to say. But before she could come up with anything, the ghost half ran, half glided through the dining room and into the kitchen. Anitra followed her.

Elizabeth stared at the avocado-colored refrigerator with the little pictures and magnets all over it and the white stove with the floral spoon rest on top and the toaster on the counter and the face-down magazine with the cigarette ad on the back and the oven mitts and the yellow sponge and the blender and the mugs. And in the middle of it all, Elizabeth turned and turned and searched for something Anitra couldn't begin to imagine. The ghost put her hands on her head and stabbed the silence with a piercing shriek.

The scream threw Anitra against the wall. Elizabeth rushed past her and tore through the dining room, through the living room, and up the stairs. Anitra caught up with her just in time to see her glide into the office and up the attic stairs.

Anitra looked up the stairs and saw nothing. Heard nothing. Her trembling foot landed on the first step, and before she could talk herself out of going up there, she was standing at the top of the attic stairs in the darkness and stifling heat. She didn't dare turn the light on this time; no need to chance scaring Elizabeth again.

"Elizabeth!" she whispered. "Elizabeth, where are you?"

No answer. She wondered if Elizabeth were hiding somewhere; all those boxes and trunks and things could hide even a big, fat ghost. But her ghostly glow would have given her away. Nothing here but darkness. In the middle of the heat, Anitra shivered. Elizabeth was gone.

Anitra stumbled as she crept back down the stairs, but she managed to reach the bottom in one piece.

"Anitra?" Grandma Charlotte called.

Anitra jumped and cupped her hand over her mouth to squelch a scream. Her heart skipped a few beats as she rushed into the hall. "Yes?"

"Is anything wrong, honey?"

"No, ma'am, I just…uh, need to use the bathroom." She hoped her voice didn't sound as wobbly as it felt.

"All right," Grandma Charlotte said.

Anitra heard their bedroom door shut as Grandma Charlotte went back to bed. How could they have missed that ear-splitting scream?

In the bathroom, Anitra splashed soothing, cool water on her face. Finally back in her room, she closed the door so her grandparents would not see the light she was going to leave on or hear the clock radio she would play for the rest of the night.

Anitra went to the dresser, changed into dry pajamas, and

kept an eye on the door. She moved slowly, rearranging the sheets, waiting for her heart to settle. Then she curled into a ball on her bed. As the DJ droned on about the heat wave, Anitra lay motionless and wondered if Elizabeth would come back. She wondered what she was supposed to do with all of this. She wondered what it all meant.

ఴ11ಐ

"Carrie! You have to come over!" Anitra insisted over the phone.

After last night, Anitra needed to talk to someone, but not her grandparents. She had gotten too close to upsetting Grandpa Jeff in the garden yesterday just by talking about a time when Elizabeth was alive. Telling them about her ghost would upset them terribly. She couldn't do that to them.

Grandma Charlotte had grown suspicious at breakfast. Anitra had slept unusually late and even turned down a shopping trip. Worse yet, her raw nerves made her jump at the slightest noise. Hard to hide that from an all-knowing grandmother. She needed Carrie.

"What's going on?" Carrie asked.

"Just come over. I have to show you something."

"Well what is it?"

"I can't tell you over the phone. You have to come over."

"Anitra, is this for real, or just another drama?"

"It's for real. Please. *Come over!*"

"Okay, okay, I'll be there. But I have to finish cleaning my room first."

"'kay. See ya."

After leaving the phone, Anitra paced a trench across her room trying to decide how to explain it all to Carrie. And how much. Grandma Charlotte would be gone until late afternoon, and Grandpa Jeff would be at work all day. She was alone in the house, and until now, that had never been a problem for her. She needed to get back to the attic, but was afraid to go alone. Carrie would have to come with her.

What a mess. With traveling through time and running after ghosts and all, Anitra's neglected room had taken on the beginnings of a seedy, radical look that Grandma Charlotte would not tolerate for long. It looked exactly like she felt. Out of order. Out of control. Out of her mind.

She flounced onto the floor and used a hanger to fish out the radio ball that had rolled under her bed. She grabbed the small hill of clothes that had accumulated on the chair, turned to the closet then the dresser then the chair again, and finally flung them onto the bed. Oh yeah, big improvement there.

Anitra rolled her eyes, crossed her arms, and began pacing again as silence bounced all over the house and began closing in on her. She decided to wait for Carrie outside, heat wave and all. She needed some fresh air or whatever that stuff was outside.

Sitting on the steps of the front porch made Anitra feel better, and she tried to convince herself that all the strange things belonged to yesterday. Wednesday was a whole new day; maybe today she could figure it all out.

The mailman came to the porch and handed her a small stack of envelopes and an *Ebony* magazine. She put the bills aside and flipped through the magazine, hoping the pictures would momentarily take her mind away from her problems. But she couldn't shake the fear that Elizabeth could come back any minute. That maybe she was inside right now, standing at a window, glaring at Anitra as she sat and waited for Carrie. Anitra shook her head to stop the craziness. The ghost was gone. She knew it.

"Okay, now what's going on?" Carrie called as she rode her bike into the driveway and took off her sunglasses.

Anitra jumped and slammed the magazine shut.

"Park your bike, and come on in," Anitra said, scooping up the mail.

At the kitchen table, Anitra poured two glasses of cold milk and unwrapped a plate of brownies with chopped pecans.

"Carrie, do you believe in ghosts?"

"*Ghosts*?!" Carrie asked. She almost choked on her first sip of milk.

"Yeah. Ghosts." Anitra nodded. "I saw one last night."

"No way!" Eyes aimed at Anitra, Carrie munched on a brownie and tried to keep the pecan bits out of her braces.

"It's true! I saw a ghost last night. Right upstairs." Anitra pointed at the ceiling.

"Anitra, look," Carrie said, waving her right hand to erase some invisible thing in the air. "You joke a lot, and most of the time it's funny, but..."

"Carrie, I'm not joking this time. I swear, I saw a ghost! It was real, and it was right upstairs in my room!" It wasn't yet time to tell her that the ghost had run around the house.

Carrie began to squirm in her chair. "That's...pretty serious." She sat, dazed.

"And I know who it was," Anitra said, ignoring Carrie's growing discomfort. She let a piece of brownie melt in her mouth as she watched Carrie's face.

Carrie stared right back, probably looking for a sign that a joke was coming. "Who?"

"My Great Aunt Elizabeth. She was my grandfather's sister, and she died when she was twelve."

"Twelve? You saw a twelve-year-old ghost?" Carrie gave up on the brownie.

"That's right. She looked just like me, too."

Carrie raised one eyebrow and smirked. "Nah, this is too much. She looked like you? C'mon, Anitra. This has got to be a joke, right?"

"No!" Anitra pleaded. "She did look like me, I mean, I look like her, I mean...It was like looking in the mirror!"

"Have you ever seen her before?" Carrie asked, suspicion flowing through her voice.

"Never. Not until last night." She finished her brownie and reached for what was left of Carrie's.

"Your grandparents ever tell you this place is haunted?"

"No, and I'm not telling them, either." Anitra thought for a moment then shook her head. "No, no, no. They might think something's wrong with me."

A sarcastic laughed popped out of Carrie. "Ya think so? You're sure making me wonder."

"Well, don't," Anitra said. She needed Carrie's support more than ever now, and she needed her to believe some incredible things. "Carrie, come upstairs with me. I wanna show you something."

"Oh, yeah, right. You, me, and the ghost can have a party. No thank you! I'll be going now!"

"Carrie, don't! Nothing's gonna happen. The ghost... well...she left." An uncertain smile invaded Anitra's face.

"Oh, she left. She left, huh? Just like that. Mm hmm. And Anitra, did she tell you when she might be coming back?

Did she leave you a schedule?"

Anitra rolled her eyes. This was going to take a lot of work.

"Well, did she?" Carrie asked.

"No, she didn't say anything. I mean, she got scared and kind of ran away."

"The ghost was scared." Carrie's eyebrows practically criss-crossed. "The *ghost* was scared?! How can the ghost get scared? *She's* the one that's dead!"

"I don't know! That's what I'm trying to figure out. See, I woke up in the middle of the night, and she was standing in the doorway of my room. When she saw me, she got scared and kind of floated to the hall, then downstairs, then back up here. Then she disappeared."

Feeling her credibility slipping further away with each word she spoke, Anitra decided to leave out the part about the attic. Carrie would never go up there if she knew. And as for the minor detail of a certain trip to the past, well, that was out of the question for now. Talking about time travel in the park yesterday was one thing. Convincing Carrie that it had really happened was completely different, almost impossible.

Carrie's eyebrows crossed even more. It looked like it really hurt. A lot.

"I bet you didn't even scream, did you?" she asked.

"I couldn't." Anitra nibbled at the corner of a brownie. "But she did."

Anitra couldn't help but laugh at the expression that took over Carrie's face. It looked like she had just seen a huge mass of leggy bugs race across the floor.

"The ghost screamed, and you didn't." Carrie thought it over, crossed her arms, and looked at the kitchen door. "Oh, but that makes sense, see, 'cause *she* was the scared one. I'da been screaming all over this house."

"Carrie, come upstairs with me. Please?"

Carrie turned back to Anitra. The bug look lingered.

"Carrie, please? Please, please, please?" Anitra looked at her friend with her best Grandma-may-I-please eyes.

Carrie let out a big sigh. "Well, the ghost isn't here, right?"

Anitra laughed. "No."

"Okay," Carrie gave in. "I don't know why I'm doing this. I should just go home right now. Don't ever try to tell me I'm not your friend! But I'm telling you, if that ghost decides to come back, I'm out! Gone!"

"Okay. Let's go."

Anitra knew Carrie's curiosity would win out; she couldn't leave something like this alone. But she didn't really believe it yet. Had she been convinced, Carrie never would have agreed to go to the attic. She was still waiting for the punch line. But there was none.

The girls climbed the two flights of stairs to the attic, and along the way, Anitra showed Carrie where she had seen Elizabeth the night before.

"Whew! Hot!" Carrie said as the heat surrounded her. "Wow, look at all this stuff."

Anitra had brought Carrie to the attic before, and she was always surprised at how much the Coles managed to pack into two rooms.

"Pretty cool, huh?" Anitra said.

"Yeah." Carrie nodded in agreement. "Pretty old, too."

"Uh huh." Anitra glanced around the room. "It's like the whole family is still here telling stories."

"Right, or haunting the place," Carrie said, rolling her eyes.

Anitra ignored the comment. She had plenty of time to explain. She pointed in the direction of the photo album that was right where she had left it.

"This is what I wanted to show you," Anitra said.

The girls sat on the floor, and Anitra pulled the album onto her lap. Flipping though the pages, she briefly recited odds and ends of the Cole family history. She stopped at the family portrait.

"Oh, my God! That's you!" Carrie's mouth dropped open as she pointed at Elizabeth.

"See what I mean? That's Elizabeth. And that's exactly what she was wearing when I saw her last night."

"Are you sure you didn't dream this? I mean you've seen these pictures over and over."

"No dream! I was walking around. You shoulda seen her, Carrie. She had this light all around her, and I could see her as clear as I can see you. Except when she moved, it looked kinda different, like she was running or walking but not really. She just glided all over the place. It was weird."

Carrie looked up from the album, and Anitra watched the truth finally sink into her friend's head.

"Anitra, you mean you really saw this ghost? I mean, you *really* saw it?"

"That's what I keep trying to tell you. Yes!" Anitra bounced up onto her knees.

Carrie put her hands on the floor behind her and leaned back. Her jaw dropped open. It made no sense to her, and to Carrie, that was totally unacceptable. She looked around nervously, probably trying to see if anything was moving around the room all by itself.

"I wonder what she wanted," Carrie finally said.

"Huh? What do you mean?"

"Well there has to be a reason why she was here. If I was a ghost, I wouldn't just come back for no reason."

"Yeah, but why come back now?"

"Well, how do you know this is the only time she's been here? You're only here for two weeks a year."

"Yeah," Anitra said. Carrie just might be right. "Yeah, maybe she's been here before."

"And your grandparents don't talk about her much, right?"

"Right!" Anitra said. Puzzle pieces started falling into place. "Maybe they see her, too! Maybe that's why they don't like to talk about it. Who'd believe it? No, wait a minute. She screamed her lungs out…uh, if ghosts have lungs…and they didn't even hear her!"

"What if they did? Maybe she drops by once a week to scream her head off. Maybe they're used to it." Carrie nodded, agreeing with herself. "You should ask them about it."

"Well maybe, but…" A thought crossed Anitra's mind and pushed her excitement aside. "Wait a minute. Wait a minute…"

"What?"

"If she's been here before, what was she so scared of? She kept looking around and touching things like she didn't know what they were. She acted like she didn't know where she was."

"Maybe she didn't."

"But Carrie, she lived in this house. All her life."

"I bet it didn't look like this when she did."

Anitra thought this over. Carrie was right. Why wouldn't Elizabeth be scared? She couldn't recognize her own home. Anitra knew the feeling; the same thing had happened to her in 1928.

"And you know what?" Anitra said. "That room I sleep in was her room. She and my Great Aunt Irene shared it. She looked in her room and saw me. Somebody that looks just like her. She sure didn't live long enough to know who I am."

"This is too weird! This can't be for real!" Carrie whispered.

"But I don't think she was here before. She might've been scared of me, but she would've seen all that other stuff before. All the changes in the house, I mean."

Carrie nodded, disappointed that they hadn't solved the case after all.

"So why would she show up now?" Anitra asked. "She died like fifty years ago."

Carrie shrugged. She had run out of things to say, and she looked confused and nervous. A little closer to believing, but she wasn't quite there yet.

"I wanna show you something." Anitra jumped up and scampered to the back of the room.

"You mean there's more?" Carrie couldn't have sounded less enthused if someone had handed her a plate of liver, but she got up and followed Anitra anyway.

"Don't worry," Anitra said as she unzipped a garment bag and pulled out the red dress.

"Oooooh! Anitra, it's beautiful!" Carrie gently touched the fabric.

"It's Elizabeth's."

Carrie snatched her hand away. "This is...*the* dress, right?" She pointed to the album.

"Mm hmm. This is what she was wearing. And, um, yesterday...I, um, tried it on."

Carrie's eyes narrowed and her mouth twisted. "Oh, wait a minute. Just wait a minute. Are you telling me that a ghost came back to tell you not to wear her dress?! All the way from the grave to protect her wardrobe?"

Anitra laughed. It was a relief to be able to laugh, even for just a second.

Carrie shook her head. "That can't really be it." She looked at the dress. "The ghost was here to get her dress back! That's a good one."

"No," Anitra said, suddenly serious. "There's...more."

"Oh, now what?" Carrie whined, sighing and stomping her foot.

"Well...yesterday I put this dress on, and...and I started dancing around for a minute, and then I...I passed out."

"Wow! But I'm not surprised. It's too hot up here for that."

Anitra nodded. "Yeah, but when I woke up, I wasn't... exactly...here."

Carrie's face went blank.

"I was...in the past. 1928." Anitra's voice shriveled to a whisper.

"No! You mean you passed out and you had a dream about the past," Carrie said. She rolled her eyes; she had reached her limit.

"No, no. I was there, Carrie. Really, *really* there!"

"Anitra, you lost me. Look, you were going through all this old stuff and trying on dresses right before you passed out. Of course it was a dream!"

"That's what I thought at first. But it was real! And why would Elizabeth show up out of the blue on the exact same day that this happens to me? Huh?"

"I don't know!" Carrie said, frowning and tossing her hands in the air. "Is this why you asked me all that stuff about time travel yesterday?"

Anitra nodded.

"Look. I can see the ghost thing. Sort of. And I can definitely see passing out and dreaming it all. But you weren't really there. That's just impossible! Now quit the joking, because you're really scaring me now." She folded her arms and looked around the room, waiting for some moldy, creepy thing to jump out of its hiding place.

Disappointment spilled all over Anitra. But she thought about how she would feel if she had heard this from Carrie, and she understood. She couldn't afford to scare Carrie away.

"That dream was so real, ya know? Like I was there. But I did see the ghost for real."

"Well, don't joke so much. This stuff's hard enough to believe in the first place."

"Sorry." She managed a weak smile.

Carrie shrugged away this latest episode of her friend's all-consuming imagination.

"Hey, help me put this on." Anitra took the hanger out of the dress.

"I don't know. *She* might get mad and come back."

Tense laughter brought a little relief. With Carrie's help, Anitra got back into the dress then put on the shoes, locket, and bow.

"That's amazing!" Carrie looked back and forth between Anitra and the family portrait. "You may as well be the same person!"

"I know," Anitra said, smiling broadly. She held the sides of the dress and demonstrated her best curtsey. "Mrs. Morgan, how are you this fine day?" she asked in a high-pitched, refined voice.

Carrie stuck her nose in the air. "Quite well, Mrs. Cole, and how are the children?"

"Oh, lovely, just lovely. My husband and I are quite pleased with their progress."

"How wonderful for you! Might you be visiting soon? We have acquired a lovely new home, and we would be ever so honored if you..."

"Oh, no!" Anitra doubled over as a sharp pain shot up

the back of her neck and attacked her head.

"Anitra! What's wrong?! Anitra!"

Anitra couldn't speak, but reached for Carrie as she once again fell to the floor.

₧—₦

Anitra awoke to the muffled sounds of voices rising from downstairs. As before, she lay on the floor in Jeff's attic room. She stood slowly, looking for the calendar. Was it April 1928 again? This time the calendar hung from a different wall, and Anitra moved closer. She read it and felt dizzy. This time, it was November 1927.

ಸಿ12ಲ

She couldn't really feel the air, but to Anitra it seemed stuffy. Heavy. It looked cloudy and desolate outside, and the room was darker than before. A deep, deep chill rampaged down her spine and made her shudder. Anitra didn't know the exact date, but she did know that sometime this month, Elizabeth would die. Was she downstairs somewhere? Or was she already dead? Anitra wanted to go downstairs, but had no idea what she would find this time.

She listened to the voices echoing in the stairwell. Lots of voices all mixed together. A party? She tip-toed down the attic stairs to the second floor. Although she knew she couldn't be seen or heard, she moved carefully. She didn't want to bump into Jeff this time.

The office had reverted back to its twenties style, and the sight momentarily trapped her. Above the party noise from the first floor, scraps of soft conversation slipped in from Irene and Elizabeth's bedroom and compelled Anitra's legs to finally move. One voice sounded like Jeff's, the other was an unfamiliar girl's voice. Elizabeth? Yes! It had to be! Anitra crept into the hall and leaned against the wall outside the room. Like the last time, she couldn't feel it.

"I can't help it," the girl said through sobs. "I miss Lizzie already!"

"I know. I do, too," Jeff said in a comforting tone so familiar to Anitra. Even so, she heard the quaver in his voice.

Anitra felt an overwhelming wave of sadness wash over her, and she wrapped her shaky arms around herself. They missed Elizabeth. She was already dead.

So who was he talking to? Anitra knew better, but she needed to look. She'd be careful; she wouldn't let him see her. Keeping her right shoulder against the wall, she rolled toward the doorway.

With one eye, she peeked into the bedroom, and right away she recognized the little cinnamon brown face of the girl sitting in front of Jeff. Her deep brown eyes seemed bigger, maybe because of the tears they sent rolling down smooth, not-yet-wrinkled cheeks that were a bit cheekier now than they would be in a few decades. Some of the tears traced the sides of the familiar round-button nose and came to rest at the edges of her trembling bottom lip.

Twelve-year-old Charlotte Thomas sat on Elizabeth's bed with a large rag doll locked in her arms. Jeff knelt in front of her and tried desperately to comfort her at a time when someone should have been doing the same for him.

"It shouldn't have happened, it wasn't supposed to happen..." Charlotte said as she compulsively rocked the doll back and forth.

Jeff sat on the floor and stared at it. "I could have..."

"No, you couldn't," Charlotte said, shaking her head and talking more to the doll than to Jeff.

Anitra sighed and wiped a tear from the corner of her eye.

Jeff and Charlotte suddenly turned and looked directly at her with weary, shocked eyes.

"Lizzie!" Jeff whispered loudly.

Charlotte just sat and stared. She didn't even blink.

It happened again! And this time Charlotte saw her, too! Anitra had stepped too far, had leaned in closer to hear them better. For a moment, she couldn't move. She said nothing, but took two quick glances behind her and backed away slowly. Without thinking about where she was going, she rushed downstairs. She just had to get away from them.

Anitra crouched near the bottom of the stairs and looked around at the large crowd of people in the living room. It looked like the whole town was there; Anitra had never seen the house so full. Lillian, Naomi, and Irene sat quietly on the sofa. Vague, lost expressions masked the softness of their faces. Papa Russell, looking tired and dazed, solemnly shook hands with a man offering condolences. Nearby, Anitra recognized his brother Marcus, who was quietly discussing the upcoming funeral.

Two people walked within two feet of her on their way to the front door. They had no clue that she was there, and when she stood, no one looked in her direction. No one. Relieved, Anitra wove slowly through the crowd, catching bits of those depressing things people always said. So sorry, such a tragedy, hard to understand, hard to believe, such a young child... She wondered why, in the next fifty years, no one would come up with anything better.

At the dining room table, Adam held Jordan in his lap and stared at some empty point in space. Jordan, his eyes and nose red, rested his head on Adam's chest. The two sat motionless, oblivious to everything around them.

On the other side of the table, a woman collected soiled plates and bowls of food. The dishes rattled in her hands.

She looked familiar. Anitra followed her to the kitchen, where Mama Sarah unmercifully scoured the stovetop.

"Sarah," the woman said softly as she placed the dishes on the table. "Sarah, dear, please go rest. I can handle this."

Mama Sarah ignored her. The jabot hanging from her collar bounced desperately, and its tip dragged on the stove as she scrubbed.

"Please, Sarah, you need to rest."

"Thank you, Lydia, but I'm fine," Mama Sarah said, her voice clear and steady.

Lydia Cole! Papa Russell's sister. She certainly had that same Cole look, though she was a little taller than most of the women in the family. Anitra remembered the sad stories about Aunt Lydia's emotional problems. But she seemed okay at the moment, not "fragile" like they'd always said she'd been.

Aunt Lydia put her hand on Mama Sarah's, halting the compulsive cleaning. "You need to rest, dear. I'll take care of this." She gently coaxed the cloth out of her sister-in-law's tortured grip.

"Thank you," Mama Sarah whispered. Her face filled with exhaustion. Patting Lydia's shoulder, she managed a slight smile, then slowly, reluctantly, left the room.

Aunt Lydia tossed the cloth into the sink, leaned on the table, and sighed. Then her back stiffened, and for a while, she didn't move. Slowly she turned and looked across the kitchen, just over Anitra's head, as if expecting some unwanted person to walk through the doorway. No one did. But she darted her eyes around the room the way people did when trying to find a fly that kept buzzing past their ears. Still finding nothing, she stared at the floor and shook her head.

"Stop it, stop it," Aunt Lydia whispered to herself. Confused and drained, she pressed her trembling hand to her forehead and braced herself as her tears fell freely. Bending forward at the waist, she gave in to deep sobs.

Anitra tried her best to keep from crying. She had always wanted to see for herself all the people and places in her grandparents' stories, but not like this. Not when they were all so hurt. But there she was, right smack in the middle of the saddest time in the family's life, and she couldn't do a thing for them. She hated this!

Unsure of where to go or what to do with herself, Anitra went back to the dining room and looked for the chair that had been positioned against the wall last time. She found it at the table and sat down. Adam and Jordan still sat as if posing for a mournful portrait, and Adam seemed to be memorizing the lace pattern on the tablecloth. Anitra sat with her arms folded and felt the sadness seep through the walls and cloud the room. She felt like an intruder.

"Papa, I'm going to walk Charlotte home now."

Jeff! He and Charlotte had come downstairs! Afraid of being seen again, Anitra wanted to run, but she was more afraid to move. She tried to sneak a quick peeked at them but could only stare intently at a bread crumb on the table. Maybe if she didn't look at them, didn't budge, didn't breathe, didn't blink, they wouldn't notice her.

"Walk her home," Papa Russell said, "but I want you to come right...Jefferson, are you listening to me?"

Anitra ever so slightly turned her head and looked. No, Jeff was not listening to his father. He was staring at her. He looked right at her, right into her eyes with his jaw hanging down to his chest. Charlotte stared, too. She looked like she hadn't blinked in a long, long time.

"Jeff!" Papa Russell demanded. He had looked in Anitra's direction and had seen nothing. So had the rest of the family.

Jeff turned back to his father. "I'm sorry, Papa. I just, it's..." He looked at his sisters' worried stares, at his brothers' questioning faces, at his mother's quiet shiver. "I'll come right back."

On the verge of melting into a helpless puddle, Charlotte continued to stare. Jeff finally managed to get her attention, and they walked stiffly toward the front door. They hastily fumbled with their coats and shot outside.

Anitra decided to follow them. At a distance. At least outside she'd have plenty of room to stay out of their way. Besides, she wanted to get away from the sadness, to get some air, even if she couldn't feel or smell it. When the next guest left, Anitra ran out while the door was still open. She hoped that someone would be near the door when she came back; she still couldn't touch anything.

Despite the sprinkling of snow and small patches of ice on the ground, Anitra felt comfortable without a coat. She kept a safe distance from her grandparents by darting between trees and fences like people did on television. All the while, she couldn't help but notice the way Fisher Street had changed. Lively, sky-blue letters spelled out "Cole Furniture" on the black truck parked outside of the Cole house. Other boxy contraptions that Anitra couldn't name replaced Mr. Arrington's pickup truck and other neighbors' colorful, gas-guzzling cars.

The pool and fence in the Gordons' yard were gone, and a large, uninterrupted lawn covered the area. She wondered who lived in the house now. There were fewer houses on Fisher Street, and these had big side porches, huge windows, and lawns for days. All of the smaller, modern houses wouldn't be built for years. Large, thick trees stood in their places. The sky was silent; no occasional jet rumbled overhead. It fascinated her, and for a moment, Anitra almost forgot to keep up with Jeff and Charlotte.

She found them on the porch of the Thomas house down the street. Anitra hid behind a tree in the yard to watch them, and she wondered if this was the one that her grandmother had talked about. This had to be the tree that Charlotte and Elizabeth had played around for hours as small children. It had been their tree, the imaginary border between Charlotte's country and Elizabeth's. Naturally, they had crowned each other queens of their respective countries and had strict rules about foreign, untrustworthy invaders like Jeff.

Anitra stared in awe at the brownish house she had only seen in faded, black and white pictures. It was smaller than the Cole house, and compared to the other houses on the street, there was nothing remarkable about it. But Anitra loved it. So many times she had imagined the house, the family that lived inside, and their future son-in-law pacing the porch with a bunch of fresh flowers in one hand.

But now here they were, Jeff and Charlotte, trying so hard to be strong for each other. She couldn't hear what they said to each other, but once more, suddenly, they were gawking at her. Not again! She had been deep in thought, and while still leaning against the tree, she had moved from behind it. Even from this distance, she could see pain all over their faces.

Jeff turned to Charlotte and rushed her into her house. She gestured for him to come in, too, but he refused. By the time he turned around, Anitra had slipped back behind the tree. Jeff quickly jumped off the porch and ran down Fisher Street at top speed. Anitra waited a few minutes, then followed.

๛

Anitra sat on her family's back porch waiting for someone to open the door. It was a long wait. She sat and sat and worried about Jeff. He already had something terrible to deal with, and now his granddaughter was appearing to him in random places. Only to him, she was his sister's ghost. She haunted him.

It was almost completely dark now. Just as she had begun to worry about sitting on the porch all night, the door opened. Adam came out, walked past her, and headed down the stairs with his hands shoved deeply into his pockets. Slowly, he paced the edge of the barren, snow-powdered garden. Staring absently into the neighbor's yard, he kicked a stone across the lawn as his white shirt sleeves flapped freely in the wind. He should have been freezing, but he didn't seem to notice.

"What happened to you, Lizzie?" he asked the sky. "What happened to you? What were you *doing* there?" The last two words stumbled and broke as his weary gaze fell to his shoes. He removed his glasses to wipe away a tear that had dripped onto one lens.

Anitra's slouched back straightened. What happened? *What happened?* What was Elizabeth doing where? Anitra had never heard any questions about Elizabeth's death. It was just something that no one said much about. Elizabeth had died, they loved her, they missed her. That was all.

After moments of silence, Adam gathered himself and returned to the house. Anitra jumped up, ran in on his heels, and hoped that Jeff wasn't in the kitchen. She followed Adam to the dining room and stopped in the doorway. Adam continued to the living room where the family, including Jeff, sat huddled together, quietly listening to the radio.

While Jeff's back was turned, Anitra ran through the room and dashed upstairs where a single desk lamp lit the attic. She looked for the green upholstered chair she had sat in before, in April 1928, but it wasn't there. Then she remembered seeing it in Elizabeth's room earlier while watching Jeff and Charlotte; it must have been moved sometime between now and next April. She sat in the desk chair and looked around. More than ready to go back to her own time, she once more looked for clues to the way back, and once again, she found none. She could only hope that it would happen on its own. Soon.

When she heard footsteps on the stairs, Anitra knew she couldn't hide. So she sat still as Adam, carrying a sleeping Jordan in his arms, reached the top of the stairs and turned to the other room. Jeff was right behind his brothers. Anitra stood, ready to speak to him. If she couldn't hide, she would have to face him. Tell him who she was.

But he didn't see her! He walked right past her and sat on his bed, staring at something in his hands. Then he got up and put the thing on his desk. He was close enough to touch her. Why couldn't he see her now?

He began to undress for bed, and she respectfully turned away. Facing the desk, she discovered what he had put there. A picture of Elizabeth standing in the sunny back yard. She wore a pretty dress that Anitra imagined as blue and held a bunch of flowers that had surely been plucked from her mother's garden. A picture of a better time. Anitra smiled.

"You okay, Buddy?" Adam called from the other side of the attic.

"Yeah," Jeff answered.

"Why don't we go to New York or something tomorrow? Get out of this house for a while." Adam sounded drained.

"I guess that's a good idea." Jeff's voice wavered.

"Get some sleep, Buddy."

Jeff came back to the desk and turned out the light. The soft stream of light flowed in through the window and fell across the room just as it had before.

෨෬

Anitra sat quietly and waited to be whisked back to the present. But nothing happened, and soon Adam's snoring flooded the attic. She sat in the desk chair with her heels on the seat, her arms wrapped around her legs, and her head resting on her knees.

To chase the fear away, she closed her eyes and thought of the happy stories her grandparents had shared with her: the young man who tried to date Irene but couldn't pass Papa Russell's inspection, the way the family pulled together and survived the Depression, the singer Naomi accompanied who couldn't carry a tune in a shopping bag, the weddings, the babies, the family gatherings. If only she could share all this with Jeff, help him see past his grief, make him smile.

When she was sure that Jeff had fallen asleep, she finally dared to move. She reached for the picture of Elizabeth and picked it up. It seemed that she could touch anything that was Elizabeth's.

Wait a minute! The tree! She didn't notice at the time, but now she remembered feeling the rough, scaly bark of that tree in Charlotte's yard. All the other trees and fences along Fisher Street that she had hidden behind were like everything else. She couldn't feel them. But that tree had been a special place for Elizabeth and Charlotte to play.

And the dining room chair! She remembered the feel of its smooth, polished wood before Jeff and Charlotte saw her.

It must have been the chair Elizabeth sat in during family meals, and they must have placed it against the wall after she died. Anitra tried to remember whether she had felt the chair during her first visit, but she had been so engrossed in the family's conversation that she couldn't be sure. So now Anitra could touch this picture. Elizabeth's picture.

Anitra strained to look more closely at it in the dim light and thought about the grieving family. She began to cry. The sadness of the day weighed her down and left her tired and restless.

"Don't cry, Lizzie." It was Jeff.

Anitra almost jumped out of the chair. She spun around and gasped as Jeff sat up in bed and looked at her. Too shocked to answer, she could only stare back and feel warm tears stain her face. Her grip on the picture tightened.

"Lizzie? Please talk to me," Jeff whispered. "Are you trying to tell me something? Do you need me to help you?"

Anitra wanted to tell him who she was and how she had gotten there, or how she thought she had gotten there. She wanted to tell him that she wasn't Elizabeth and that he didn't have to worry. She needed him to know that things would get better and that the family would be okay again, that he would marry and have children and grandchildren, that he would be happy. But she couldn't. She couldn't get her mouth to work, and even if she could tell him all of this, he would never understand.

"Lizzie, please talk to me," he repeated. "Are you, um... lonely?"

Anitra blinked several times and forced her jaw to open. "No. I'm not lonely at all," she whispered as soon as her nerves would allow.

Her eyes had long since adjusted to the darkness, and she noticed that he almost looked relieved.

"Why are you here, now?"

"I...I don't know..." That was the truth.

"Um...Lizzie, can you forgive me?" he blurted out.

"What?" His words almost shoved her to the floor. Forgive him for what? What had he done?

He said nothing. He waited.

"Forgive you?" she asked, confused.

"Can you forgive me?" he repeated. "Please?" His usual calm fell apart.

Seized by confusion, she could think of nothing to say before she felt another sharp pain attack her neck. The last thing she remembered was Jeff yelling, "Lizzie? Lizzie?"

ം13ൽ

"Anitra? Anitra?"

Anitra slowly opened her eyes and found herself tightly curled on the floor. A faint, hot breeze rushed across her face as Carrie vigorously fanned her with a feeble piece of cardboard. Anitra looked around the room, waiting for the cobwebs in her head to break apart. She looked up at Carrie's worried face.

"Thank God!" Carrie said. She stopped fanning and sighed. "You okay?"

"How long was I gone?" Anitra asked, her words slurring.

"Gone? Well, you were passed out on the floor for a minute."

"Passed out? I was here? The whole time?" Anitra propped herself up on her elbows. A battering ram pounded incessantly on the inside of her skull, but she was suddenly wide awake and fully alert.

"Yes, Anitra, you were here! Were you expecting to be somewhere else?" Carrie looked ready to call the mental hospital people.

Anitra closed her eyes and covered her face with her hands. "I was."

Carrie's eyes narrowed. "Huh? What do ya mean? What happened to you?"

"Tell me. What did you see happen to me?"

Carrie studied her friend, still searching for that missing punch line. A small rain cloud of a frown spread across her face.

"We were talking," Carrie said, "and you all the sudden bent over like you were really hurt. You grabbed the back of your neck and your eyes rolled all the way to the back of your head! You looked like you were dying or something!"

So that was what it looked like.

Carrie's flailing hands propelled her to continue. "Then you started to fall and I caught you and helped you to the floor. I got scared when you wouldn't wake up, and I was gonna go downstairs and call for help. But then you started moving, so I fanned you. You were *out cold*! Now you tell me what's going on!" Carrie sat on the floor, winded.

"It happened again! Carrie, it happened again!" Anitra's memory came into focus. "I put this dress on, and it happened again! And Jeff, he was trying to tell me something, and he thought I was..."

She stopped speaking, suddenly realizing that she was holding something. She sat straight up and opened her hand.

"Oh, Carrie!"

It was Elizabeth's picture.

Carrie's eyes darted back and forth between Anitra and the picture. There had been nothing in Anitra's hands when she fainted. And this picture was newer than the ones in the photo album; there were no creases or tired edges. And Anitra was sure she had never seen this one in any of the albums before.

As soon as she got used to the hot, stale air again, Anitra stood and looked at her paralyzed friend.

"Carrie, help me change out of these clothes," she said with an uncontrollably shaky voice, "then I'll tell you exactly what's going on."

œ)∞Œ

The girls sat cross-legged facing each other on the wicker sofa on the side porch as Anitra recounted the events of the last two days, sparing no details. She talked about the photo album, the dress, the first trip back in time, the family, and the way the house looked. She told Carrie about the book on Irene's shelf and the bookmark that fell out of the dress when she woke up and changed her clothes. She told her about the cold breeze in the woods, the dream, and the ghost of Elizabeth Cole. Then she talked about this last trip: the sadness, the fear, the confusion when Jeff and Charlotte thought she was Elizabeth. Then she stopped talking. Her story was done.

Carrie had listened silently, moving only to keep the vinyl cushions from sticking to her legs. When Anitra finished, Carrie looked at Anitra, then outside beyond the porch screens. The hot, thick air remained motionless as if it, too, waited in helpless suspense for Carrie to speak. A card in bicycle spokes created the only stir as two little boys coasted down Fisher Street.

"I'm not kidding anymore," Anitra said. She couldn't stand the silence any longer. "This is really happening to me, and I don't know what to do about it."

Carrie said nothing.

"Carrie, you gotta help me!" She grabbed Carrie's arm.

"It's too weird," Carrie finally said. "If it wasn't for that picture, I wouldn't believe any of this. There's got to be some explanation besides this. There has to be!"

Anitra let Carrie's arm go and shook her head. There wasn't any.

"Anitra, I just don't know about this! It's scary. I think you should tell your grandparents."

"No! I can't! They never talk about this. They tell all these stories about every single part of their lives. *Except this!* They never, never talk about it." Anitra pounded her fists on her knees. "If I bring it up to them, it'll upset them. I just can't do that."

"C'mon why not? It can't be that bad," Carrie said. "Can it?"

Anitra looked out beyond the porch screens at Fisher Street. "Maybe something happened that they don't want me to know about, you know? I mean, Adam acted like he didn't know what happened to her, and Jeff *begged* me to forgive him." She shook her head. "I can't tell them."

"But what can *I* do to help you?" Carrie asked. "I don't know anything about all this. Your grandparents are the ones who know what happened."

Anitra stared at the floral pattern on the sofa cushions, then looked up. "That's what I'm afraid of."

Carrie frowned. "What do ya mean?"

"Jeff asked me, I mean, he asked Elizabeth, to forgive him. Like he did something he felt all guilty about. Grandma, I mean Charlotte, kept saying that it shouldn't have happened or it wasn't supposed to happen, something like that. It sounded like they did something wrong. Carrie, it was...it scared me. Especially at the end. I mean, Jeff was *begging* me to forgive him!"

Carrie studied her fingernails. "Ya think they...you know..."

"What?" Anitra shut her eyes.

"...um, killed her?" Carrie whispered.

"No!"

Carrie jumped.

"Carrie, how can you say that?!"

"I...I just...well, 'cause of how you said they were acting..."

"You can't say that!"

"Well, *you* did!" Carrie put her hands on her hips.

"No, I didn't!"

"Uh huh! You're the one saying Jeff thought you were Elizabeth and wanted you to forgive him. You said there was something they didn't want you to know, like they did something wrong."

"Yeah, but...but no, not that!"

"It had to be something really bad for him to beg like that."

"They didn't kill her, Carrie!" Anitra shouted. Sometimes Carrie made her so mad!

"I thought you wanted me to help you!"

"I do! But that doesn't mean you can go around accusing them!"

"Well, what am I s'posed to do?" Carrie's whole face frowned.

"I don't know!" Anitra jumped up and paced in front of the wicker sofa. "Just not that."

"But what if it's true?"

"No!"

Carrie popped off the sofa and paced behind Anitra. "C'mon, what else would they have to feel all guilty about?"

Anitra stomped her foot with enough force to make the screens shake. "Shut up, Carrie! Just shut up! You don't know what you're talking about!"

Carrie stepped back with her mouth slightly open. Anitra crossed her arms and felt red seep into her face.

Carrie looked like she might cry. "I told you I didn't know what to do!" she shouted. "I told you to talk to them, but, no! You didn't wanna do that. Now you're all mad at *me* 'cause I'm telling you something you don't wanna hear. That's not fair!" She pointed at Anitra. "And you know I just might be right! You know it!"

Anitra clenched her jaw so tight, she thought her teeth might break.

"I'm going home!" Carrie said, as she marched to her bicycle.

"Good!" Anitra shouted.

"Good riddance!" Carrie fired back.

Anitra walked over to the window and looked into the living room at Grandpa Jeff's favorite chair with the little burn mark from his pipe. Then she peeled away from the window and flopped onto the sofa. Picking at a tiny hole in a vinyl cushion, she let go the tears she'd been holding back. Suspicion broke her heart.

ഇറബ്

A couple of hours dragged by, and Anitra might have dozed off for a minute or two. But now she sat alone on the sofa. She wanted to pound her head against the wall for yelling at her best friend in the whole world. Carrie had just wanted to help, like Anitra had asked.

Anitra put her head in her hands and tried to think up the best apology ever before going to Carrie's house to fix their friendship.

"Hi." It was Carrie!

Anitra got up. Surprised. Relieved. "Hi."

They looked at each other.

"Carrie, I'm really, really sorry!"

"Me, too!"

"I didn't mean…"

"Me neither…"

Apologies tripped over each other and eased the girls into a hug. They sat quietly for a moment, letting their friendship settle back into place.

Carrie traced the sofa cushion's floral pattern with her fingers. "So, um, you decide what to do? I still wanna help you, ya know."

"I know," Anitra whispered, smiling. She thought Carrie's question over and had to think twice about what came to mind.

"Well?" Carrie said.

Still silent, Anitra looked at Carrie.

"Uh oh, what's going on up there?" Carrie asked, pointing at Anitra's head.

"Carrie?"

"Yeah?"

"Would you stay here with me tonight? Sleep over?"

"Huh? *Are you crazy?* You keep jumping back and forth in time, and you got ghosts! And you want me to stay here? Yeah, right!"

"*A* ghost. Just one. A little one. C'mon, Carrie, please! I don't wanna stay alone."

Carrie sighed. "Can't blame ya. Why don't you come stay at my house tonight? We don't have any ghosts. Least not unless you bring yours!"

She smiled a little at Anitra, who forced a slight smile of her own.

"I can't," Anitra said.

"Why not?"

"Because I think it's time to hear some more stories. Maybe they'll tell me something that'll help. And if you stay, you can hear them, too. With you here, I can ask them to repeat some I've heard before 'cause you've never heard them. Maybe I'll hear something I didn't pay attention to before."

"You sure do ask a lot of somebody."

"Only my very best friend!" Anitra smiled her most persuasive smile. "C'mon, Carrie, spend the night. I mean, I really wanna know why all this is happening. I need to know. But I'm scared, and I really don't wanna stay in that room by myself. Would you ask if you can sleep over?"

Carrie raised an eyebrow.

"Please?" Anitra asked. "My grandmother won't mind if you sleep over."

"Carrie, you're welcome to stay for dinner, too, dear." Grandma Charlotte stood on the porch with a large shopping bag in her hand.

Anitra jumped up and gave her grandmother an anxious hug.

"Well, what brought this on?" Grandma Charlotte asked, laughing.

"Just glad to see you, Grandma," Anitra said, remembering the teary-eyed, twelve-year-old girl from the past.

"Thanks, Mrs. Cole," Carrie said, smiling at Grandma Charlotte, then secretly glaring at Anitra.

"Well, you just let me know, and I'll set a place for you." Grandma Charlotte went inside.

Anitra turned to Carrie. "Well?"

"Tell ya what. I'll stay for dinner, and maybe we can watch some TV or something. But then I go home."

Anitra threw Carrie a pouty, disappointed look.

"Oh, no. Don't try that on me! I'm sorry, Anitra, but I can't stay. Too many weird things going on. Like I said, I'll help you and all, but I can't stay here. I mean, look at me," she said, holding out a shaky hand, "I'm a wreck!"

Carrie meant what she said, but Anitra knew she was curious. Just too afraid to stay. She had seen the old picture appear in Anitra's hand in perfect condition. Carrie was hooked.

"I'm sorry," Carrie said in response to Anitra's silence.

"It's okay. I understand."

"I'll be here for dinner, but first sign of a ghost, and I'm gone!" Carrie tried to make Anitra smile.

"Deal," Anitra said, halfway smiling.

"Hey, come swimming with me," Carrie said as she walked to her bike and lifted the kickstand.

"Okay," Anitra said. She needed to cool off; the heat wave made this mess worse. "I'll meet you at your house."

As she went upstairs and changed her clothes, Anitra felt sick. She loved her grandparents dearly, but now she was suspicious, and the stories she loved so much had become just a way to find out something they didn't want her to know. What could these two wonderful people possibly have done almost fifty years ago to cause Elizabeth's death? Whatever it was, they couldn't have done it intentionally. She hoped.

❧ 14 ❧

"That was great!" Carrie said as she finished a piece of Grandma Charlotte's doubly chocolate cake.

Over dinner, the girls filled the Coles in on the drama at the pool, but the whole time, Anitra was trying to think up a way to make answers miraculously tumble out of their mouths.

"Did you swim a lot when you were kids?" Carrie asked.

Anitra glared at Carrie; she had planned a more subtle approach.

"Well, not very much," Grandma Charlotte said. "There was no pool at Grant Park at the time, and even if there had been one, we wouldn't have been able to use it."

"Why not?" Carrie asked.

Grandpa Jeff explained. "Colored people were not allowed to go certain places and do certain things."

No one in the family had succeeded in getting either him or Grandma Charlotte to say "black."

"I thought that was just in the South," Carrie said.

"Oh no, dear," Grandma Charlotte said. "Don't let anybody tell you that. There might have been more of it in the South..."

Grandpa Jeff completed her thought. "...but there was plenty of it right here in Louiston!"

The two always got on a roll and started finishing each other's sentences. The familiar spectacle comforted Anitra and helped her to at least act happy.

"Then what did you do in the summer?" Carrie asked.

"Oh, we could swim," Grandpa Jeff said, "but we had to go to certain beaches. We couldn't go to just any beach we wanted."

Anitra grinned. "Yeah, and they wore these cool bathing suits that covered up *everything*! They looked like they were dressed for work!"

Everyone laughed.

"Well, not quite everything," Grandma Charlotte said, "but there was none of those teeny tiny string bikinis back then."

"And no skinny dipping," Anitra informed Carrie.

The girls giggled.

"Absolutely not!" Grandma Charlotte said, frowning.

"Oh, now you've done it, Peanut," Grandpa Jeff said, tugging Anitra's hair. "You got her going!"

"Now, Jeff, you know how I feel about these things. All those young girls parading around with their backsides on display for all the world to see!"

Grandma Charlotte waved her hand in the air to make absolutely sure they understood her point. Then she placed both hands on the table and leaned forward. "And where are their mothers?"

Anitra mouthed the words "and where are their mothers" as her grandmother spoke them, and the girls laughed.

"And they didn't go streaking, either!" Anitra said.

Grandma Charlotte scowled at her granddaughter. "You may think this is funny, missy, but I'd better not hear of you getting involved in any of those things!"

"Yes, ma'am," Anitra said. Funny how Grandma Charlotte had a way of making her feel guilty when she hadn't done a thing.

Grandpa Jeff laughed. "Oh now, Charlotte, you know the child has more sense than that."

"So, what else did you do in the summer back then?" Carrie was engrossed. "I mean, no pool, no television, what was there to do?"

Anitra knew that Grandpa Jeff was anxious to explain that, contrary to popular belief, they did not go out and play with dinosaurs. This one would take a while. The girls would just have to sit back and watch her grandparents volley the story back and forth, because the answers they wanted were a long way off.

"Well, you know, dear," Grandpa Jeff began, "we did have a lot of things to do. We didn't just sit hypnotized in front of a television set watching people shoot everything and everybody that moves." He hammered the table with his index finger.

"That's right," Grandma Charlotte said. "We played outside and pretended just like you children do, but we had to use our imaginations more."

"These days, you kids have toys for everything. Plastic this and plastic that…"

"…and dolls that do everything but cook your dinner and wash your clothes!"

"Our toys were simple. A toy boat was a toy boat. A doll was a doll…"

"…and we made up whatever stories we wanted for them.

Now that was a healthy way for a child to play." Grandma Charlotte nodded resolutely.

"So, what games did you play?" Absorbed in the stories, Carrie wanted to know more.

"Well, Carrie," Grandma Charlotte said with pride, "Dr. Cole was quite a baseball player in his day. He played third base!"

"First base, dear," Grandpa Jeff said, correcting his wife, "first base."

"Oh, whatever it was, he was quite a ball player."

Grandpa Jeff blushed a little. "My friends and I put a team together and called ourselves the Louiston Monarchs, after the Kansas City Monarchs."

"Who? I've never heard of that team," Carrie said.

"That's because they were a Negro League team. Has anybody ever told you about the Negro Leagues, Carrie?"

Carrie shook her head; it didn't register at all.

Anitra sighed. She loved this story, but tonight she could barely stand to hear it.

"Remember when I said colored people weren't allowed to do certain things? Well, we couldn't play on the professional sports teams, including baseball. So we formed our own. Had teams like the Monarchs, and the Chicago American Giants..."

Grandma Charlotte joined in. "...and the Baltimore Black Sox. And my favorite team name was the Birmingham Black Barons!" She laughed.

Carrie laughed and nudged Anitra, who made herself smile.

"And those players," Grandma Charlotte continued, "well, they had some names a person had to live up to."

Grandpa Jeff laughed. "Mm hmm. Like Cool Papa Bell, Bullet Joe Rogan...and...and...Satchel Paige." Staring into the air, he said that last name with great reverence.

Grandma Charlotte patted his hand and fanned his face. "Come back to us, Jeff," she said. "Come on back, now."

Anitra clung to their smiles and laughter. It was hard to believe that only hours ago, she had sat in this very dining room and helplessly watched panic distort their childhood faces.

"I'm here, Charlotte," Grandpa Jeff chuckled. "Oh, they were something to watch. I remember Papa taking my brothers and me to New York to see them play. I had to be about fifteen or so at the time. Best baseball I'd ever seen. For the longest time I wanted to be just like them, even long before I ever went to one of their games. So I practiced and practiced. And so did all my friends."

Anitra thought about Jeff playing baseball with his friends during her first trip to the past. Then she remembered the pain that had spread across his face at the dinner table. Anitra looked at him now and searched for the boy who had begged to be forgiven. She begged herself to believe that Elizabeth had died some kind of explainable, understandable death that had had nothing to do with him. Turning away from the group at the table, she blinked at a tear.

"Are you okay, Peanut?" Grandpa Jeff asked.

"Um, yeah," she said. "Eyelash in my eye. Got it." She wiped away the imaginary eyelash.

"So, Dr. Cole, were you a really good player?" Carrie asked.

He nodded. "Well, Carrie, I'd say I was pretty good."

"Oh, he was better than that!" Grandma Charlotte said with tremendous pride. "The whole family would come and watch him play sometimes."

"You had a big family, Dr. Cole?" Carrie asked.

"Yes, indeed," Grandpa Jeff answered. "There were

seven children in my family. Three boys and four girls. All growing up right here in this house."

"Wow. It must've been crowded," Carrie said.

Suddenly Anitra interrupted. "Oh, hey, it's getting late. The Tony Orlando and Dawn show will be on soon." Despite Carrie's confused look, Anitra needed to stop the conversation. This was wrong, and as much as she wanted to know more, she suddenly needed to protect her grandparents.

"All right, dear," Grandma Charlotte said, looking a little confused herself. Anitra had never stopped them in the middle of a story before.

"We'll clear the table, Grandma."

"Why thank you, ladies! Leave the dishes in the sink. We'll get to them later," Grandma Charlotte said.

"Oh, that's okay. We'll do it."

Grandma Charlotte looked both pleased and surprised as she and Grandpa Jeff went to the living room. She didn't know that guilt had forced Anitra to volunteer.

The girls finished clearing the table and stacked the dishes by the kitchen sink.

"What'd ya do that for?!" Carrie whispered. "We were close!"

"Maybe, maybe not. 'Sides, I can't do that to them. It's sneaky. It's just not right."

"Yeah, I guess," Carrie agreed after some thought.

What Anitra didn't say was that deep down, she was very much afraid that they might confirm something she truly didn't want to know.

"We need to go look through the stuff in the attic," Anitra whispered, squeezing too much yellow dish washing liquid under the running water.

"The attic?" Carrie asked. She looked at Anitra as if a big, giant zit had suddenly materialized right between her eyes. "You sure we need to go up there? Are you really, really sure?"

"Yeah."

"Uh, um, why?"

"Don't worry, we can go in the morning. It won't be so hot then."

"It's not the heat I'm worried about!" Carrie lowered the dishes into the sink.

"There's gotta be something in all those boxes that'll tell us something."

"Like what?"

"Well, there's all kinds of stuff. Toys, books, clothes..." Anitra formed fluffy little animal shapes in the soap suds.

"That's not gonna tell you anything."

"Yeah, but there's other stuff, too. Like pictures. And scrapbooks with things people in the family wrote and even newspaper articles. Stuff like that."

"Think there'll be some articles about what happened to her?"

"Well, they've got everything else up there. Everything about everybody."

"You think they keep stuff about people dying up there? No wonder you got a ghost!"

Anitra laughed. "Hey, I can show you the picture of my great-grandfather in his coffin." She held her sudsy hands up like claws.

"Eeewww!" Carrie hit Anitra with a dish towel. "No thanks!"

Anitra hadn't really thought about it before, having seen that picture among others so many times. "It is kinda gross, huh. Look, I just want to see if they have some articles or something up there."

"Then why don't you just go to the library? It's gotta be a lot easier than digging through that old attic."

"How will that help?"

"There's a ton of newspaper articles up in the attic about people in your family, right?"

"Yeah."

"I bet lots of 'em are from the *Louiston Times*. I bet that paper goes all the way back to the twenties and even before."

"You think the library has them?"

"Yeah!" Carrie stopped to think for a minute. "They have the *New York Times* on microfilm. I had to use it for school last year. I know they have the *Louiston Times*, too."

Anitra looked at Carrie, startled but hopeful. "And maybe there'll be something about Elizabeth."

"Yup."

"Well, we still have to go to the attic in the morning. It won't be so hot, and Grandma will be out. We can go to the library after that."

"You still wanna get up in that attic, huh?" Carrie frowned and almost rubbed the finish off the bowl she was drying. "Well, okay, but let's be real quick about it."

Anitra smiled and nodded. "Then we'll go straight to the library."

"Yeah...oh, no!" Carrie rolled her eyes. "I gotta watch my neighbors' kids part of tomorrow. So, let's see. I'll go up to that attic with you, then you can wait for me, and we can go to the library."

"No! I can't wait. I wanna just go."

"Okay, okay! Take it easy. I'll meet you there. You know the way to go to avoid that big hill?"

Anitra rinsed the last plate. "Nope."

"I'll give you directions when we finish the dishes. But you just remember the rule about the attic. Any ghosts, and

I'm gone."

"Okay! No problem," Anitra said as she and Carrie put the dishes away.

୫୦୯୫

Anitra awoke curled up on the living room sofa. It wasn't any cooler than it had been all day; the air remained hot and dead. One lamp tossed dim light around the room, and a dull gray test pattern filled the television screen. She could barely hear the high-pitched whine that accompanied it.

Her watch said 2:24. Anitra had asked her grandparents to allow her to stay up and watch a late movie, and they had agreed. She'd had no interest in the movie, of course, but was simply afraid to go to her room and try to sleep with that sharp, ghostly scream still echoing in her head.

Like Tuesday, Wednesday had lasted way too long. Having lived so many extra hours in the past, she felt unbearably tired. She had been determined to stay awake with the television and lights on, but she'd fallen asleep some time during the news.

Anitra wondered what was on at 2:24 in the morning. She looked toward the end table to find the remote, but something else caught her attention and forced a quick, painful gasp. A figure standing not more than two feet away, surrounded by soft, glowing light.

Elizabeth.

ॐ15ॐ

The heavy air Anitra suddenly sucked in burned her lungs, and she felt almost faint from popping straight up on the sofa. Her limp hand dropped the remote control, and it tumbled to the floor, clicking off the television with a light *ping*. Slowly she eased herself to the farthest corner of the sofa, drawing her knees to her chest. Not once did she dare to take her eyes off the ghost standing almost close enough to touch.

Those suffocating ghost eyes, now too familiar, trapped Anitra and made her feel so crushed into the sofa, she thought she'd become a part of the cushions. Unlike last night, Elizabeth stood close enough for her surrounding glow to make the wispy little hairs on Anitra's arms stand on end. What was she doing here? Again. Now.

"Who are you?" Elizabeth said, her eyes raking Anitra's face.

Anitra swallowed the chalky dryness in her mouth.

"Who are you?!" Elizabeth insisted, those eyes now clawing.

Anitra scrounged frantically for her voice, and a sickly "Um…" seeped out. "I…I'm… um…" If she could keep her chin steady, if she could make her tongue move right, if she could just seal her eyes closed and make the clawing-raking-scalding stop…

But it didn't stop.

"Family," Anitra wheezed with what little air she had left. "I'm family."

Elizabeth leaned barely a hair closer and frowned deeper. "What family?"

"Uh…yours." Anitra clung to her words and begged them to work.

Elizabeth clamped her jaw so tightly, Anitra swore she saw it pulse.

"I never saw you before," the ghost said.

"Only in the mirror," Anitra muttered. Oh no… Elizabeth heard that…

Elizabeth cupped her hands over her mouth. "Are you… me?" She glared at her parents' portrait and back at Anitra.

The eyes lost their grip on Anitra, who scrambled for new words. Words that could fix the last ones.

"Well…no…I mean…"

Elizabeth backed away and turned toward the stairs.

"No! Don't go!" Anitra hissed. She couldn't let her go this time, not this time.

Elizabeth stopped, still facing the stairs.

"Are you…looking for Jeff and Charlotte?" Anitra asked. She peeled her back away from the sofa cushion and planted her uncertain feet on the floor to stand.

Elizabeth turned, and her face became a blinding mix of rage, fear, and unbearable sadness.

"They were wrong," Elizabeth said, shaking her head. "They were wrong! They were so mean! Why did they…*Who are you?!"*

Anitra's eyes grew so wide they began to hurt, and a slimy chill slithered all over her body. *Oh, God, what had they done?* She wanted to ask it, needed to ask it. But she couldn't stand to hear the answer, whatever it might be.

"Why are you here?" Anitra asked, remembering the question Jeff had asked her.

Elizabeth's frown deepened. "I...I don't...know." Angry, milky tears rolled down through the glow in her face.

"Do you...need help?" Anitra almost wanted to reach out and hug the poor ghost. Almost.

Elizabeth nodded as she looked at the floor and wiped glistening tears from her cheeks. But then she looked straight at Anitra and shook her head.

"No! No!" She shot up the stairs before Anitra could collect herself and chase after her.

Mindful of her sleeping grandparents, Anitra crept up the stairs. It took forever, and the whole time she had to fight herself to keep from running and making enough noise to scare everyone in the house, ghost and all.

Regret stung her as she thought of what she had let Elizabeth hear her say. *Only in the mirror.* What was she thinking? No wonder the ghost ran away. How was anybody supposed to understand that? Anitra had missed her chance to find out what was going on. Why Elizabeth needed help. Why Jeff needed to be forgiven.

Anitra crouched outside the doorway to her bedroom and watched as Elizabeth moved around in the darkness with a twitchy, panicky glide. Like last night, she seemed to be looking for something, but this time, Anitra wouldn't turn on the lights. She wouldn't say a word or do anything to startle the ghost. Elizabeth was scared enough. Maybe if Anitra just watched, she would learn something.

But Elizabeth left the room and glided through the office to the attic stairs. Keeping a safe distance, Anitra watched Elizabeth disappear up the stairs. And though she was disappointed to see Elizabeth leave, Anitra at least knew that the ghost needed help.

Anitra had finally lost her battle with fatigue. Instead of staying in her too-quiet room, she had gone back downstairs and tried to let the television distract her. But as she awoke Thursday morning, Grandpa Jeff found her on the sofa. She pretended to sleep. He turned off the set and walked quietly to the kitchen while she peeked at him with one open eye.

After hearing him drive away, she sat up and found a note on the end table. Grandma Charlotte had already left and would be working with those girls at the Community Center until late afternoon. Alone in the house again, Anitra showered hastily with the curtain partially open and her radio blasting. Later, in the kitchen, she gulped her orange juice and bowl of cereal as she demanded to herself that Carrie get her butt there in the next two minutes.

She stomped into the living room, turned on the television, and tried to drown out pestering thoughts by watching some stupid game show contestant yell her face off. But all that obnoxious cheering and jumping couldn't erase the fact that two days ago Anitra had landed in April 1928, that yesterday she had ended up in November 1927, that Elizabeth's ghost had made a habit of prowling the house each night, and that Jeff had begged to be forgiven for something that couldn't have been anything but terrible.

Anitra paced the living room floor and waited and waited for Carrie. When the doorbell finally rang, Anitra flew to the back door.

"Let's go!" she said, grabbing Carrie by the arm and yanking her into the kitchen.

"Hey!" Carrie protested as she stumbled into the house, barely missing the edge of the table.

"Sorry. We got a lot to do today." Her nerves hurt.

Anitra snatched the small electric fan from the kitchen and took it with them to the attic. At the top of the attic stairs, Anitra pointed to a set of boxes and trunks in the room on the right.

"Let's start there," she said.

She plugged the fan into a nearby outlet, and it whipped the oppressive, stale heat into something a little more bearable. She decided not to tell Carrie about Elizabeth's latest visit. At least not yet. Anitra was already terrified of what her grandparents might have done. She didn't want to scare Carrie and risk losing her, too. The thought of being completely alone in this was unthinkable.

Anitra opened a rickety brown trunk and carefully pulled out the seven dolls in their faded dresses that would normally be the objects of her attention. Two were in faded red dresses, two in dusty green, two in what used to be yellow, and one in a dim blue.

"Ooh!" Carrie said, carefully taking them from Anitra. "They're so pretty! And old!"

Carrie placed them gingerly on top of the ancient sewing table for safekeeping and gently whisked any hint of dust from their brittle clothes.

After removing a layer of paper, Anitra smiled as she recognized Jordan's wooden horse. It looked ready for the wood pile now, but it was definitely the same horse she had seen during her first trip to the past. It was surrounded by other toys that had entertained more than one generation of

Cole children. She removed them all from the trunk and watched Carrie grin.

"Look at all this stuff!" Carrie said, fascinated by the discovery of buried treasures.

"I saw that horse in my Great-Uncle Jordan's room when I went back, Carrie. It looked like new. It *was* new."

"What else is in there?" Carrie asked, eager to see more.

Anitra pulled out three children's books, and the smell of rotting paper filled her nose. She put two of the books on the floor but held on to the third one, the book of fairy tales that she had picked up in Irene's room.

"What?" Carrie asked, noticing the special attention Anitra gave the book.

"This was Elizabeth's book." She showed Carrie the writing on the inside of the front cover. "The one that had the bookmark in it. Remember the bookmark I told you about?"

"The one that fell out of the red dress, right?"

"Right." Anitra opened the book and gently shook it. The other half of the bookmark fell to the floor. The girls stared at it, then at each other.

"Wait here. I'll be right back!" Anitra said as she got up and rushed to the stairs.

"Hey! Don't leave me here!" Carrie yelled. But Anitra was already downstairs.

A minute later, she came back with the other half of the bookmark. She handed it to Carrie, who put the two pieces together. They matched perfectly at the tear, except Anitra's half was much newer.

"Wow!" Carrie whispered.

"You know, when I touched this book," Anitra said, "well, it was the first time I found out I could touch Elizabeth's things. It scared me at first, but it was...it was kinda cool, in a way."

Carrie looked at Anitra with a raised eyebrow. "Cool, huh?"

"Well, yeah. I mean, it was scary and all, but it really was cool. Touching something from back then...when you're right there...*back then.*"

Carrie just stared. She didn't get it.

"Anyway," Anitra said, giving up, "It was the first thing I could touch."

Carrie thought for a moment. "But didn't you say someone was in the room? Didn't they see you pick it up?" Carrie asked.

"No, Irene was in another room, and..."

Carrie looked up. "And what?"

"Wait a minute! I think I just figured something out! Nobody ever saw me but Jeff and Charlotte. And even they didn't always. Only..." Anitra began to think.

"What? *What?*"

"Jeff saw me when I was sitting in that chair near the dinner table, Elizabeth's chair, and again after Elizabeth died when I was in the same chair. They saw me standing in the doorway of Elizabeth's room...and when I was touching their tree...and when I was sitting in her chair that they moved to Jeff's room...that was the first time when I thought Jeff was sleep...and when I held her picture...Carrie!"

"So they only saw you when you touched Elizabeth's things, right?"

"Right! And only Jeff and Charlotte. Never anyone else. Never! And Irene noticed the book out of place, but she never saw me. And I was right there!"

"And the only things you could touch were Elizabeth's?"

Anitra nodded.

"This is deep," Carrie said. "But why's it happening? What does it mean?"

ഇൻറ

The girls sat on the attic floor, exhausted. They had spent over two hours continuously digging, moving from one box or trunk to the next, all the while repositioning the fan to keep from being reduced to two puddles of sweat. They found scrapbooks with newspaper articles about family members, including graduations, weddings, awards won in school, and funerals. Lots of funerals. They read an article describing Jordan's death in World War II, something about Papa Russell's funeral, every family obituary. They found them all.

Except Elizabeth's. Here and there they uncovered some of her things or a picture of her. But it seemed that anything surrounding her death had been removed from the carefully nurtured family archives.

"So now what?" Carrie asked as the girls worked to carefully put everything back in place.

"I don't know," Anitra answered, deep in thought.

She had reached another unsettling dead end. The family was just too careful about keeping its memories intact to let information about Elizabeth be accidentally lost. Someone had left or taken it out on purpose. Who? Anitra hated the possible answer floating through her head. She desperately wanted to know, but even more desperately wanted to believe that it had nothing to do with her grandparents. But the attic had no clues, and things were looking worse.

"This is scary," Carrie said. "I mean, there's nothing here in all this stuff. All this stuff! Anitra, do you think..."

"No!"

Carrie started to say something, but after yesterday's fight, thought the better of it.

"I *have* to know what happened!" Anitra said. "I have to know!"

The girls sat in silence for several minutes, each trying to come up with an explanation, another idea, anything.

"I guess I better go the library," Anitra said. She picked at the buckle on her sandal.

"Yeah, I guess so," Carrie said, brushing the dust from her butt. "I'll meet you there in about an hour. When you get there, ask for Mrs. Taylor and then ask her for the *Louiston Times*. Mrs. Taylor's real nice. She'll help you."

Anitra rushed to her grandparents' office and grabbed a handful of paper and some pens. She met Carrie back in her room, put on her sneakers, and stuffed everything into her backpack.

The girls headed to the kitchen and briefly reviewed their plans over glasses of ice water. After Carrie left, Anitra plugged her ears against the awful silence that came rushing back into the house.

₮ↂↃ

Damned lock! She couldn't remember the combination to her bicycle cable, and it was hard to reach anyway because it was all twisted behind the tire. Zero...two... What were the last two numbers?

"Come on!" she yelled, beating on the handlebars.

The bike tipped over. Anitra caught it right before it hit the ground, but not before the metal pedal scraped her from her ankle to her knee. Just some scratches, no blood, but it sure did hurt her feelings. She kicked the front tire twice for revenge, then set the bike back on its kickstand. Her backpack, jostled by the battle, felt scratchy on her back, and she jabbed it hard with her elbow to make it behave, too.

"One…four!" Shaky, clammy hands pushed the last two numbers into place, yanked the cable away, and coiled it below the handlebars. It took forever to remember that combination. How she could forget her own birth date was beyond her. Dumb!

The battle over, she climbed aboard and paused for a moment to wipe a drop of sweat that had rolled from under her sunglasses and down her cheek. Actually, it was a tear.

‪‬

As she rode into town, Anitra wished that she had gotten an earlier start. It was already ninety-five degrees, and the temperature was still rising. Humidity stuck to her skin like thick paste, and by the time she reached the corner of Fisher Street, she was soaked from pony-tailed head to red-sneakered toe. She stopped and took a few sips from the bottle of ice water she had stashed in the bicycle's bottle holder. As she waited to cool off a little, the sweet, heavy smell of honeysuckle drifted by. She reached into her pocket for the directions to the library, but it was empty.

"Ohhhh!" Anitra stomped her red sneaker into the ground.

Why couldn't she remember to pick up a little piece of paper along with all the other stuff? Closing her eyes, she tried to recall the directions she had written as Carrie recited them last night. There were just a few streets to remember; she could find it. It was just too hot to be rolling around on the wrong streets wasting time. Riding slowly, she continued her trip into town and found every shady spot along the way.

Anitra passed the center of town and its mix of old and new shops, churches, and a large brick town hall building. On the next street, older buildings gave way to a cozy neighborhood set at the bottom of a hill. Thinking through Carrie's directions, she detoured around the hill and reached a modern two-story brick building with a "Louiston Public Library" sign in front.

She gratefully slipped off her bicycle and locked it in the racks. Taking one last sip of water, she removed her sunglasses and entered the building. The air conditioner mercifully blasted instant relief. She went directly to the front desk and asked for Mrs. Taylor.

"That would be me," the woman responded. "How can I help you?" Mrs. Taylor was a large woman, about Anitra's mother's age, with brilliant red hair pinned neatly in a French roll. She seemed friendly enough.

"I'm looking for some information from 1927," Anitra said. "Do you have copies of the *Louiston Times* from back then?"

"Those are on microfilm. Come with me, dear. Have you used microfilm before?"

Anitra nodded. "Yes, ma'am."

"Okay, I'll show you where they are."

They walked through the stacks and stopped in front of a row of beige metal file cabinets with shallow drawers. Mrs. Taylor scanned the drawers and opened one.

"Now, exactly what dates are you looking for again?"

"Well, I'm not sure of the exact date, but it's November."

"And it was 1927, right?"

"Right."

Mrs. Taylor pecked through two drawers for a moment. "Here we go," she said as she removed two small boxes. "Both of these are from the time you're looking for."

She led Anitra to the row of microfilm machines, and reviewed instructions for the proper use. "Is this for a summer school project?"

"No, it's sort of a family project," Anitra said, making herself smile.

"Okay, well if you need any more help, I'll be at the front desk," Mrs. Taylor instructed. She patted Anitra on the shoulder and left the room.

"Thanks," Anitra said as she began exploring the pages of the past.

Starting with November 1, 1927, Anitra slowly made her way through the first two weeks of the *Louiston Times*. Thousands of articles and advertisements raced across the screen, and Anitra couldn't help but slow down and skim a few, like the one describing the arrest of two local men for liquor violations and another about an accident involving a child. It wasn't Elizabeth. She pushed the film forward past the society pages announcing parties that the well-to-do of Louiston were attending and the sports section summing up local rivalries.

The ads fascinated her. With Thanksgiving coming up, there were plenty of ads for New York City plays and concerts for the holidays, and clothes were on sale for all who wanted to look their holiday best. Ads for candy and cigarettes covered almost every page, and tons of ads for ointments and remedies claimed to cure anything anyone ever had. For a grateful minute or two, it all slowed her down long enough to forget what she was making herself do.

Finally, Anitra sped past the classified ads to the obituary page and found nothing at all about Elizabeth.

Anitra had been searching the paper for over an hour when she reached the fourth week of November. Early in the week, there were articles about the unusually early snow that had found its way to the area. No more snow was expected, but it would remain colder than usual for a while longer. Thanksgiving was a few days away, and the area hotels advertised elaborate menus at three dollars a plate. Anitra passed more quickly through the pages; she was getting tired of finding nothing.

But then she reached the front page for the twenty-third. She clutched the sides of the machine. There on the bottom half of the page, near the middle of the second column, glared the headline: "Negro Girl Found Dead in Grant Park."

☙16❧

"Hey! Did ya find anything?" Carrie asked as she bounced into Anitra's view.

Anitra looked up, and the expression on her face made Carrie rush to the machine. She looked at the headline and stepped back.

"Oh, my God! Did you read it yet?"

"No. I just found it." But Anitra had been staring at the headline for fifteen minutes, mesmerized by the black print, unable to read further, hoping the letters would scramble and form some other headline she could understand.

"Well, print it out, and let's look it over."

Anitra dropped a nickel in the coin slot, pressed the print button, and a few seconds later a piece of paper slid calmly out of the machine. She moved closer to Carrie, and the two read through the article:

> A routine evening of walking the dog turned to horror for Mr. John Bartholomew last night. Mr. Bartholomew, of Porter Street,

was strolling through Grant Park with his dog, as he had done every night for the past two years, when the dog began barking uncontrollably. After trying in vain to calm the animal, Mr. Bartholomew finally allowed the dog to lead him to an area just inside the woods. It was there that he found the body of a young negro girl.

The girl was identified as twelve-year-old Elizabeth Cole, daughter of Mr. and Mrs. Russell Cole of Fisher Street. According to Officer Ronald May of the Louiston Police Department, the cause of death has not yet been officially determined, but the girl's neck appeared to have been broken, and a large rock covered with blood was found near the body. Officer May said that the family had reported her missing earlier that evening, and they did not know why she would be in the park. She was not wearing a coat despite the cold weather. Foul play has not been ruled out, but there are no suspects at this time.

Foul play.

Anitra clutched her stomach to keep it from turning upside down, and her heart beat faster than she thought possible. Carrie sat motionless with her mouth dangling open.

"Foul play?" Anitra managed to say.

"This is not what I was...expecting," Carrie said, gingerly picking her words.

"What were you expecting?" Anitra asked. She fixed her gaze on the article, wishing more information would pop up on the page.

"I don't...I don't know. An...accident or something. Not this," Carrie said.

"Yeah. Me, too."

"Anitra, are you okay?"

Anitra nodded. "Now what?" There was too much blur in her head to say or do anything more.

"Well, there's got to be more," Carrie said. "Another article or something. Let's keep looking. There's got to be some kind of explanation here somewhere."

Anitra simply nodded again and continued to stare at the article in front of her. Why weren't those letters scrambling and forming a different set of words with a nice, logical reason for all this?

"Anitra, it's going to be okay. We'll figure it out. C'mon, let me sit there and work the machine."

The girls switched places. Carrie continued to search the microfilm as Anitra sat silently beside her and stared absently at the screen. Pages and pages of the past whirred by, spinning any intelligent thoughts she may have had into one big, airy froth. Anitra wondered if she wanted to know any more. She wanted to help Elizabeth, Jeff, Charlotte, her grandparents, but the more information she dug up, the worse things became. She regretted going to the attic two days ago; she should have listened to her grandmother and gone back to the pool.

"Anitra, look at this," Carrie said, pulling her friend out of her fog.

Between Thanksgiving ads, an article in the next day's paper read: "Negro Girl's Death Still a Mystery."

The Louiston Police report no additional evidence in the death of twelve-year-old Elizabeth Cole. Despite extensive questioning

of family members and neighbors, the police
have no new information, and no witnesses
have come forth. According to Captain Ed-
ward Forsythe of the Louiston Police Department, the family discovered that the girl was
not at her friend's house as expected and began looking for her. Later that evening, the
police received the call from Mr. John Bartholomew, who found her body in Grant
Park.

The article went on to say that Elizabeth's funeral would
be held on Friday morning at the Carver Street Baptist
Church. Carrie printed this page and continued through two
more weeks of papers, finding only one small article tucked
away in the far corners of the paper. The *Louiston Times* had
apparently lost interest; no more clues had been discovered,
and the case had never been solved. Carrie printed this last
article, removed the microfilm from the machine, and placed
the microfilm box on a shelf near the file drawers.

As Carrie shut off the machine, Anitra sat with her head
in her hands and felt her heart sink. No answers here. Just
more questions. Just more suspicions. And less hope.

Carrie tapped Anitra's shoulder. "Hey, why don't we go?
I think we've got enough."

Anitra nodded and stuffed the pages into her backpack.

As they passed the front desk, Mrs. Taylor waved. "Did
you find what you were looking for?"

"Yes, ma'am," Anitra said. "I guess we did."

"Wonderful!" Mrs. Taylor said. "Well you have a nice
day, now."

"Thank you," Anitra said with a forgery of a smile on her
face.

৪৩৫৩

The girls sat at a table in their favorite downtown deli eating lunch. Anitra had been silent from the time they left the library until the deli clerk asked for her order. She had a decision to make.

"I have to go back," Anitra said.

"You what?!"

"I have to go back."

"After everything that happened?" Carrie asked. "Why would you want to go back there?"

"They need me," Anitra said. She gnawed on the straw in her drink until it was completely flat.

"But how do you know? Did they ask for your help?"

"Well, yeah. Sort of."

"What do you mean, 'sort of'?"

"I didn't tell you this before 'cause I didn't wanna scare you."

"Oh, try me."

Anitra stopped torturing her straw and looked up at Carrie. "She came back."

"Who...came...back?"

"Elizabeth," Anitra said. "She came back last night."

Carrie hesitated for a minute, but she looked surprisingly calm. "Still looking for her dress, I guess."

"I fell asleep on the sofa last night, and I woke up at, like, two in the morning. She was practically standing over me! Staring at me!"

"Well did you at least scream this time?"

"Almost. Sort of. I mean, I jumped. It was weird. She was right there in front of me. I coulda touched her."

"You didn't, did you?" Carrie's lips barely moved.

Anitra shook her head. "No way! Even *I'm* not that crazy."

"Yes, you are. So, then what?"

Anitra spilled every detail of Elizabeth's latest visit, sending Carrie deep into her watching-a-good-movie trance.

"You talked to a ghost," Carrie said. "I can't believe it. You talked to a ghost."

"Yeah."

Carrie thought this through. "Anitra! *You talked to a ghost!*"

Anitra had to laugh.

"So you really think she wanted help?" Carrie asked.

"Well, she did nod when I asked."

"Yeah, but then she said 'no,' right?"

"Just 'cause she was scared."

"Hmm. Maybe." Carrie fanned herself with a little square paper napkin.

"She really needs help, Carrie."

"Yeah, I know, but maybe she didn't mean you."

Anitra chomped on the flattened straw. "Who else is there?"

Carrie nodded. "But what would you do?"

"I don't know. But I can't do anything here. I have to go back, Carrie. If I just sit here and do nothing, well, I'll just never forgive myself if it turns out I coulda done something and didn't."

"Anitra, are you sure? I mean it's not like you can control it. You don't know where, I mean when, it'll put you. It might be too late to do anything."

"I'll take that chance. It's better than doing nothing."

Carrie twisted her paper napkin. "I guess you're right."

Anitra sighed, grateful that Carrie understood.

"So when're you going?" Carrie asked.

"Today. As soon as we get back."

The ceiling fan directly above them swirled the aromas of oil, vinegar, and spices around in the humid air and sent it sailing around the room. The girls sat silently and finished their sandwiches, then raced back to the attic.

With Carrie's help, Anitra stepped back into the red dress and the shoes, put on the locket and red bow, then sat on a trunk and waited.

"Good luck," Carrie said with a tremble in her voice.

"Thanks."

About a minute later, Anitra felt the familiar sharp pain in the back of her neck. This time she felt Carrie catch her as she slumped over.

ഇറ

Once again the heat was gone, and once again Anitra found herself lying on the attic floor waiting for the haze to clear from her mind. She sat up and looked for the calendar. November 1927. Not again! The last thing she wanted was a repeat of the last trip. She hoped it wasn't the same day. One thing was certain: this time, she absolutely could not let Jeff see her.

Footsteps on the other side of the attic startled her. Carefully, she peered around the stairwell to find Adam standing in front of a mirror busily brushing his wavy hair and humming a cheerful tune. Free of the numb, devastated look he'd had the last time, he adjusted his suspenders, grabbed his cap, and headed for the stairs.

Anitra followed him down to the second floor but stopped at the bottom of the stairs and peeked around the corner. The office, the whole house, felt empty. No voices from below, no footsteps other than Adam's, no grieving sighs. Just a tempting stillness.

"Good morning, Mama," she heard Adam say as he reached the kitchen.

Anitra went to the doorway of the office and glanced cautiously into the hall. Not one Cole on the second floor. After inching down the stairs, she crept through the empty rooms and into the kitchen where she found Adam working diligently on a plate of eggs and sausage. Nearby, Mama Sarah ironed a basket of clothes with the most ancient iron Anitra had ever seen. Judging from her great-grandmother's efforts, it had to be a little bit heavy.

"Did you sleep well, Adam?" Mama Sarah asked.

"Yes, ma'am. Nothing like sleeping in your own bed, even if it's on the wrong side of the attic. I guess Jeff finally wanted his own room."

"Actually, your father and I finally gave in. He'd been pestering us about it since you left for college."

Anitra sat in a chair in the corner and wondered where the rest of the family could be. Where Elizabeth could be.

"I'm surprised you didn't wake me," Adam said. "You never let us sleep this long."

"Well, it was so late when you came in last night. You needed your rest, and I know you don't get enough sleep at school."

"Sure I do, Mama."

"Oh? And I suppose you had those dark circles under your eyes when you were living here?"

"I've been studying very hard."

"Mm hmm. And going to parties."

All this normality made Anitra squirm. She looked at the ceiling and begged these people to tell her where everyone was.

Adam smiled. "Mama, it's all a part of the college experience."

"College experience? You can get the college experience at Bailey and live right here at home. And you certainly wouldn't have to go around running yourself ragged." She snapped one last wrinkle out of a shirt.

"Mama..." he groaned. He'd undoubtedly heard this many times before. "Did we get a newspaper today?"

Anitra perked up.

"Your father left it in the living room."

"Papa still can't leave for work without reading the editorials first," he said as he walked into the dining room.

As Adam returned to his seat, newspaper in hand, the telephone jingled lightly.

"I'll get that, Mama," Adam said.

"No, you finish your breakfast." Mama Sarah placed the iron on its platform and left the room.

Anitra eyed the newspaper and dared to get up and look over Adam's shoulder.

"...Lydia, how are you this morning?" Mama Sarah's voice floated into the kitchen. "Yes, he came in Sunday night...I don't think he's been getting enough sleep, but he seems just fine otherwise...Yes, we're almost ready...Adam will be here to help..."

Anitra tried to find the date on the paper, but Adam had it folded so the date didn't show.

"Yes, that will be just fine, Lydia," Mama Sarah continued. "No, it's not a bother at all...I'm looking forward to it, too, dear...All right. I'll se you soon."

Adam looked up from the paper when Mama Sarah returned, and Anitra jumped back a step or two.

"Adam, I'll need you to drive me into town this afternoon. I need a few more things for Thanksgiving dinner, and Lydia would like me to visit."

Anitra's heart picked up its pace as she looked up at Mama Sarah. Which day was it? It was close to Thanksgiving. But if they were acting like this, Elizabeth couldn't have died yet. Where was she? *Which day was it?*

"Yes, ma'am," Adam answered. "How's Aunt Lydia these days?"

"Oh, she has her good days and her bad days," Mama Sarah said, returning to her ironing. "Lately more bad than good."

Adam shook his head. "Is that why we're having Thanksgiving dinner here this year?"

"Mm hmm. I told your father and uncles it was a bad idea to let their sister host this year. She just couldn't cope." Mama Sarah's lips tightened, and her ironing became a little less orderly.

"She's not getting any better, huh?"

Mama Sara shook her head and slammed the iron onto an unfortunate shirt. "This may be an unkind thing to say, and please don't mention this to your father, but she puts such a terrible strain on the family. She wants to be included, and she seems fine for a while. Then for no reason, no reason at all, she behaves as though she's terrified of everything and everyone: me, this house, something on the radio, even you children. I'm just glad she has no children of her own. I don't want to think of what the poor things would…"

"Mama?!" Adam looked shocked.

Mama Sarah suddenly needed to pay strict attention to her chore, and Adam found something of great interest in the newspaper. In the long minutes that followed, they shared only an occasional glance.

With the folded paper still in hand, Adam stood and stretched. "Mama, let me know when you're ready to go."

"As soon as I finish this, I'll be ready. Oh, and Adam,

you won't need to come back for me, dear. Your father can bring me home when he finishes work for the day. I'll leave a note for the girls to start supper when they get home from school."

"Call me when you're ready, Mama." Adam left the kitchen, tossing the paper onto the table.

With an eye on Mama Sarah, Anitra went to the table and looked at the *Louiston Times*. At the top of the page was the date: November 22, 1927. The day of Elizabeth's death.

ᔰ17ᔱ

Anitra collapsed into her chair and waited for the shock to melt away. Of all days to come back. The day Elizabeth died! But right now, right this moment, Elizabeth was still alive. Anitra knew exactly why she had returned. To save Elizabeth!

Thankfully, Mama Sarah and Adam would be leaving soon, giving Anitra a way out of the house. Anitra would have to go to the school, find Elizabeth, and stay with her. Keep her from whatever or whoever was about to kill her. If only Anitra knew what that was.

Anitra watched, waited, and paced as Mama Sarah finished her work and strolled upstairs with the freshly ironed clothes. She followed her to the master bedroom and felt no chilly excitement over this first look at the room as it appeared in 1927. Heavy drapes, furniture with fine curves and patterns carved into it, delicate tins and boxes. None of it mattered. Because today Elizabeth was going to die.

Mama Sarah hummed softly as she put the clothes away and stopped occasionally to banish a bit of dust from her husband's dresser or rescue a piece of jewelry from some-where other than its rightful place. Anitra sat on the floor and rocked. She stood up and paced. She stomped her foot on a slightly worn blue rug. She considered hating Mama Sarah and her calm.

Satisfied that everything was in place, Mama Sarah picked up the basket and headed for the attic. Anitra rolled her eyes and followed.

"Adam, I'm coming upstairs, dear," Mama Sarah said. At the top of the stairs she turned to Jeff's room.

"Can I give you a hand, Mama?" Adam asked.

"Oh, if you would take Jordan's things and put them away," she said, handing the smallest clothes to Adam.

Anitra paced faster. A dark, achy cloud formed in her head.

"Well, Adam," Mama Sarah said after filling Jeff's ward-robe, "give me a few minutes to put myself together, and I'll be ready to go."

"I'll be waiting downstairs, Mama," Adam said.

From the tone of his voice and the expression on his face, Anitra knew it would be a long, miserable wait. How much time did she have left? It couldn't be much. She'd go crazy if Mama Sarah didn't pick up her clunky-shoed feet and get a move on.

Five times Anitra ran up and down the stairs between the kitchen, where Adam now waited in his coat and cap, and Mama Sarah's room, where this oh-so-slow woman meticu-lously rearranged the short curls that sat snugly against her face. Anitra would have been exhausted had there not been so much at stake.

"Let's go, people!" Anitra yelled from the bottom of the stairs, wishing they could hear her.

Finally, finally, *finally* Mama Sarah flowed into the kitchen arranging her hat and scarf. When Adam opened the door for his mother, Anitra scrambled out behind her.

§)Œ

Anitra ran down Fisher Street, away from Charlotte's house and Grant Park, and toward the Archer Street School. Grandpa Jeff, his brothers and sisters, Grandma Charlotte, Anitra's father, and even Carrie had all gone to this school. In earlier summers, she and Carrie had spent plenty of time there running around on the slides and swings, playing kickball and duck-duck-goose with Carrie's friends, and sitting on a bench pigging out on the strawberry licorice and candy necklaces bought from the store across the street.

They had looked into the school windows so that Carrie could show off the classrooms she'd been assigned to, and they even managed to go inside once when the janitor left a door open. It had been fun walking through an empty school, hiding behind empty desks, and writing cryptic messages on the blackboard for a confused janitor to find. Well, it had been fun until he had found them and chased them out with a big, hairy mop in his meaty hand. They hadn't gone back there in a long time; since they were both now in junior high school, it was just too uncool to go to the elementary school and play unless they were baby-sitting somebody's kid.

At the end of Fisher Street, Anitra turned left and ran the remaining three blocks to the school. She couldn't help but stop, momentarily shocked by the stunning view. The three houses that stood across the street in the seventies weren't there. In their place were two larger, weathered houses and a vacant lot loaded with weeds that had lost their battle with the early cold.

"C'mon, snap out of it," she told herself. She didn't have time for this.

Anitra tore herself from the scene and ran the rest of the way to the school. It must've been lunch time, because bunches of kids, bundled in their winter coats, shot out of the school. Little boys in knickers darted around while girls with short, boyish haircuts jumped behind the school's flagpole dodging tiny snowballs packed from the remaining snow. Anitra smiled at the familiar scene; some things never changed.

She remembered Grandpa Jeff saying that they sometimes went home for lunch. She was sure that Jeff and Elizabeth wouldn't today; Mama Sarah wouldn't have gone out if she knew they were coming home. But Charlotte might. Anitra ducked behind a tree in case she came out and joined the crowd.

While she waited, Anitra stared at the two story building that she knew would be much bigger in about forty years. Grandpa Jeff had said an addition had been attached in the sixties to handle the town's growing population.

As kids ran in every direction, Anitra cautiously picked her way across the street, into the school yard, and around the left side of the building. Across the yard a small crowd of kids slid back and forth across a sheet of ice in the middle of the playground. No Jeff, no Charlotte, no Elizabeth.

The school yard was much smaller than the yard she remembered, and a row of small houses stood behind a wooden fence in an area where she knew the lower grades' playground to be. Staying close to the building, Anitra ran toward the back of the school to find the cafeteria, then remembered that it was in the newer part of the building. The part that wasn't there yet.

She sighed and shook her head. With her luck, her grandparents and Elizabeth would be in a room way up on the second floor where she couldn't find them. She sat on the ground against the wall and thought things through. There had to be a cafeteria somewhere in this building. Didn't kids eat lunch at school in the twenties? She'd just have to walk around the building and look into each window to find it. Hopefully Elizabeth, or at least Jeff or Charlotte, would be somewhere on the first floor.

She peered into each window. Classroom after classroom was filled with frail wooden desks neatly arranged in rows of four. She looked at dim lights hanging on long cords from the ceiling, small blackboards that didn't even cover the entire front walls, dark wooden teacher's desks covered with nicks and scratches, and books with plain, dull covers instead of the bright, pictured ones she had. Most of these rooms were empty except for an occasional teacher cleaning a blackboard. The kids had to be in a cafeteria. Wherever that was.

Anitra rounded the corner and heard lots of voices. Through a slightly open window above her head, she heard the sound of kids in recess. Finally! This had to be the cafeteria, and Elizabeth had to be in there. She had to.

Grabbing the window ledge, Anitra stood on top of a large rock and hoisted herself up to look in. Inside, several long rows of tables covered a gym floor, and kids packed the tables talking, yelling, and laughing as they ate their lunches. Large windows covered the length of the wall, almost all of them partially open. Anitra understood why; she could imagine the heat seeping out the window from the huge radiators or whatever ancient contraptions they had in there cranking it out. Had to be hot with all those kids in there.

Anitra sighed and smiled. At the table nearest the window, just to her right, she spotted Jeff and Charlotte facing the window and Elizabeth sitting across from them. It felt so good to see them smiling! She had hated seeing her grandparents so hopelessly sad last time, and Charlotte was so much prettier now that she wasn't tormented by grief.

Anitra wanted to go inside, but she didn't dare take that chance. There wasn't anything of Elizabeth's for her to touch, so Jeff and Charlotte couldn't see her. But no telling what Elizabeth would be able to see. Anitra had to play it safe and stay outside by the window.

Although she had seen Elizabeth's ghost twice, this was Anitra's first chance to see the real Elizabeth. Alive, well, happy, and looking so much like Anitra in a green plaid dress. Anitra watched her talk and laugh with a girl sitting next to her. It was just like watching herself from a distance. Amazing.

"I'll trade you three cookies for that," Elizabeth told the girl, starting a round of lunch trading.

"Not my mama's cake," the girl said, frowning deeply. "I should get at least four o' them."

"Oh, applesauce! Look at these cookies!" Elizabeth insisted, waving one under the girl's nose. "Three cookies. That's it!"

The girl thought for a minute, shook her head, then nodded, officially completing the trade. Elizabeth placed the cake in front of her and momentarily examined the spoils of her victory. She bit her bottom lip and looked somewhere across the room.

Anitra smiled. Elizabeth was good at this.

"What's wrong?" Charlotte said.

Elizabeth shook her head. "Oh, nothing," she said as she rose from her chair and skipped across the room with the cake nestled in her palms.

She sat next to a small girl at another table and gave her the cake. Anitra couldn't hear what she said, but the little girl smiled as she accepted the gift. Elizabeth returned to her seat.

"What'd ya do that for?" Jeff asked, almost pouting.

"She was hungry. She didn't have much for lunch."

"Her family doesn't have much of anything," Charlotte said. "She never eats much. No wonder she's so little." Charlotte smiled her approval. "That was nice, Lizzie."

Jeff frowned. "Well, some of those cookies you traded were mine, so I should get that last one."

"Oh, no," Elizabeth said, taking a huge, protective bite out of the remaining cookie. "You were mean to me this morning."

"I was not!"

"Were too!"

Charlotte interrupted and turned to Jeff. "You can have some of mine."

Jeff smiled at Elizabeth, who glared back at Charlotte.

"Well, he wasn't mean to me! Don't cast a kitten!" Charlotte said.

The girls both laughed. Then Elizabeth suddenly stopped laughing and looked around the room with a frown.

"What?" Jeff asked.

Elizabeth shrugged. "Just thought...just this feeling like... nothing."

Anitra wondered what that was about. She hadn't been seen, she was sure, and she hadn't made a sound. Whatever it was, it must have passed, because Elizabeth plunged right back into talking and laughing once again. But only yards away, two boys on a serious mission slunk behind Elizabeth. One of them looked very familiar, but Anitra couldn't place him. They whispered to each other as they closed in. Then one grabbed Elizabeth's hair and yanked.

"Tin Lizzie!" he yelled.

Anitra laughed. She knew Elizabeth would hate being compared to those clumsy old cars that Grandpa Jeff had described over and over again in his stories.

"Oww! You...!" Elizabeth flew out of her chair, grabbed the boy by the arm, and spun him around before he knew what was happening.

Anitra was impressed.

"What?" the boy asked with as much innocence as he could manage. He was trying very hard not to laugh.

"Didn't you learn your lesson? Or do I have to win another running race against you to get you to stop pulling my hair? Do you want to lose to a girl again?"

Elizabeth's face was all twisted and scrunched up, and Anitra expected hot, red flames to *whoosh* out of her ears. Anitra scratched her head; this whole thing sounded way too familiar.

"Well...I..." the boy tried.

"And you!" Elizabeth turned on the other boy. "You should know better, Alvin Cole!"

Anitra laughed again; this was Great-Great Uncle Marcus's son. In the seventies, he was alive and well and living the artist's life in California. But right now he was forced to suffer the wrath of his cousin Elizabeth.

"Lizzie," Jeff said grabbing her arms. "Mrs. Casey is watching. She'll come over here if you don't stop. You don't want Mama to come get you again, do you?"

Elizabeth's back stiffened. Anitra understood; Mama Sarah didn't seem like the type who enjoyed picking her daughter up from the principal's office. Giving the boys one last fiery glare, Elizabeth let her brother lead her back to the table.

"You have to stop this!" Jeff said as he sat his sister down. "I'm tired of getting you out of trouble all the time!"

"Why are you so jumpy today?" Charlotte asked.

"He pulled my hair! He's such a goof!" Elizabeth said, startled that Charlotte would even ask such a thing.

"That's not what I mean. You've been jumpy all day. Is something wrong?"

Elizabeth whispered to Charlotte, and the two girls stood and put on their coats.

"They're coming outside!" Anitra whispered. She looked around frantically for a place to hide and ducked behind a bush next to the wooden stairs that led from the gym.

"What do you mean, you got it back!" Charlotte said as the girls walked down the stairs and sat on the last step.

Anitra crouched as low as possible. They were too close. Too close.

"It was Jordan," Elizabeth said. "We were...out there... and he found it. He started running and running all the way back there and I had to go run after him. You know how he is. By the time I found him...he...he had it in his hands." Her voice began to tremble.

Charlotte gasped. "He did?"

Elizabeth nodded.

"But Lizzie, why didn't you leave it?"

"I had to pull it out of his hands. He got mad and started to cry because I wouldn't give it back to him. He'd go back and get it if he knew it was still there. I *had* to take it."

"So...where is it?" Charlotte didn't seem to want an answer.

"Home. I hid it in a safe place. Until I know what to do. Until *we* know what to do."

"Lizzie, I hope *we* means Jeff, too! Wait here." Charlotte jumped up and ran inside.

Anitra held her breath. She was alone with Elizabeth, and she didn't dare make a sound. She watched silently as Elizabeth sat and stared out across the school yard and watched other kids spin and glide freely on wide patches of ice. Anitra remembered the eyes of Elizabeth's ghost and wondered if those kids out there could feel her searing eyes blister their shouts and laughter.

"You didn't tell anybody, did you?" Jeff said as he exploded out the door and down the stairs with Charlotte behind him. He stood facing his sister.

Elizabeth shook her head. She hadn't told.

Jeff stood silently for a moment, staring at the ground in deep thought. When he looked up, his jaw tightened.

"After all that, you brought it back," he blurted out. "You were supposed to leave it alone!"

Elizabeth looked surprised. "But Jeff..."

Charlotte frowned, confused.

"No. I'm not getting you out of this. I did that last time, I just got you out of trouble today. No. 'Sides, it's not hurting anything now. I told you before *if you just left it alone* nothing would happen. Nobody would know. So leave it where it is."

"Are you sure?" Elizabeth asked.

"Just leave it alone, Lizzie. Look, it's almost time to come in, and Mrs. Casey still has her eye on you!" He pointed at his sister and stomped back inside.

"He's right, Lizzie," Charlotte said.

Anitra was close enough to see Elizabeth shudder.

"You think so?" Elizabeth asked.

Charlotte nodded.

"But what if...?"

"It won't." Charlotte put her hand on Elizabeth's arm.

"Guess I'll leave it there, then." A frail little smile tripped onto Elizabeth's face.

"We'd better get inside," Charlotte said.

They got up. Elizabeth stopped at the door and turned

around, looked in all directions, shrugged, and went inside with Charlotte.

When she was sure it was safe, Anitra stood and shook the cramps out of her legs. Her heart had picked up speed, and she had a vague, prickly feeling that wouldn't go away. What was that all about? What was "it" supposed to be? And how could it hurt Elizabeth?

This mysterious thing had to be connected to Elizabeth's death. It had to be, she hoped. It sounded like they couldn't tell anyone about it, so maybe it was something valuable. Something someone wanted badly enough to hurt someone else for it. Badly enough to kill a young girl and leave her body for some stranger to find.

Elizabeth would die tonight unless Anitra could figure out what "it" was and stop it from hurting her. "It" waited somewhere in the house, hidden away. She was going to find it.

ക18ര

A nitra ran all the way back to the house on Fisher Street and reached the back steps feeling drained. A car sat in the driveway; someone had to be home. Mama Sarah was supposed to be gone all day, so it probably wasn't her. Adam, maybe. Anitra bounded up the back porch stairs and peered into the kitchen. She didn't see him. Where was he? She ran to the front of the house and looked through every window accessible from the porch. No one in the living room, either. She jumped up and down to calm her nerves. She didn't have all this time to waste, but right now she could do nothing but watch and wait.

At least an hour passed, and Anitra had already gnawed the nails on one hand and started in on the other one. Jumping from one window to the next and back, she kept herself sane by working out a search plan, imagining what "it" could possibly be, focusing on getting it away from Elizabeth, and picturing Elizabeth happy and safe at the family's Thanksgiving dinner table. Anitra would do this. For Elizabeth and for the family.

"Come on!" Anitra yelled, banging noiselessly on the

window. "Open the door! Open the door, please!"

Faint footsteps answered her cries as Adam reached the bottom step, strolled through the living room, paused to straighten a chair in the dining room, and disappeared into the kitchen.

"Yesss!" Anitra screamed as she raced to the back door and pressed her face against the window panel. Or against that mysterious barrier between her and everything else.

In the kitchen, Adam took a piece of bread from the pantry and held it in his mouth while he put on his coat and cap.

"Come on! Come on!" Anitra said, boiling over.

Adam paused for a bite, then walked to the door.

"Oh please oh please oh please..." Anitra chanted. She crouched, ready to pounce.

Adam finally opened the door. She leapt in and blew a puff of relief. She had to give him credit; Adam was the most reliable door opener in the family.

It felt good to be alone in the house, free to roam. Even though most of the family couldn't see or hear her, she was still afraid that she might touch something that belonged to Elizabeth and make a noise. But in an empty house, she could think.

Elizabeth had said "it" was in a safe place, and Anitra figured the basement would be the best place to hide something. The door was open just enough for her to wiggle through, and Anitra cautiously stepped down the dark stairwell, allowing her eyes time to adjust to the dim light that peeked in through short basement windows. She wondered if it smelled as musty and leaky now as it did in the seventies.

"Wow, look at all this stuff!"

When she reached the bottom of the stairs, Anitra had to smile. The uncluttered basement she knew didn't have much more than the washer and dryer and some shelves with

Grandpa Jeff's tools. But this basement burst with the trunks and boxes that, in Anitra's world, lived in the attic. Like the attic, the basement had a room on either side of the stairs, and both rooms held the beginnings of the Cole family's museum.

A strange machine in the corner of one room demanded Anitra's attention. A large, round wooden tub. Metal frame, bunch of knobs, wringer. The washing machine, just as Grandma Charlotte had described it. Anitra welcomed the laugh that sneaked out. Like the iron Mama Sarah used earlier, this thingamajig looked like way too much work. It wasn't even electric.

"May as well go out and beat the clothes against a rock," she said, as she picked a cluster of boxes to start her search.

Anitra ran her hands across the boxes until she found something she could touch. She rummaged through two boxes with Elizabeth's old clothing inside. Then she stopped at a small wooden trunk in the second room that had Elizabeth's name burned into its lid. It was a little over two feet long and about a foot deep, light enough for Anitra to carry to a table and pry open.

"Why haven't I seen you before?" she asked the trunk.

Just a few old dolls and small toys that Elizabeth had surely outgrown by now. Near the bottom, Anitra found pictures drawn and words written by a child's unsteady hand, and she carefully studied each and every one. Nothing helpful here. The only unusual thing about this trunk and its contents was that they no longer existed in the seventies.

Finding nothing else she could touch, Anitra went back upstairs to the kitchen and squinted as her eyes readjusted to the bright light. Mama Sarah had left a note, instructions for the girls, and some money on the kitchen table. The note was folded, and Anitra couldn't open it.

"This couldn't be it," she told herself, shaking her head. Probably not, but she'd listen carefully if the girls came home, just in case.

She slowly explored the rest of first floor, looking on shelves and under the furniture for the slightest hint of something unusual. But everything looked as if Mama Sarah had precisely arranged it with her own elegant hands. There was just a lot of nothing, nothing, nothing on the first floor, and Anitra was running out of time. So far, the newspaper provided the only clue, and it wouldn't have that story about Elizabeth until the next day. Too late.

She went upstairs and sat on the top step to think away the tension that crowded her head. When she got up, she noticed that her stomach didn't get up with her. Jumping up and down a few times calmed the queasiness enough for her to start searching the second floor. As usual, the master bedroom door was closed, and the hand mirrors, small bottles of cologne, and tins of powder that sat delicately atop Lillian and Naomi's dresser told no secrets. Neither did anything in the office.

In the bathroom, small tubes of toothpaste and shaving cream, bottles of mouthwash and medicine, and a few other things were all visible through the half-open medicine cabinet. Soap, a family of toothbrushes, white towels, and Papa Russell's shaving mug and brush were the only other things there.

"This is going nowhere!" Anitra stomped her foot on the bathroom floor and listened for the sound it didn't make. "What am I supposed to do? What am I s'posed to look for?!"

In Elizabeth and Irene's room, she sat on the floor and rested her head in her hands. "Why'd I come back here if all I can do is just look at stuff? There's gotta be something here!"

Pulling herself up, Anitra looked around the room to find a good spot to start looking again. But if that thing was supposed to be "safely hidden," and Elizabeth was so afraid of it, why would she put it in her own room? It didn't make sense, but neither had anything else for the last few days. At least this room would be a lot easier to search; she could touch things. She would just have to be careful to put them back in place.

The room was spotless, not surprising for any of Mama Sarah's children, and nothing weird immediately jumped out at her. She opened the closet door. Stepping inside, she looked over the dresses, accessories, and those blouses that Grandma Charlotte called "middies," and concentrated on the smaller clothes that would have fit Elizabeth.

"Oh, my God!" Anitra gasped.

The red dress with its pristine cream lace trim stood out from among all the others. The crisp, brilliant red dress hanging neatly in the closet was the very same as the dulled, mothball-scented red dress she was wearing. She gingerly touched the sleeve. How could both dresses be there...how could they both *be* at the same time? Wasn't the world supposed to explode or something?

She walked out of the closet scratching her head, still confused about the red dress, and turned her attention to the desk where a few books, a lamp, and a cup filled with pencils sat on top. She flipped through the books she could touch hoping some slip of paper might fall out and give her all the information she needed. No luck there. Anitra looked through everything in the bookshelves, on top of and behind the desk and the dresser, and pulled all the stuff out of the desk. More of the same.

"C'mon, c'mon, c'mon, c'mon!" Anitra said. "Something

has to work here! Now!"

She went to the dresser. She couldn't touch the top two drawers. Irene's. The bottom two opened easily, and Anitra gratefully reached in. She pulled heavy cable knit cardigans out of the bottom drawer. In the drawer above it, she pushed aside soft, warm undershirts, complicated slips, and the bloomers that she always teased Grandma Charlotte about. They weren't very funny today.

The sound of the back door closing interrupted her. Someone was home! Anitra placed the clothes neatly back in the drawer and closed them quickly, silently. Then she crept into the office, sat on the floor, and tried to hear what was going on downstairs.

"Mama, are you home?" It was one of the girls. Which one?

"There's a note on the table." Another girl. *Which one?* "She's visiting with Aunt Lydia. She wants us to go to the store, then start supper. Here's her list. Look, she left us some money. She'll come home later with Papa."

"Well, no need to take our coats off." *Who said that?*

The phone jingled. "...No, Mama's not here. She's with Aunt Lydia, so we're going to make supper...You could come home and help, you know...Ha ha, funny...Oh, I suppose it's all right, but you'd better talk to her about it. Swell. That was Lizzie. Mrs. Thomas invited her to stay for supper with Charlotte."

"That girl! Let's go, then."

Anitra heard the girls leave, but did they all go? She crept into Lillian and Naomi's room and looked out the window to see all three girls walking toward town. Elizabeth was with Charlotte. Was she safe? Was Jeff there, too? And where was Jordan? Anitra had to be more careful, now; it was getting late, Elizabeth was no longer safely tucked away at school, and everyone would be home soon. Anitra wanted to get to the Thomas house and stay close to Elizabeth, even show herself if she had to. Anything to keep Elizabeth safe. But Anitra had missed her chance to get through an open door when the girls left.

Anitra went to the attic. And then she remembered. The first time she traveled to the past, Jeff had hidden something in his dresser drawer. But that day wouldn't happen until after Elizabeth's death. Was it in the drawer yet? Trying to keep up with all this twisted time battered her head.

What if that thing in Jeff's dresser was "it?" Although she knew better, Anitra tried to open the drawer. Naturally, it didn't budge. She searched both attic rooms, but they were just like the rest of the house. Innocent.

She returned to Elizabeth's room; she hadn't really finished looking through that last dresser drawer. She opened it quietly, placing the clothes neatly on the floor out of her way, hoping that Elizabeth hid things in her dresser like her brother did.

Under the last sweater, tucked way back in the corner of the drawer was a small, white cotton cloth. She pushed the cloth aside to reveal a little tattered box. For a moment, Anitra froze and stared. Jeff's box! This was it!

Slowly, gingerly, Anitra reached for the box, dreading that it might jump up and bite her at any second. She felt her hand shake as she removed the cloth and picked up the small box wrapped in dirty, worn strips of crumpled paper. Anitra swallowed hard. This was "it." Had to be. But how could something so small cause a tragedy? One she had to prevent.

After shaking the jitters out of her unsteady right hand, she slowly reached for the box that sat in her left palm and began to open it. But a loud, sharp noise jarred her, and the box dropped to the floor. Anitra looked up. And screamed...

☙19❧

"NO! NO! NO! NO!…"

Anitra sat straight up with her hands tangled in her hair, the incessant screams startling her until she realized they were her own. They forced Carrie to back away as Anitra scrambled across the floor and wedged herself into a corner formed by the old dresser and a large, cardboard box. The loose box top *shooshed* abrasively as her body quivered.

Anitra wondered if she was still screaming. Had she stopped, or was that just the memory of it ricocheting inside her head?

"Anitra! Anitra, stop!" Was that Carrie kneeling in front of her and grabbing for her wrists?

The screaming fell away, and Carrie let go.

"Anitra, what happened?" Carrie asked, her voice muffled and distant.

"No…no…no…no…" Rocking back and forth, Anitra heard her screams turn to faint muttering. But where was it coming from?

"Anitra, *please* talk to me," Carrie sniffled. "C'mon. Say something!"

Anitra had to listen carefully to be sure she actually heard Carrie. And even then, the words dissolved into a foreign jumble. She scanned the attic, hoping to recognize the familiar disorder she had cherished all her life, but instead, chaotic debris surrounded her.

Wrapping her arms around herself, Anitra felt the satiny arms of the red dress. She looked down, shocked to see the dress on her, and jumped as if it burned.

"Get it off me! Get it off me!" She lunged out of her corner, flailing and scratching at the dress. "Get...this...off me!"

Carrie reached for her. "Okay, okay," she panicked, "I'll help you. Please, please, let me help you."

Anitra struggled out of the dress, almost knocking Carrie over in the process, and flung it across the room. It floated to the floor and settled in front of the garment bags. She ripped at the red bow, tearing a few hairs out of her head as she sent it tumbling after the dress, and snatched off the locket, leaving a stinging scrape on her neck before it followed the bow. Then before she could pull off the shoes, her legs gave out, and she flopped onto the floor. Free of the dress's horror, she rocked herself again and cringed from the thoughts that scratch-scratch-scratched the inside of her head, trying to escape.

Carrie wiped tears from her cheeks. "Anitra, please talk to me," she whispered. "Please tell me what happened."

But Anitra kept rocking, still listening to the scratching.

Carrie scooped up Anitra's shirt and shorts and timidly held them out to her.

Still rocking, Anitra whispered "nnnooo" to the rhythm of the scratching.

A sob shook Carrie and spilled tears all over her face. "Anitra, c'mon. You gotta let me help you get dressed."

Anitra stopped.

Carrie moved closer and held out the shirt, and Anitra glanced at it from the corner of her eye. Carrie moved even closer.

"No!" Anitra shouted, crawling to the red dress.

Carrie jumped, and the shirt fell out of her hands.

"I gotta go back," Anitra said. "I gotta go back, I gotta go back."

"What...what're you doing?" Carrie cried.

"I gotta go back," Anitra barely whispered. For the first time, she looked at Carrie.

"No," Carrie said. "Don't go! Please don't go!" She tried to pry Anitra away from the dress.

Anitra waved her away and pulled the dress back on as Carrie's voice echoed.

"I gotta go back," Anitra repeated. She sat, waiting for the past to tear her away.

Stunned, Carrie just watched.

"Take me back, take me back," Anitra chanted. Five minutes passed. "Take me back!" Ten minutes. "Please! Take me back! Now!"

"It's not working!" Carrie whispered.

They waited. And waited.

"Nothing's happening!" Anitra's voice wobbled.

"Nothing at all?"

"NO!"

"Okay...okay, calm down." Carrie held Anitra's hands.

"But it worked every other time!" Tears rolled down Anitra's face as she looked up at Carrie. "It's not working! It's not working, I can't get back, why won't it send me back?! Carrie! I HAVE TO GET BACK THERE!"

Carrie grabbed her friend and hugged her tightly. "It's okay..."

"NO, IT'S NOT!" Anitra screamed.

She pulled away, and the girls looked into each other's reddened eyes.

"It's not!" Anitra whimpered. She collapsed back into Carrie's arms and sobbed.

⊰⊱

It was too bright in Carrie's room. Afternoon sunlight piled in and made the pale yellow walls glow, made the metal knobs on the eight-track tape player fire little light beams across Anitra's nose, and made the paralyzed gawks of the stuffed animals seem way too intense.

Anitra stared at the patchwork quilt she sat on and pushed her toes into the spiky fibers of the pea-green shag carpet. It helped her concentrate on the words that spilled from her mouth, repeating horror, reliving torment. The words were too soft and muddled for her to piece together their meaning, but Anitra was pretty sure they were the cause of the bulging eyes that threatened to fall out of Carrie's face.

Gradually the words came into focus as Anitra began to hear herself speak clearly, her voice confident, as if some calm, unworried person had taken her over.

"...so I'm going to tell them," she said.

"Tell your grandparents? Oh, no you don't!" Carrie jumped off the bed. "You can't, Anitra! You can't do that!"

"I'm telling them," Anitra repeated as if merely explaining that she had ten fingers and ten toes.

Carrie ran her fingers through the fringe in her macramé wall hanging. "But, why?"

"Because," Anitra said, "I want them to know that I...

know."

Carrie eased back to the bed and sat. "You scared?"

"Yes."

The girls sat quietly, and Anitra stared down the beady-eyed elephant on top of the stuffed animal pile.

"Carrie?"

"Yeah?"

"Would you come with me?"

ഇരു

Anitra and Carrie walked down Fisher Street back to the Cole house. They had gone back to the deli, where Carrie had insisted that Anitra eat at least a little bit, to wait for Grandpa Jeff and Grandma Charlotte to get home and settle in. Every evening, they needed their helping of Watergate news and a half an hour or so to gnash and slash it before they were truly comfortable. But the wait had given Anitra too much time to think, and she wasn't so sure about talking to her grandparents now that the haze was clearing from her mind.

Anitra's whole body ached as she walked. This was the longest walk down Fisher Street she had ever taken, and it seemed the road stretched longer with every step she took. Maybe the road would keep going and never end. She would just keep walking to the end of time and never reach the family house.

She tried not to practice what she'd say, because the words brought with them the images of that last, terrible trip to the past. But the words kept reforming and replaying anyway, and they tore through her, wrapping themselves around her neck until she thought she'd pass out right in the middle of endless Fisher Street.

As the girls entered the house, Carrie squeezed Anitra's hand. "You can do it," Carrie whispered.

Anitra looked at her and nodded.

In the living room, Grandpa Jeff and Grandma Charlotte sat watching one of those new "Bicentennial Minute" things Channel 2 was going to show for the next two years until the actual Bicentennial.

"Hi, girls!" Grandma Charlotte said.

"Hey, Peanut!" Grandpa Jeff said, smiling at the girls. "Hello, Carrie. You two have fun today?"

Their smiles assaulted Anitra, and she backed away until Carrie nudged her forward.

"Grandpa? Grandma?" Anitra began. "Um, I have something I need to tell you." Her throat felt dry.

"Sweetheart, what's wrong?" Grandma Charlotte replaced her sweet smile with worry.

"Peanut, has something happened?" Grandpa Jeff asked, turning off the television.

The girls perched on the edge of the sofa.

"Well, sort of," Anitra began. "It's just that...I mean, nobody's hurt or anything, but... well some things have been going on the last few days, and it's all been really confusing, and, um, well, you know how I keep sleeping late a lot?" Not at all what she had thought to say.

Grandpa Jeff and Grandma Charlotte waited.

"Anitra..." Carrie whispered, squeezing Anitra's hand again.

"It's about Elizabeth," she finally blurted out. She tried to stop herself from saying it, but it came out too fast. Too late.

An itchy blanket of discomfort suddenly smothered the room.

"Elizabeth?" Grandma Charlotte said.

"Yes," Anitra said. It was out now. "See, um, I know what happened."

Grandpa Jeff leaned forward in his chair. "You...what?" he asked.

Anitra nodded very slowly. "I know what happened to her."

"How...what...I don't understand..." Grandma Charlotte sputtered. Her words came out so slowly, they almost got stuck in the air. Her face, her frown looked foreign.

"I know...because...I saw..." Anitra winced as she saw the incredulous looks on her grandparents' faces. In the middle of the blazing heat wave, the room became suddenly cold.

Carrie sat motionless with her eyes fixed on the floor.

"Child, what are you talking about?" Grandma Charlotte asked. The patience that usually floated through her voice suddenly disappeared.

Anitra looked at her grandparents, and with an unsure hand, she held out the picture of Elizabeth. It should have been wrinkled, yellowed, and faded.

"I...I was there," she said. She felt weak.

Grandpa Jeff took the picture, and his hand shook like the picture weighed a ton. He recognized it. With deepening furrows in his brow, he looked back and forth between Anitra and the picture.

"Where did you get this?" he asked, barely above a whisper.

"From your room. In the attic."

"This picture is not in the photo albums." He rested his elbow on his knee. "It was lost a long, long time ago. Where did you find it? In one of those boxes?"

Anitra felt accused. "I got it off your desk. In the attic."

No one moved.

"Grandpa, that was me that night. In your room. You

thought it was Elizabeth, her ghost. Remember? You asked if I was lonely, and I said no."

"Jeff?" Grandma Charlotte turned to her husband, her eyes pleading.

Grandpa Jeff stared intently at the picture as if trying to coax answers out of it. He passed his hand over his thinning, graying hair and said nothing.

"It was me, Grandpa."

"Now that's *enough*!" Grandma Charlotte said, her jaw tightening.

Both girls jumped. Grandma Charlotte had never spoken to Anitra that way. Ever.

"But Grandma..."

"No! Now I don't know what kind of game this is supposed to be, but it's going to stop right now!"

"But..."

"I'm surprised at you! And you, too, Carrie!"

Carrie sat up straight.

"This is not like you, Anitra," Grandma Charlotte said. "Not like you at all."

"Grandma, please…"

"I said that's enough! You come in here playing this silly game, upsetting everyone. I've heard enough." She stormed into the kitchen, and dishes angrily clattered as she yanked them from the dish rack.

Grandpa Jeff calmly placed the picture on the end table and followed Grandma Charlotte without saying a word. Without looking at Anitra.

Anitra couldn't pry her hands loose from her knees. She couldn't get her head to turn or her ears to listen to Carrie.

"Maybe they just need some time…or something," Carrie said.

Carrie's words lingered in the space between them as they

stared at the floor.

ℬↃↄℬ

In Anitra's room, Anitra curled into a ball on the bed. Carrie sat next to her, and they listened to the dish clatter in the kitchen until a low rumble of muffled voices took its place.

Carrie perked up. "What're they saying?"

"I don't know."

"Don't you wanna listen? Maybe we can find out if…"

"No."

Carrie frowned. "But I thought you wanted…"

"No," Anitra repeated.

Carrie folded her arms and sighed. "Anitra, we both knew this would be hard. But I didn't know they'd be like this. They're never like this. I mean, they're always so…"

"We were talking about Elizabeth," Anitra said.

"Well, maybe you should leave it alone," Carrie said. "They were really mad."

"No. I have to do this." Anitra sat up, grabbed a tissue, and slowly shredded it.

"I don't know, Anitra. Don't you think they might get even madder?"

"They might." Anitra pushed tissue bits around on the bed. "Maybe you better go, Carrie. I think I have to do this by myself, now."

"You sure you'll be okay?"

"Yes," Anitra lied.

"Maybe you're right," Carrie said, heading to the door. "Maybe they don't want to say anything around me. Like it's too private and stuff."

Anitra shredded another tissue.

Carrie's eyes welled. "Okay, um, call me later and…and

tell me *exactly* what happened. Or, um, if you need some… help…or something."

Anitra kept shredding.

"Bye," Carrie whispered.

Anitra offered Carrie a weak smile and watched her leave. Then she pressed the tissue bits into her palm, rolled them into a tight ball, and tossed them into the trash can. She tried to make herself think clearly, but the sound of footsteps on the stairs interrupted her thoughts.

Anitra looked toward the door and worried. What were they going to say? Were they going to punish her for playing a cruel joke on them? She tried to keep her panic at bay as her grandparents reached the top of the stairs and came into her room.

"Anitra, honey," Grandma Charlotte said, sounding like Grandma Charlotte again, "I'm so sorry I raised my voice to you that way." She sat next to Anitra on the bed.

Grandpa Jeff stood just inside the doorway with his hands in his pockets, his face a blank slate. Anitra had no idea what could have been drilling through his mind.

"I didn't mean to upset anybody," Anitra said. "I just wanted to help."

"We know, Peanut," Grandpa Jeff said as he moved two T-shirts from the chair and sat down.

"I saw some things, and…" Anitra began.

"That picture. You found the picture in the attic?" Grandpa Jeff asked.

"Well, yeah, but something happened when I went up there the other day," Anitra said. She spoke slowly, torturously aware of every word.

"What happened, Anitra?" Grandma Charlotte asked, her face contorted with worry.

"Well, I was up there looking for those pictures like you

said I could, Grandma. And...and it was really hot...and I was looking at the photo album..."

They tried hard to follow her random thoughts.

"I kinda got distracted...and...and I kinda passed out and woke up in..."

"Passed out!" Grandma Charlotte gasped. "You fainted?"

Grandpa Jeff sat up straight in the chair. "Did you hurt yourself, Peanut?"

"No, I didn't hurt myself," Anitra said, "but something happened. I saw these things happening, and I saw you, Grandpa, when you were my age, and..."

Grandpa Jeff smiled. "Oh, Peanut, no wonder you're all confused. You fainted up in that hot attic, and you dreamed all kinds of things." A quiet, relieved laugh slipped out. "I'm sure it seemed real to you."

Grandma Charlotte shook her head. "I told you it wasn't good for you to go up there, now didn't I, honey?" She flashed her maybe-next-time-you'll-listen-to-me look.

"Well, yes, ma'am, but..."

"Now that's it," Grandma Charlotte said. "No more going to that attic until this weather breaks. Do you understand me, missy?" She gave Anitra a hug and kissed her forehead.

"Yes, Grandma, but something really happened..."

"Oh, I'm sure it seems that way, Peanut," Grandpa Jeff said. "You wake up and you think something you dreamed was real. But it was just a dream. Don't you worry."

"But, Grandpa..."

Grandma Charlotte gave her a reassuring squeeze. "Honey, we tell you so many stories, no wonder you started dreaming about them. But that's all it is, baby. A dream. Just a dream."

"You get some rest tonight," Grandpa Jeff said. "You'll feel better in the morning, and everything will make sense."

"Okay," Anitra whispered as she let herself melt into her grandmother's arms.

So they had it all figured out. It had all been a dream. She would wake up the next morning feeling refreshed and ready to go back to the pool and bike rides with Carrie. Just like that. No one had anything to worry about.

ೞ20ര

A light spring breeze puffed through Carrie's living room window and played with the blinds.
Laughter from a small group of mountain bikers
and the scent of freshly cut grass drifted in and mixed with
the silence inside. Quietly huddled together on the sofa, the
two women protected each other from the rage of twenty-
two-year-old memories.

Anitra had cried herself empty. Nothing seemed real anymore. It seemed this life, this present, was the dream and
those days in the twenties were the only reality. The wall she
had built around those menacing memories had come crashing down on her in a pile of rubble and fine, stifling dust, and
she now had to find a new, safe place to keep them. To deal
with them.

Carrie wiped her eyes with the last tissue in the box. "Oh,
Anitra, it's been so long since I really thought about all this. I
remember trying to bring it up a couple of times right after
that summer, but I couldn't because...I guess because it
would mean it really happened. And that was just too much.

Besides, you weren't going anywhere near the subject. So I just left it alone."

Anitra leaned forward and rested her head in her palms.

Carrie sighed loudly. "Seems like more than twenty-two years. Seems like forever ago."

"I wish it was *never*," Anitra whispered. Her voice, dry and flat, seemed to be coming from some other place.

"All that mess bottled up inside you. Girl, it's a wonder you haven't exploded from the pressure!" Carrie placed a shaky hand on Anitra's shoulder.

Anitra sat up and tried to think back over the past twenty-two years. "I don't know. I guess I just never remembered any of it. And, Carrie, I mean I really didn't remember. But now I remember that day when I decided not to send the letter. I knew there was nothing either of us could do, and I knew no one else would believe me. My grandparents were certainly off limits. So I guess I just let it sink, and somehow I just stopped thinking about it."

Anitra looked up through the silence and found Carrie examining the intricacies of her front lawn. "Carrie?"

"Hmm?" Carrie snapped out of her trance and looked at Anitra.

"What's going on up there?" Anitra asked, pointing at Carrie's head. Carrie's gears were cranking; Anitra could almost hear them.

Carrie twirled the cord to her blinds and watched the plastic ends plunk against the window frame.

"I think you need to talk to someone," she said.

"What, a psychiatrist? You think I'm telling this little problem to some stranger?" Anitra smiled slightly. "Oh, no, I don't think so. They'd put me in a straight jacket."

Carrie shook her head and smiled back. "I mean your grandfather."

Anitra rolled her eyes and groaned. "You can't be serious!" She raised her hand and let it drop listlessly onto her lap as she watched Carrie move away from the window and face her on the sofa.

"Oh, yes, I'm very serious. You need to talk to him. I bet he needs to talk to you, too."

"Carrie, I think the last thing he needs is to talk about something like this. Look how hard it was for the two of us just now. Damn near killed us. Besides, I don't think he can handle it. He and Grandma wouldn't discuss it back then, and now he's alone and a lot older, you know."

"He's the youngest eighty-something-year-old I've ever met! He's a strong man, Anitra, but I bet he needs to talk about it. I mean, all those years. Think about it!"

Anitra shook her head so fast it gave her a headache. "No. No way in hell."

Carrie moved closer to her friend and looked directly into her eyes. "Anitra, don't you realize what this can do to you if you don't face it? Right away? Now? You think you were having trouble before with all those memories locked away all nice and neat?"

"No, Carrie!"

"Anitra, who else are you going to talk to? He's the only one left who can help you deal with this. And it's not just you. Who does he have to talk to? What's he got all bottled up? Girl, if you don't do this, it will eat away at you for the rest of your life. You can't push it to the back of your head anymore. And besides, you can help him too, don't you think?"

Reluctantly, Anitra nodded.

"Mm hmm," Carrie said. "If you don't talk to him, he'll always have it hanging over his head. Anitra, your grandmother took it to her grave. Please don't let that happen to him."

Anitra began to wake from her self-imposed stupor. She turned her thoughts over and over in her head and waited for them to fall into place. She knew Carrie was right, but she still wanted it all to return to that hiding place that had kept her safe all this time.

"Call him, Anitra," Carrie said, holding the black cordless phone out to Anitra. "Do it now before you talk yourself out of it."

Anitra sighed and stared at the phone in Carrie's hand.

Carrie gently placed it in Anitra's lap. "I'll drive you there, stay there with you, whatever you want. Anything. Just call him."

Anitra held the phone with both hands to steady the trembling. "Thank you so much, Carrie. I don't know what I would have done…"

"Don't you worry about it. You came through for me every time I needed you. Every single time. It's just my turn to be here for you, that's all." Carrie smiled. "Now stop procrastinating and dial."

Anitra took a deep breath, dialed the number, and waited. "Hi, Grandpa. It's me, Anitra…"

ഇൽരൂ

The two mile drive to Fisher Street was much too short. Not nearly enough time to piece together any coherent thoughts. To figure out some clever thing to say to make it all make sense. To prepare to accept whatever her grandfather might say. Damn, there had to be some other way. Maybe she wouldn't bring it up at all, and they'd just chat about unimportant things the way they always had since that summer.

She lowered the driver's side window and took in the

sweet spring air that lightly brushed her face and calmed her heart. Sticking her hand out the window, she stretched her fingers to let the wind rush through them. But when she turned onto Fisher Street, her stomach turned, too. Over the years, this place she'd so loved had become a place to avoid, to fear, to try to forget.

As she pulled into the driveway, she sat for a moment and watched her grandfather work in his garden. Preparing the soil, no doubt. His favorite spring chore. When he stood in his garden at least thirty years melted away from his face, his back, his knees, his hands. The arthritic creaks and gnarls lost their grip any time he broke the soil to wake it from its winter hibernation or when, months later, he picked rich, red tomatoes from vines that left that pithy green smell on his hands.

He looked up from his work and waved at her. Wiping the soil from his clothes, he slowly made his way toward the house.

⚮

Grandpa Jeff brought two tall glasses of lemonade from the kitchen and placed them on the coffee table in front of her.

"Well, Peanut, how have you been these days?" he asked.

Anitra sighed and smiled. "Oh, fine. I'm just fine."

"Thaaat's good," he said with a grunt as he settled himself into his recliner.

Anitra sipped her lemonade and let it sit on her tongue for a minute. Strong enough to yank a man out of a coma. Just like Grandma Charlotte used to make. But this time Anitra's Aunt Maryanne had made it. She'd moved in not long after Grandma Charlotte had died.

"So, uh, how 'bout you, Grandpa? How are you doing?"

That came out a little too perky.

"Oh, well, I'm doing just fine, too, Peanut." He reached over and patted her hand. "Mm hmm…that's right. Juuuust fine."

They nodded at each other, happy to have established that they were both "just fine."

Grandpa Jeff sat back in his chair. "It's so good to see you, Peanut! What brings you to town?"

"Well, I'm giving myself a week of vacation time. Drove down to Mom and Dad's this morning and I thought I'd stop by to see you and Carrie while I was in the area."

"Vacation!" Grandpa Jeff plastered a shocked look on his face and laughed. "You mean somebody finally pried you loose from that office of yours?"

Anitra's laughter surprised her.

"Now when was the last time you took a vacation?" Grandpa Jeff asked.

"Oh, c'mon. John and I went to the islands a few months ago."

"Yeah, I heard all about that," he chuckled. "Poor fella had to drag you kicking and hollering away from work."

"Oh, he did not!" Anitra blushed.

"That's what I heard. Almost tore your fingernails off trying to hang on to your desk! 'Sides, that was one of those long weekend things you kids like so much. That doesn't count."

"Sure it does." She laughed quietly to herself and sighed.

Grandpa Jeff laughed quietly to himself and sighed.

They sat, sipped lemonade, glanced at each other, and waited for some other person to come along with a witty comment.

"So, Peanut, how is John these days?"

Why did he have to ask about John? Damn. "Okay, I

guess," she said.

"Oh? 'Okay, I guess?' What does that mean?" His smile faded a bit.

Anitra sighed. "John and I...we...we broke up."

"What happened, Peanut? Did he do something to you?" he asked, ready to pounce and defend his granddaughter's honor.

"No, Grandpa. No, things just weren't working out."

"Hmm. I see." He thought it over. He thought it over some more. "Well..." A little more thinking. "...you just take your time."

"I will. Thanks." Anitra nodded absently and studied the melting ice in her glass.

Grandpa Jeff twirled the ice cubes in his glass and made them clink.

"Aunt Maryanne made some serious lemonade," Anitra said, desperately changing the subject.

"Mm hmm." Grandpa Jeff agreed. "This'll kill a lesser human being, all right." He couldn't help but laugh at himself.

"It's just like Grandma's. Did she finally give up that secret recipe of hers?"

"I'm afraid so, Peanut. And your Aunt Maryanne seems to think I don't want to drink anything else. Ha!"

He made Anitra laugh again. "She taking good care of you, Grandpa?"

"Oh, yeah. Although sometimes I'm pretty sure I'm the one taking care of her!" He winked at Anitra. "But don't tell her I said so."

"You got it," she said. That secret was safe. "Do you think Grandma gave her any more of her recipes?"

"Mm hmm. All of them."

"Guess they aren't secrets any more," Anitra said.

"Well, you know, Peanut, you get older, and keeping secrets just doesn't mean as much anymore."

What? Could he have opened the door any wider? What was he doing? Did he know?

"What do you mean, Grandpa?" she asked.

"When your grandma was sick, well, she and I talked a lot about wanting to make sure nothing was lost. You know, things like her recipes and those instructions, or patterns, or whatever you call them for all those…those little things she used to knit for the children." He sat back, savoring the warmth of his wife's memory.

As she watched the smile spread across his face, Anitra thought she saw the look he always got in his eyes whenever he told one of his family stories. Grandma Charlotte would now take her rightful place in those stories.

"She wanted to make sure someone had them. Someone who'd use them properly. So she gave the recipes to Mary-anne and those instruction things to your sister."

Anitra let the same warmth wash over her. "She sure wasn't going to leave them to me. I remember she tried to teach me to knit so many times…"

"But you could never sit still long enough for her to put the needles in your hand." He tugged at her hair just as he had when she was a child.

"That's right. Guess that's why she left me all those Thomas family photo albums instead."

"Mm hmm." He slowly closed his eyes; he was away somewhere with Grandma Charlotte. "She knew you'd take good care of them, Peanut."

"You know, Grandpa, I haven't seen the Cole photo albums in so long."

His back stiffened just barely enough for her to notice. "Oh…they're still up there. Everything's…still…there…" His voice flattened.

With the exception of a few mercifully quick errands for Grandma Charlotte, Anitra had not been to the attic since that summer. So many years. It didn't seem that long.

"Yeah, I suppose they are all there," she said. "I still have all those pictures memorized."

"I'm sure you do, Peanut. You used to live up there." A speck of sadness tainted his smile. He retrieved his pipe from an ashtray on the end table.

"Especially that family portrait," Anitra said. She suddenly felt that old, creepy chill. "That was my favorite. It was so beautiful."

Grandpa Jeff stared at the air. "Yes, that it was, that it was."

"Your parents looked so proud of all of you."

"Yes, indeed, they most certainly were," he nodded.

Anitra watched his eyes as she spoke. "And I loved the clothes. Especially the girls' dresses. They were so pretty." How far was he going to let her take this?

Grandpa Jeff nodded and contemplated his pipe. "I'll be right back, Peanut." The pipe clinked into the ashtray, and he gently touched her cheek as he stood and headed for the stairs.

In the several minutes he was gone, Anitra tortured herself with worries that she'd upset him enough to make him need to leave the room to recover. Years ago it had changed her relationship with her grandparents for good and had made her believe that she could never stay with them again.

Grandpa Jeff returned with an old, worn shoe box tucked under one arm. He sat next to Anitra and placed a picture on the table in front of her. It was the picture of Elizabeth from that summer night, the picture she had brought back from the past.

ഇ21ൽ

nitra put her hand to her mouth. She had forgotten. That night, she had left Elizabeth's picture in the living room after her disastrous attempt to tell Grandpa Jeff and Grandma Charlotte what had happened. It looked worn, but not by the seventy years it should have endured. In the strange reality of the family home, this picture was barely more than twenty years old.

Grandpa Jeff put his finger on the picture. "It's about this, isn't it, Peanut?"

Anitra blinked away the shock. "Uh, yes. Yes, it…it is." She couldn't take her eyes off the picture. It made the lemonade taste suddenly dry and bitter. And those damned chills ran her down.

"It's all right, honey. You go ahead. It's all right."

The door was wide open. He put it right in front of her, where she never thought it would be, and invited her to stroll on through. And now she had no idea what to say. This time she hadn't rehearsed.

"It's all right," Grandpa Jeff repeated, enveloping her

hand in both of his.

Anitra sighed. "I was there, Grandpa," she whispered to the picture. There. It was out. And it came out so easily.

"Where, Peanut?"

"There with you in 1927 and '28. The summer of 1974, when I was thirteen, well, somehow I ended up back in the twenties. With you." She paused to let that sink in. She could hear him frown.

"With me?" he asked.

"That picture...I got that picture...I found it on your desk in the attic. But not in the attic like it was in '74." She paused to search for the right words. "It was your bedroom, Grandpa. When you were a child, about the same age I was at the time."

Anitra waited a moment for the dust to settle and imagined his head spinning. His gaze alternated between the picture on the table and their intertwined hands. He was so quiet.

"Grandpa, I know how hard this must be to believe. But...but I was there! I was really there! It was that dress."

"Dress?" His frown deepened.

"The red one. Elizabeth's red dress in the attic. See, Grandpa, one day I went up to the attic and started looking at the old pictures, like the family portrait." Anitra felt her voice waver, but she gave up trying to control it. What she was saying sounded crazy anyway, even to her.

"I was looking at the dress Elizabeth wore in the portrait, so I got it out of the garment bag and put it on. I mean the whole outfit. Dress, shoes, locket, bow, everything. I wanted to see how much I looked like her, and I did." Anitra smiled at the memory. "I looked exactly like her. But then I passed out, and when I woke up, everything had changed."

"Changed?" Grandpa Jeff asked as he closed his eyes.

"It was 1928. In April."

Grandpa Jeff opened his eyes to stare at the wall. Anitra wasn't sure, but she thought she felt his hands begin to tremble ever so slightly.

"It really did happen, Grandpa. Really."

He didn't argue. In fact, he hardly seemed surprised. He just sat there and listened as if she were giving him gardening tips.

"Go on, Peanut."

"Well, I started to walk around the house, and everything was different! The furniture, the rugs, the old radio and stove, Aunt Naomi's piano. And the attic was two bedrooms."

"Your grandmother and I told you about all that, Peanut, and you used to look at those pictures all the time. You said you fainted. Maybe you dreamed the whole thing." He didn't sound confident. It sounded more like testing. Or hoping.

The memory of old suspicions made her squirm.

"I know," she said. "I thought that, too, at first. But it was real. And, Grandpa, I saw them all."

"Who?"

"The whole family! Jordan, Lillian, Naomi, and Irene were all right there in the kitchen making dinner. Your parents were bringing Adam home from college for Easter. Even you, Grandpa. I saw you, too. You came home from playing baseball, and the girls teased you about Grandma Charlotte. I watched all day, and nobody could see or hear me. And I couldn't touch anything."

He listened intently, but as usual, his face was hard to read.

She continued, "When everybody got home, you all had dinner in the dining room. You were talking about Naomi going to college and who would run for president. Mama

Sarah didn't want Naomi to go so far away. I was sitting in a chair against the wall, and I watched the whole thing. Nobody knew I was there until I laughed at something somebody said." She paused and looked into her grandfather's eyes. "You heard me, Grandpa. You saw me."

That was it! She studied his face and knew. He remembered!

"Sitting in Lizzie's chair." he whispered. Yes! He knew!

Anitra pressed on, encouraged by her grandfather's reaction. "Later that night, I went to the room I used to stay in, and I could touch things. Elizabeth's things. I picked up her story book and touched her bed. Then Irene came in, and I went upstairs. I sat in that green chair in your room while you were sleeping, and I started crying because I was tired and didn't know how to get back. You called me 'Lizzie' because you thought you heard her cry. But it wasn't her, Grandpa, it was me." Her eyes pleaded with his. "It was me!"

Grandpa Jeff stared at her.

"Then I woke up, and I was back here maybe a minute after I passed out. Grandpa, don't you believe me?"

"…hard to say…" he whispered.

"Every time I put on that dress, it happened." She had to keep going.

"Every time? This happened more than once?"

"That's right. I put the dress on the next day to show it to Carrie, and it happened again. I passed out right in front of Carrie and woke up in the past again. Except this time it was 1927, right after Elizabeth died. That's when you saw me again, Grandpa. You and Grandma Charlotte were in her room, and Grandma was holding a doll and crying. You both looked so sad, and I wanted to cry, too. I stood right there in the doorway, and you both looked up and saw me. Don't you remember, Grandpa? I was wearing the red dress. Elizabeth's dress."

His eyes widened, and Anitra worried that it might be too much for him. But he remembered.

"No one knew," he said. "No one knew."

"Are you okay, Grandpa? Can I get you something?" Anitra asked, afraid to continue.

"No, Peanut," he said, patting her hands. "You go ahead now."

Why wasn't he shocked? Why didn't he run from her as fast as he could? How could he listen to all this? Despite her confusion, Anitra found herself feeling the old burden start to lift just a little bit.

"Okay. Well, I got scared because you saw me, so I went downstairs, and the room was full of people. And, oh, it was so sad." Anitra shook her head at the memory. "All those people. But nobody saw me. Just you. You saw me again at the dining room table."

"Sitting in Lizzie's chair," he said. "And by the tree!"

"Yes!" Anitra almost came off of the sofa. "That was me, Grandpa! I followed you and Grandma."

"And in my room later that night," he said.

"Right. But you only saw me when I touched that picture." She pointed to the picture on the table. "Grandpa, I was right there, and you never saw me until I touched something that was Elizabeth's. That time it was the picture, and that's...that's when you asked me if I was lonely."

"That was you," he whispered. He sounded as if a lump had formed in the middle of his throat.

Anitra nodded and ran a shaky hand through her hair. "That's how I got this picture. I still had it in my hand when I woke up. I brought it back with me. That's why you couldn't find it."

Grandpa Jeff remained silent.

"Grandpa, do you believe me?"

He closed his eyes and nodded slowly. "Yes I do, Peanut."

Relieved and grateful, the burden felt a little lighter still. Yet something nagged at her. This was too easy. How could he accept something so bizarre so quickly? Because she was telling him things she should have no way of knowing? Maybe, but it was strange all the same.

She thought about what to tell him next. She was definitely not ready to talk about her final trip to the past. She couldn't. Not now.

"There's more," she said, breaking a brief silence.

Grandpa Jeff stared and waited for the next bizarre revelation. He clearly wanted, no, needed to know what she had seen back then, no matter how painful it might be.

"Go ahead, honey," he said.

"After that first time, I woke up in the middle of the night, and...I saw...Elizabeth's ghost."

Grandpa Jeff abruptly looked up. "Her ghost?"

Anitra nodded. "Yes. She was upstairs in the bedroom I used to use, and she wore the same red dress. I watched her and followed her all over the house. She looked scared... well, for a ghost. She was looking at everything in the house like she was trying to figure out what everything was."

Anitra pointed to the portrait of Papa Russell and Mama Sarah. "And that portrait, well, she kept staring at it. She even touched it once. It scared her, and she started to cry."

"Where did she go?" Grandpa Jeff asked.

"She finally ran upstairs into the office and disappeared up the attic stairs."

"Was that the only time you saw her?" A gray cloud spread across his brow.

Anitra looked at her grandfather. Why would he ask that?

How did he know to ask that?

"She came back the next night. I fell asleep on the sofa after watching a movie because I was too scared to go back to my room. And I woke up, and there she was practically standing over me. She kept asking me who I was. She thought I was her, and I can't say I cleared things up for her."

He still didn't look surprised.

"I...I asked her if she was looking for you," Anitra said, "and...she...she got upset."

Squeezing her eyes shut, Anitra longed to put her fingers in her ears and run far away. Outside, a group of neighborhood kids laughed and chattered past the house. Anitra clung to that sound, wishing the red dress could transport her into their child world of bicycles and bubble gum.

Grandpa Jeff ran his hand across his face but said nothing. He was locked in the past.

"I asked her if she needed help," Anitra said. "She acted like she did. Then she just ran...glided...up the stairs and disappeared."

"It can't be...it can't be..." He spoke barely above a whisper.

What had she done? This was too much for him. Too much.

"But, Grandpa, she wasn't that upset, really." She gently squeezed her grandfather's hand. "I'm sure she's been safe and happy in Heaven all this time. Maybe she knew I'd been to the past and...and wanted to visit me."

She couldn't do this any longer. It was time to just let it go. But before Anitra could say another word, Grandpa Jeff opened the old shoe box and pulled out a small, wrinkled piece of paper that had had several decades to yellow. Anitra immediately recognized it as the mysterious, crumpled paper that he had kept hidden in his dresser drawer back in the twenties. The same piece of paper that had upset him so. He handed it to Anitra.

Trying to control her shaking hands, she gingerly unfolded the brittle paper, terrified to finally see what it was. She gasped, and her heart pounded as she read the contents. At the top of the page was printed: "*From the Desk of Dr. Jefferson M. Cole.*" Below, in her own thirteen-year-old handwriting, were the directions Carrie had given her to the Louiston Public Library.

҂22҂

"Peanut," Grandpa Jeff said softly, "there are some things you need to know." He moved to his favorite chair and sat back as he always did when it was time to tell a story. Satisfied that he had reached optimum comfort, he began to tell the most important story of all.

҂҂

"Hey! What are you two doing in there?"

Jeff had come upstairs to look for the baseball glove that always managed to stay hidden from him. As he reached the top step, he heard the familiar sound of giggling little girls. Strangely, it was coming from his parents' room, so he went in to investigate. And there were Lizzie and Charlotte. Caught!

"We're not doing anything!" Lizzie said. A lie. Her hands were full of the paper she had pulled out of the decorative box that sat on the floor just outside the closet door. The two girls hovered over it like it was a brand new puppy, guilt smeared all over their faces.

"You know you're not supposed to play in here, Lizzie. Mama's not going to like this," he said. "Not one bit!" He smiled. He was so good at this.

"She won't know if you don't tell her," Lizzie said. "So what do you want this time?"

Ah, the music of her words. That's right, no arguments, just get right to it. "Clean my room."

"Fine, I'll clean your room," she said, rolling her eyes.

"For two weeks," he said, jutting his chin into the air.

"Two weeks!" She was not happy about this at all.

He stared at her, giving her time to think about what their mother might do if she found out. Not a pleasant thought.

"Two weeks," she said. "But only two!"

"Deal," he said, pleased with his quick victory. These little battles were getting too easy. But he didn't feel bad about it; she just had to learn to stay out of trouble. He doubted she ever would. And this time, winning in front of Charlotte Thomas was a great big bonus.

"So what is that anyway?" he asked.

"It's her Christmas present," Charlotte said as she daintily lifted a bright red dress out of the box, "and it's beautiful!"

All right, it was nice and all, but nothing to drool over. Girls were not easy to understand, especially these two.

"You opened your Christmas present? Ooooh! Somebody's getting her hide tanned today!" He smiled broadly as he tortured his sister.

"Jeff!" Lizzie was getting annoyed. She knew another week of room cleaning was coming her way.

"Give me one more week, and I'll help you put the wrapping back on. No one will ever know."

"Forget it!" she said defiantly. "We'll do it ourselves."

"Well, fine, but if it doesn't look just right, Mama will know..."

"Mama will know what?" Mama asked.

Jeff jumped and spun around to see his mother standing behind him with a set of neatly folded sheets resting in her arms. He knew that this was not one of Sarah Cole's favorite things to hear.

"Oh, hello, Mama, uh..."

"Elizabeth!" she shouted, looking at the box on the floor.

Lizzie quickly jumped up, ran to her mother, and hugged her tight. "Mama, it's beauuuutiful! It's the most beautiful dress I've ever seen! Thank you so much! Thank you, thank you, thank you!" She knew she had to work quickly.

As he watched, Jeff rolled his eyes and groaned. This was pitiful.

"Elizabeth Sarah Cole! What have you done this time?" Mama was just beginning to boil. She put the sheets on her dresser and placed her hands firmly on her hips.

Lizzie had to talk fast to get out of this one. "Mama, we didn't mean to open it. We came in to find some beads. The ones you let us play with. We couldn't find them, so I went to the closet. I thought they were in your old hat box on the shelf, and when I tried to reach it, that box...that box fell right on the floor, and...and the ribbon came loose, and, well, I saw my name on it, and, well..."

"And the ribbon untied itself and you just *had* to open it," Mama said, hands still on hips.

Lizzie nodded eagerly. "I did," she said with great remorse. "But Mama, it's so beautiful. Everything you make is so nice, but this, this is the prettiest. All for me! Thank you Mama!" Lizzie hugged their mother so tightly that Jeff expected her eyes to pop out and roll down the stairs.

But Mama was unmoved; she barely raised an eyebrow at her daughter's fine performance. "Now, Elizabeth, you listen to me. You take that dress, fold it neatly, and put it back in that box. Then you put the wrapping back on and put it back where you found it."

"But Mama, do I have to put it back?" Lizzie pleaded. "I've already seen it. Can't I have it now?"

Mama's face turned a special shade of red saved especially for Lizzie and sometimes Jordan. "You do as you're told. I have half a mind to give it away to some other little girl who knows how to wait for Christmas for her presents."

Lizzie's soft, brown eyes began to fill with tears. "Oh, not my dress! Please, Mama, may I keep it, please? I *promise* I'll take very good care of it. And I won't ask for anything else for Christmas. Nothing at all. Please?"

Jeff shook his head and rolled his eyes again. Lizzie's wide, brown, innocent eyes worked magic every time. His mother's face softened, although the left corner of her mouth still strained with annoyance.

"Well, all right. But this will be your only present. Do not expect anything else, do you understand?"

"Yes, ma'am," Lizzie said dutifully.

"Hang it up neatly in your closet right away."

"Yes, ma'am."

"And Elizabeth, if anything happens to that dress between now and Christmas day, if you get yourself into any more trouble..." She didn't need to finish. Lizzie knew.

Mama turned and left the room, and Lizzie stood with eyes wide thinking over the very serious warning. She would have to be very careful for two whole months.

"You were lucky," Charlotte said.

Lizzie shook her head and looked at Charlotte. "No, not lucky at all," she said woefully. "Mama will have a sharp eye on me every day until Christmas morning."

"That's right," Jeff laughed. This was almost worth losing the room cleaning service.

Lizzie glared at him then turned to Charlotte. "Let's go, Charlotte."

She draped the dress over her arm with great care, and she and Charlotte marched out. Lizzie gave her brother the coldest look she could manage, but as Charlotte passed him, she briefly flashed a shy little smile.

Jeff smiled, satisfied with the outcome, and headed to his room to find his baseball glove.

⁪⁫

A crisp autumn breeze whisked bright red and yellow leaves in front of Jeff and Adam as they strolled the Manhattan sidewalk. Jeff pulled on the collar of his heavy, cable-knit cardigan sweater and pulled his gray wool cap further down on his forehead. He had been sure that the sweater would keep him warm enough, but he hadn't counted on the occasional breeze that came along when the sun momentarily ducked behind puffy white clouds or a row of tall buildings. Had he listened to his mother, he would have brought his coat, and he'd be warm. Why did she have to be right all the time?

Jeff always looked forward to Adam's trips home from college. Each trip, Adam made time for the two of them to do something together. This usually meant a train ride to the city and a lot of food. Today, they had gone to Harlem to visit one of Adam's friends and just walk around. Before they left, they had had to convince Irene to stay home. She had jumped at the mention of Harlem; she wanted to see for herself all of the famous writers and musicians that lived there. But this trip to the city belonged to Adam and Jeff.

This afternoon, the street was packed with people. As he followed Adam out of the apartment building on the north side of the street, Jeff watched as dozens of cars and trucks rattled along, children darted in and out of doors, and adults milled around the shops on the south side of the street. The boys passed a small crowd of women gathered outside of a huge church discussing the important events of the day. Across the street, a young mother stuck her head out of a fourth floor window and called for her daughter to come back in and finish her chores.

Jeff loved these trips to Harlem. Even the largest church in Louiston was tiny and cramped compared to the one he and Adam had just passed. And the shops! Barbers, pharmacies, grocers, restaurants, beauty salons, night clubs that his mother would never want him to go near, and shops for anything else a person could ever want. They were all crowded with customers staying long enough not only to buy what they needed, but to share the latest neighborhood gossip, too. This place was alive! Here, he could go into a store and not be watched suspiciously by the owners. Even if they didn't know his parents. Things were different in Louiston.

Adam and Jeff drifted slowly down the street ducking in and out of shops along the way. The sweet, inviting aroma of fresh pastries grabbed them and coaxed them across the street to Adam's favorite bakery. Well, *every* bakery was Adam's favorite. Minutes later, they left the bakery with full stomachs and a little less change in their pockets.

"Hey, Buddy, look at that," Adam said as they continued down the street. He pointed at a store window.

Jeff stopped, paralyzed by the vision in the window. Behind the window, sitting on an upended black trunk, was the most beautiful thing he had ever seen. The world's most perfect baseball glove! Eighty-four cents!

"Adam!" Jeff said, pressing his nose against the glass to get as close to the glove as he could. "You think the Monarchs use gloves like that?"

"Maybe," Adam said, smiling.

"Someday I will, too."

"You should've earned enough for that by now."

"Not yet. Soon, though. Probably by the next time you come home."

Jeff sometimes worked for his father on Saturdays, and so far he'd saved enough for a new baseball bat and a few other things he'd had his eye on. He added the glove to his list of things to buy.

"Then we'll have to come back and get it," Adam said.

The boys smiled in agreement and strolled a few more blocks. Another store window caught Jeff's attention and pulled him to it. On the window, it said, "Jewelry." No store name, just "Jewelry." He had to look. He wasn't sure why; he couldn't help it.

"What're you doing, Buddy?" Adam asked. There were no baseball gloves in this window.

"Look at these, Adam. Mama and the girls like things like this. Maybe we can find something for them for Christmas."

Adam looked completely confused. "Don't you think it's a little soon for that?"

Jeff shrugged and looked up at Adam like it was normal to want, to need, to go into a jewelry store.

Adam pushed his glasses up on his nose and shrugged back. "All right. Let's take a look."

They went into the store and had to wait for their eyes to adjust to see where they were going. It was dark, and the only sound belonged to a faintly ticking clock. Jeff exchanged suspicious looks with his brother. This place was different, all right.

"Welcome, boys. I've been waiting for you! May I help you?" asked a voice with a syrupy, southern accent.

Adam and Jeff jumped. An old, excessively-wrinkled woman came from behind a curtain and scurried to a glass counter filled with all sorts of jewelry. She was no taller than Jeff and surprisingly quick for someone so wrinkled. Jeff wondered why she'd been waiting for them. Probably didn't have many customers; they were the only ones there.

"Um, yes, ma'am," Adam managed to say. "We'd like to look at some of your jewelry."

"For a lady friend?" she asked. Her voice was low and raspy, like she had spent too many years smoking or even drinking at shady speakeasies.

"No, for our mother and sisters. For Christmas."

The old woman's wrinkles made room for a smile. "A little early for Christmas, don't you think, boys?"

"Never too early if you see just the right thing," Adam said, trying to smile back at the woman. Adam seemed slightly unnerved, and that made Jeff fidget.

"Well, then. Let's see what we have for you boys today." The old woman folded her hands on the counter and craned her neck up to look thoughtfully into Adam's face. "And how old are your sisters?"

"The oldest is seventeen, and the youngest is twelve," Adam said.

She showed the boys delicately patterned pins, brooches, rings, chains, beads, and even purses. Soon Jeff's head was spinning. Even Adam looked overwhelmed as his glasses slid to the tip of his nose. Quickly overcome, Jeff realized that this was well beyond their understanding. After all, these were girls' things. They had stepped into some other country. The boys looked at each other, scratched their heads and shrugged.

Adam pushed his glasses back into place. "Ma'am, we're not so sure what we want. We'll just have to come back some other time."

Jeff said nothing; he had a headache.

"Are you sure, boys?" the woman drawled.

"Yes, ma'am," Adam said, and he and Jeff turned to leave.

"Oh, boys," the woman said, her drawl thickening just a bit, "why don't you wait here. I have something I think you'll like."

She disappeared behind the curtain and dug around in a back room. She returned, looking slightly dusty, and held up a delicate silver locket. It spun lazily as it dangled from its chain.

The boys turned to look, and Jeff felt himself drawn back to the counter.

"Any little girl would be very happy to have this for Christmas," the old woman said. "A special locket for a special girl."

Jeff watched intently as the silver locket bounced and swayed in front of him. "But it's old," he said noticing the tarnish that had collected in the etched pattern on its surface.

"That's what makes it so special," the woman replied. "This is over one hundred years old!"

Adam raised an eyebrow and stifled a laugh. "I'm sorry, ma'am, but I don't think we have enough money for something like that."

"And how do we know it's really from way back then?" Jeff chimed in.

The old woman laughed, making her wrinkles dance around her face. "Look at this, child! This is from the early 1800's! You can tell by the pattern. It's been with me since before I came up here to Harlem. Brought it all the way up from Georgia. It's special, I'm telling you."

"What's so *special* about it being old?" Jeff asked. He was already getting tired of her calling the thing "special."

"Well, now. The last person to own this locket was a beautiful young girl. A very special girl who owned it, some twenty or twenty-five years ago. Sad to say, she couldn't keep it. Hard times and all, you see. It's been waiting here ever since for just the right person. Something like this is meant to stay in a family. Get passed along. Never leave the family."

Jeff sighed. Wasn't she done yet?

"I wouldn't let it go to just anybody," she continued. "I haven't even *shown* it to anyone until today! It's been in that back room all this time! That's how special it is!"

Well, with all that talking and all those "specials," she still hadn't answered his question. It sounded like a lot of baloney to him. But he couldn't tear himself away from that locket.

The woman pointed an arthritic finger at Jeff. "You can have it for just one dollar."

"One dollar?" Adam laughed. "Ma'am, I don't mean to be rude, but if it's as special as you say it is…"

"It most certainly is special, dear." The woman was so busy defending her claims, she abandoned her drawl. "But I can see this young man is taking great interest in it. I wouldn't want to deprive him of this…opportunity," she said, reclaiming the drawl and putting it solidly back in place behind her wiry smile.

Adam rolled his eyes in disbelief.

"Lizzie would like this, Adam," Jeff said, thinking of the red dress she had coaxed from their mother. Lizzie wouldn't just like it; she'd love it.

Adam pulled his brother aside. "Jeff, listen to me. She's lying. There's nothing unique or special or anything else about that thing. Not if it costs a dollar! I bet it was made a couple of months ago. In fact, a dollar is probably too much. She's just trying to take your money."

"You sure?"

Adam nodded. "She wants your money," he repeated.

Jeff turned back to the woman. "I'll give you fifty cents."

Adam groaned.

The woman let out a scratchy laugh. "Oh, I can't give this to you for just fifty cents, son," she said making the locket spin in front of his face. "Not this one. It's just too precious."

She paused to give Jeff a moment to think. "But I can give it to you for ninety cents."

"Sixty," Jeff said resolutely. He felt confident now; she was caving in.

Adam shook his head.

"I'm sure your Lizzie is a pretty little girl. Even prettier wearing this." She continued to swing the locket in front of him.

"Sixty-five cents."

"Jeff!" Adam said.

"I know what I'm doing!" Jeff said. Well, not really, of course, but he wanted to show Adam that he could handle such an important matter on his own.

"I'm sorry, dear," the woman said as she placed the locket back in its box. She shook her head in disappointment. "I can't sell this for so low a price."

Her face suddenly lit up as a brilliant idea magically popped into her head. "But if you agree to seventy cents, I can part with it. But only for you, dear, because you're so nice to your sister."

She held the locket up again. That smile crawled across her face and made him want to run. But he couldn't. He felt triumphant.

"Seventy cents, it is!"

He reached into his pocket, pulled out fifty cents, and groaned. He looked at Adam.

Adam rolled his eyes and shook his head. "No!"

"Please, Adam," Jeff whispered. He had to get that locket for Lizzie.

Caving in, Adam gave Jeff the twenty cents he needed.

As the boys waited for the woman to box and wrap the locket, Adam gave his brother a disapproving look and shook his head again. Jeff ignored the look. He had struck a deal.

ಬ23ಛ

"Children! Is everyone ready?" Mama called from two flights down.

Jeff sat in his room trying to help Jordan tame the unruly brown curls that covered his head. It didn't seem to matter how short his hair was cut. It had a mind of its own.

"Hold still, Jordan!" Jeff said.

"I'm trying," Jordan said impatiently.

"You'd better let me do this. If Mama sees you all messy, you know she'll get upset."

Jordan stopped wriggling and submitted to the torture.

"That's better. Take a look." He handed Jordan the mirror.

Jordan nodded and smiled approvingly then bounced down the stairs. Jeff looked in the mirror and adjusted the jacket of his best Sunday suit then gave his own hair one last brushing before heading downstairs himself.

He stopped in Lizzie and Irene's room and found Lillian struggling to get Lizzie's thick, perfectly curled hair into the large red bow that she had given her sister to match the prized red dress she now wore. Charlotte Thomas stood nearby handling hairpins like a nurse assisting a doctor with a life-saving procedure. Irene stood by and dished out instructions. To Jeff, it seemed strange that it took three people just to fix Lizzie's hair. He would never understand girls.

It was time to take the family portrait, and everyone was dressed up for the special occasion. For Lizzie it was her first chance to wear the red dress, and it had taken a whole day of begging and whining for her to convince Mama to allow her to wear it. Jeff had to admit, though, it did look nice on her.

"Hi, Jeff," Charlotte said with that familiar sweet smile on her face.

"Hi," Jeff said shyly, painfully aware that his sisters were watching him with wide, toothy grins on their faces.

"Well, that should hold," Lillian said. She inspected her work and took Elizabeth's chin in her hand. "You look pretty, honey."

"Thank you," Lizzie said. She was all smiles.

"Children!" Mama called. "Hurry!"

"Let's go," Lillian said, and she and Irene went downstairs.

"It's so pretty, Lizzie," Charlotte said.

"Come with me," Jeff said. He had an idea.

"Why? Mama wants us downstairs now," Lizzie said.

They followed him to the bottom of the attic stairs.

"Wait here a minute."

He ran upstairs to his room then called the girls to come up. As they reached the top of the stairs, they found him standing with a small box in his hand. He gave it to Lizzie.

"What's this?" she asked. She and Charlotte looked at each other.

"Merry Christmas!" he said, proudly grinning.

"Christmas? In October?"

"Well, you already opened one Christmas present. You may as well open this one, too."

Lizzie smiled mischievously, tore open the wrapping, and slowly opened the box. Her jaw dropped, and a smile spread across her face as she removed the locket.

"Jeff! It's beautiful! Look, Charlotte!"

"Oh! It's so pretty!" Charlotte said.

"I thought you might like it with your dress," Jeff said.

Lizzie pried it open.

"It's empty for now," Jeff said. "But you can put a picture in later, when you fall in looooove!"

"Stop it!" Lizzie pushed him and laughed.

"Put it on, Lizzie," Charlotte said, smiling at him. "It's very nice, Jeff."

He blushed and smiled at the floor.

Charlotte helped Lizzie put the locket around her neck and held her hair aside to fasten it in the back.

"There. Let's see how it looks, Lizzie," she said.

Lizzie looked at herself in the mirror, pleased with what she saw. "Thank you, Jeff," Lizzie said, hugging her brother.

"Welcome," he said, so proud to have done this for his sister. "Let's get downstairs before Mama comes to get us." He turned to go downstairs.

"Lizzie?" Charlotte said. "Lizzie, what's wrong?"

Lizzie bent over in pain. Her left hand clasped the back of her neck.

"Lizzie!" Jeff cried. He held his sister as she slumped to the floor. "Lizzie!"

ဢℭ

"What happened?" Lizzie said, lying on the floor looking

like someone had hit her over the head.

Charlotte fanned her with a piece of paper.

"We don't know," Charlotte said. "You fainted. We were going to get your mother. Are you all right?"

"Yes," she said, but she didn't sound sure.

Jeff looked worried. "Lizzie, do you feel sick?"

"No," Lizzie said.

Suddenly she sat up and threw her arms around Jeff's neck. "Jeff! Something happened! Something terrible!"

"What?" He loosened her choke hold so he could breathe again.

"I was here. In this room. But it wasn't really this room. It was dark, and there were boxes and things all over. I couldn't see what they were because it was too dark, and I couldn't touch them. I tried, but I couldn't. So I went downstairs to find you. I thought you were playing a trick on me. But even downstairs looked different. There were all sorts of strange things there. And, oh, everything looked so...odd. Things I've never seen before."

She grabbed Jeff's shoulders and shook him. "Jeff, we've never seen things like the things I saw! Things in the kitchen that...I don't even know what they were. And there was a big rug all over all the floors. I couldn't feel it, but...but no one has rugs like that! I was scared because I didn't know how to get out of there. Or how to get back here."

"You must'a been dreaming," Jeff said.

"No, Jeff, it was real. It was happening! I saw all sorts of odd, scary things. And I couldn't touch most things. Just a few. And...and then I saw..." She was shaking now.

"Saw what?" Charlotte asked. She looked a little shaken herself.

"Me," Lizzie said.

Jeff and Charlotte both stared blankly at Lizzie.

"You saw *you*?" Jeff asked, confused.

Lizzie nodded. "It was me, but I looked different. And I, or she, was in the strange house wearing strange clothes."

"Lizzie, it was a dream. Now let's go before we get in trouble!" Jeff was getting impatient with his sister's story. It was one of many.

"Jeff, please believe me! It was real!" she pleaded.

"Jefferson! Elizabeth!" Papa called from the bottom of the attic stairs. He had come up one flight of stairs to yell at them, and it wouldn't be long before he started on the next flight. "Come downstairs right now! We're all waiting! Mr. Lloyd is expecting us in twenty minutes."

"Yes, Papa! Now, see?" Jeff said. "Papa's yelling at us, and we're going to be in trouble. Get up! Let's go before he comes up here with his belt!"

Charlotte helped Lizzie stand up and wipe off her dress.

"Charlotte, this thing is stuck in my hair. Can you help me?"

Jeff noticed that she was still trembling.

Charlotte struggled with her own shaky hands but finally unhooked the locket.

"Children!" Papa yelled. Jeff knew this was their last warning.

"We're coming right now, Papa! Hurry up," Jeff said. "I'm going." He ran down the stairs.

The family gathered in the living room and prepared to pile into the family car for a ride to Mr. Lloyd's studio.

"I'm sorry, Papa," Jeff said as he joined the family.

"Where is your sister?" Papa asked. His mouth formed a straight line under his mustache, an unmistakable sign that his patience had worn down to nothing.

"Right here, Papa," Lizzie said as she reached the bottom of the stairs. She still looked worried.

"Put your coat on, Elizabeth," Mama said. "Right now."

Lizzie rushed to follow her mother's instructions.

As Papa counted heads, Jeff looked across the room and saw Charlotte. She stood near the piano bench putting on her coat, and Jeff noticed that she wore Lizzie's locket. It looked even nicer on her than it did on Lizzie.

"All right, everybody," Papa said, "get in the car."

"Charlotte," Mama said, "we can take you home on the way."

"Thank you, Mrs. Cole." Charlotte said, smiling at Jeff.

››‹‹

After the family returned home, Jeff, Lizzie, and Charlotte sat in Jeff's room.

"Are you sure you're feeling better, Lizzie?" Jeff asked. "You've never fainted before."

Lizzie nodded. "I feel fine. Really, I'm fine."

Charlotte removed the locket and gave it back to Lizzie.

"Oh, I forgot to put this on for the portrait," Lizzie said, disappointed.

Charlotte laughed. "I almost forgot I was wearing it."

But Jeff hadn't forgotten. As the family began to pose, he had thought about the locket around Charlotte's neck and smiled.

"But I still say I saw something real," Lizzie said.

Jeff groaned. Lizzie never gave up on her stories. Sometimes she kept going on and on until it made him sick.

"I'm sure it seemed real, Lizzie," Charlotte said. "Dreams can seem real sometimes. Mine do."

"No! I saw something," she insisted. "The cabinets out in the hall downstairs had paint on them. White paint. And there were these…loud things in my room. And I was standing there watching myself, I mean her, look at me. And the pictures...you should have seen them. You wouldn't believe..."

"Lizzie, please," Jeff said. "It was a dream! A dream, Lizzie! Stop playing before we start thinking something's really wrong." He pointed to her head. "Like Aunt Lydia," he whispered.

Lizzie was getting upset. "Why don't you believe me? And you, too, Charlotte. Do you think it was a dream, too?"

Charlotte nodded slowly and looked guilty for not believing her friend.

"But it was real!"

"Baloney!" Jeff said. He was used to her stories.

Pouting, Lizzie stood up and went to the mirror on the dresser. She smoothed her hair, gently touched the lace collar on her dress, and put the locket back on. Charlotte and Jeff looked at each other and smiled. They knew she would get over it soon. She was wearing her favorite dress, and she had a beautiful locket to go with it. She was already smiling again.

"Well," she said reluctantly as she turned to face them, "maybe it was a dream."

"A very strange dream," Charlotte said, nodding.

Suddenly, Lizzie's eyes grew wide, and she grabbed the back of her neck again. "Oh, Jeff, what's happening to me!" she said as her eyes rolled back, and she once more dropped to the floor.

ഇറര

"Go get my mother!" Jeff shouted.

"No! No, don't," Lizzie said. She had awakened more quickly than she had the first time.

"Lizzie, we have to tell Mama and Papa. You're sick,"

Jeff said. He was very worried now. This had never happened to his sister before today.

Lizzie sat up slowly. "I'm not sick! Something happened again, Jeff! It happened again!"

Jeff rolled his eyes and sighed. If this was one of her jokes, it was a terrible one.

"Lizzie, you can't keep on playing like this!" he said.

"That's right. You're scaring me, Lizzie," Charlotte said. Even she was annoyed. "Please stop it!"

"I'm *not* playing!" Lizzie said. "It happened again! I was in this house, and all the strange things were there again. I went downstairs, and that's where I saw...me again. Sitting there."

"Lizzie..."

"I did! I tried to ask her who she was. And I think she said she was me."

Jeff's and Charlotte's faces filled with disbelief.

"No, Jeff, please! It really happened to me. I saw myself, and I talked to her...me. I...she...asked if I was looking for you. She knew who you were. I was scared, but I was mad at you, too, 'cause *you* wouldn't believe me the first time it happened!"

Her face clouded up. "I kept trying to ask her who she was, but then I got real scared and ran back upstairs. I was wishing I could come back to you, then I woke up! Jeff, I'm so scared! Something awful is happening to me!" She began to cry.

"Stop it!" Jeff yelled. "This is not funny anymore. You fainted twice, and you're making a big joke and scaring everybody! You might be sick, and we need to tell Mama. You weren't there. You had a dream when you fainted, and that's all it was!"

Lizzie glared at Jeff and Charlotte. "Then how did I get

this?!" she yelled, shoving a small, crumpled piece of paper into his hand.

It felt strange. The paper was smoother, crisper, and whiter than any paper Jeff had ever seen. He opened it and read the unfamiliar black print at the top: *"From the Desk of Dr. Jefferson M. Cole."*

෫෨ᘰ

It felt like hours had passed while he stared at the paper and waited for the shock to burn off and for the paper to explain itself.

"Lizzie! Where did you get this?" Jeff said. He'd never seen anything like this before. Where could it have come from?

"Let me see," Charlotte said. She gasped when she looked at the paper and read the handwritten notes. "It says, 'Louiston Public Library. Fisher Street, right on Highland to town. Pass Louiston Town Hall, left on Ross Street, right on Pine Street.' Ross Street? Where's that? And the library is in the middle of town, not on some Pine Street. Lizzie, what is this?"

Jeff continued to stare at the paper trying to find an answer between the printed words. It bore his name, but he had never seen paper like this before. And "Dr." sat confidently in front of his name. He knew what that stood for, but what was it doing there?

Lizzie watched them stare. "I found it in my room. The room that looked different. It was on a table all folded up, and it was one of the things I could touch. So I took it. It was the only way to prove that I'm telling you the truth!"

Jeff and Charlotte couldn't say a word. They just stared. Listened.

Lizzie continued. "I saw things in that place...this place...I don't know what to call it. This time, there was someone else in the house. A man. An old man. I saw him in the hall when I came downstairs from the attic. I didn't see his face, and he was going into Mama and Papa's room. I was hiding in my room, so he didn't see me. He was talking to somebody, but I couldn't see who. He said he was tired, and he wondered how long someone else in the house would stay up. I didn't know who he was talking about, so I waited a long time, and I went downstairs.

Then I saw me...her...again. She asked me if I needed help. I tried to say something, but I was too scared. So I ran upstairs to my room. That's when I saw this piece of paper. I picked it up and held on to it." Lizzie stopped and thought for a minute. "There's something else."

"Lizzie..." Jeff said. What more could there be to all this? What was wrong with her?

"When I first got there and came downstairs, I...I was in Papa's office. The things there...the books, and some machine on the desk..." Lizzie leaned closer to Jeff and Charlotte. "But Jeff, Charlotte, there was a calendar on the desk. It was *1974*!"

Jeff laughed. She had him going for a while, but this was a little too much. "Oh, it was 1974, huh?" He asked, laughing again.

"Yes!" Lizzie said.

Charlotte smiled. "That's a very, very good story, Lizzie. You should tell it at school!"

"It's not a story!" Lizzie insisted. "It happened! Look at that paper!"

"Well, I can't figure that part out," Jeff said, "but 1974? I was following you until that part, Lizzie."

"Don't you see?" Lizzie said. "That was our house! In

1974! And I was there!"

"Oh, banana oil!" Charlotte said, laughing. "People don't just go to another year. And how could you be there seeing *you?* You plan to stop growing up and stay a girl until then? That's a long, long time to wait! You've been reading too many stories." Charlotte couldn't help but laugh again.

"I don't know! I don't know!" Lizzie said. She was getting upset again. "I just know that I was there. Both times I put that locket on I got a bad headache and fainted. And when I woke up, I was there! I was *there!*" She stomped her foot on the floor.

"But Lizzie," Charlotte said, "I put the locket on, too. I wore it for hours, and nothing happened to me."

"I don't know!" Lizzie started crying. "I can't wear that locket again. It makes scary things happen!"

Her words stung Jeff. He thought he had done something nice for his sister, and he had worked so hard to get it. But now it was scaring her. She had no reason to keep up a lie. Something had happened to her, and none of them knew what.

"Lizzie, it's going to be all right," he said. "You don't have to wear the locket. Just keep it in your jewelry box."

"No! It might happen again! I can't do that again!" She was really crying now.

Charlotte hugged her friend to calm her down. "Jeff, don't you think we should go get your mother? Now?"

"No! No, you can't," Lizzie said. "She won't believe me, either. I can't tell her."

"Lizzie," Jeff said, "I'll keep the locket up here. I can take it back to the store the next time we go to New York. I promise."

"No, Jeff, it can't stay here! It might happen again. I don't want it in the house! I don't want it anywhere near the

house! Near me! We have to get it out of here! Now!" All the
crying was making her cough.

"Throw it away in the trash, Jeff," Charlotte said, her
voice trembling.

"No!" Lizzie said. "That's too close! Too close! Get it
away from the house!" Her face had turned bright red, and
Jeff worried that she might faint again just from fear.

"All right, Lizzie," Jeff said.

He was feeling more and more worried and helpless, but
he had to do something to fix this. She would never rest until
it was completely gone.

"Lizzie, how 'bout we throw it in the woods? That's far
away, right?"

"Yes," she said, sounding a little better.

"We can take it right now, Jeff," Charlotte said. "We can
take it to the park and throw it away in the woods. Then you
won't have to worry about it anymore. Right, Lizzie?"

Lizzie nodded, and the three agreed to change their
clothes and meet in front of Charlotte's house.

࠮ꙮ࠰

Jeff, Lizzie, and Charlotte stood in Grant Park at the edge of
the woods. Jeff held the locket in its box and torn wrapping.
He was convinced that his sister had been dreaming, but the
dream seemed real enough to her. He didn't understand, but
he'd never seen her so upset.

"Are you sure this is what you want to do?" Jeff asked.

"Yes," Lizzie whispered. Still shaken, she gathered her
coat closer to her chin.

With an arm accustomed to throwing a baseball, Jeff
threw the box into the woods with all the strength he had.
The small box sailed through the cold, breezy air, and they

heard it bounce off a tree in the woods and land in an unseen place.

"There! It won't hurt you anymore," Charlotte told Lizzie. "It's gone. All gone."

Lizzie looked relieved. "Thank you," she said timidly. For a moment, she stared off into the woods still confused and afraid of something she couldn't explain.

"Let's go home now," Jeff said.

Lizzie nodded. Jeff put his arm around his sister and guided her out of the park. On the way home, the three agreed to keep this to themselves. No one would believe them, and they wouldn't know how to explain it anyway. It was their secret for life. They walked in silence the rest of the way home. And though Jeff wondered if he would ever truly understand what this was all about, he was just happy to know that whatever it was, it was over.

ॐ24ॐ

"*That was her?!*" Anitra was floored. "That
was her! Oh, my God!"

Anitra jumped off the sofa to pace the liv-
ing room floor as her grandfather's revelation ricocheted in
her head. "She wasn't a ghost! Oh, my God!"

Grandpa Jeff, still numb from telling his own story, followed her with tired eyes.

On her fourth lap around the room, Anitra stopped to
snatch a tissue out of a nearby box and began twisting and
shredding it. Then she paced some more.

"But that light. Grandpa, she had this...this yellowy glow
all around her. And...and when she moved, it was more
like...like gliding or something."

"So did you," Grandpa Jeff said, his voice small.

"What?"

"So did you, Peanut. Every time we saw you, you had
that same light glowing around you. And you moved just like
you said she did."

"So I looked like a ghost to you?" An occasional tissue

remnant sprang from her churning hands.

"Yes, that's what we thought. Looks like you thought the same about Elizabeth."

"Yeah. Yeah, I sure did."

A jumble of thoughts fired in her head so fast, they piled up and clogged her brain before she could sort them out. No wonder Elizabeth was so scared when she appeared in 1974. Poor thing had no idea what was going on.

Grandpa Jeff, tired of watching Anitra tennis-match style, grabbed her arm and guided her back to the sofa. She left a trail of tissue bits along the way.

"And it was the locket that did all this," Anitra said, staring at the picture on the table. "It wasn't the dress after all."

"Yes, Peanut," Grandpa Jeff said. "It was the locket I gave her. It did something strange to her. I...I suppose it did the same to you."

Grandpa Jeff opened the shoe box once more and pulled out the locket. He handed it to Anitra.

She jumped at first, and a sharp ache rumbled through her stomach. She was afraid to touch it, afraid that it might rip her away and toss her back into the past once more. But it didn't. She pulled herself together, took the locket, and flipped it over in her hands, studying it.

"Doesn't look like it could do all that, does it?" he asked.

"Sure doesn't. But you said Grandma put it on once, and nothing happened to her. Why Elizabeth, Grandpa? And why me?"

"There's one more thing," he said. He pulled an old book from the shoe box and gripped it with both hands.

"What's that?" Anitra whispered, afraid of the answer.

His face clouded as he paused to find the right words. "I found this in the attic not long before your grandma died."

He handed it to Anitra. "My Rememberings, 1902"

reached across the diary's worn cover in large, artistically handwritten letters. Confused, she looked at Grandpa Jeff.

"Look inside. Then read the pages I bookmarked." He stood. "I'm going to go make some tea. Would you like some?"

"Uh...no...thanks..."

He was in the kitchen by the time she said "thanks."

Alone in the living room, Anitra opened the book. Inside the front cover, Lydia Alice Cole had written her name in bold ink. Anitra gasped quietly, shut the cover, and thought about Aunt Lydia in the past. It made her shudder. She remembered what she'd heard of Aunt Lydia's bouts with mental illness. Depending on who told the story and when they told it, it was severe depression or breakdowns or paranoia or some combination of the three that started in her late teens or early twenties and worsened every year until she took her own life back in the thirties.

Anitra wished she had the guts to put the book down and leave and live the rest of her life without any answers. The thought of reading the diary pages made her feel no better than she had when trying to read her letter to Carrie. But she had to reopen the book.

On the first page was a picture of Lydia. Creased and spotty, it still had a warm, yellow-brown tint. Anitra recognized a lot of herself in this picture: the caramel complexion, heart-shaped face, wavy hair covering her shoulders, and the distinct Cole-shaped nose. Lydia wore a light-colored dress or blouse and...Anitra almost choked on a sip of lemonade. Around Lydia's neck was the locket!

How could that be? Twelve-year-old Jeff had bought that locket in 1927 from a store in Harlem. He hadn't gone looking for it. He had just walked in, and the woman had coaxed him into buying it. How could it be around Lydia's neck in

1902?

Anitra held the locket up to the picture. Yes, it was the same one. Or at least it sure looked a lot like it. Managing to take her eyes from Lydia's picture, she turned the page and skimmed the remarkably perfect handwriting.

> January 1
>
> My name is Lydia Alice Cole, and I am fifteen years old. This is my fourth Rememberings book. Today is the beginning of a brand new year...
>
> My brothers pestered me while I wrote my poetry. Mama finally shooed them out with a broom, and I couldn't stop laughing at the sight...
>
> I am ready, ready, ready to go back to school. Miss Harrison asked me to read some of my poetry in class! Imagine!

Nothing about the locket. She turned to the first bookmarked page.

> June 14
>
> Today is my birthday! Sixteen! My brothers made me a jewelry box, and my sister put some pretty hair combs in it. Mama and Papa gave me some new writing supplies for my poetry. But my favorite birthday gift came from Aunt Ruth. I couldn't believe she came here! We never see her.
>
> She hates Mama! Her own sister! I'm not supposed to know this, but she thinks Mama stole Papa from her way back when they were

girls. She never forgave Mama for that. She's been so hateful for years.

But today she said she's been wrong all this time. She brought me a birthday gift as a peace offering. Mama was so pleased! Aunt Ruth gave me a beautiful silver locket. I gave her a big hug! I tried it on, but then my neck started to hurt! Mama made me lie down. For a minute I felt like I was dreaming, like I was somewhere else, but then I woke up with a headache. I felt fine after a nap. Papa said it was all the excitement.

Anitra shivered. No doubt now. This was the same locket. And Lydia had no idea what was waiting for her.

June 15

I'm very frightened. I put on my new locket, and that terrible pain came back to my neck just like yesterday. Then I had the most awful dream! I was in someone's house. It had things I have never seen before, and I couldn't touch a thing. And I tried. There were a woman and some children in the house, too. I stood right in front of them, I even tried to talk to them, but they didn't see me!

But the most amazing thing happened when I went upstairs. There was a calendar for 1918! Imagine! 1918! Sixteen years from now! What a dream! Then I walked into one of the bedrooms and saw a little girl, about three years old, playing with her dolls. She reminded me of my sister. It made me smile because I remember when she was about the same age.

This little girl looked at me and said hello! I was surprised that she could see me, but I smiled at her and said hello right back! I asked her for her name. Lizzie. A pretty name, but she almost couldn't say it right.

Lizzie called me Auntie! I laughed and told her I was not her aunt, just her friend. She handed me one of her dolls. It was a pretty little thing about the size of a real baby. And I held it like a real baby, too. She liked that. Then I woke up, and I was still holding Lizzie's doll! Something evil is happening to me!

Anitra's head spun. So Elizabeth had had an earlier encounter with the locket. But she had been too young to know Lydia didn't belong there, too young to remember.

Then Anitra wondered if the adult Lydia had actually seen her, or at least sensed her presence, in the kitchen during her second trip to 1927! Stunned, Anitra continued to read the girl's increasingly deteriorating handwriting.

July 23

Mama wanted me to wear my locket for the photograph today. I wanted to tell her it was broken, but she pulled it out of my jewelry box. I didn't want to lie to her, but how could I tell her that evil things happened when I put it on? That I hadn't been able to look at it since the day after my birthday? I told her I would put it on later so nothing would happen to it on the way.

When we arrived, Mama had to put it around my neck because my hands shook too much. I told her I was just nervous about the photograph. As I started falling out of the chair, I think I heard her tell me not to worry. In my dream, I played with Lizzie. When I woke up, Mama said it had only been seconds. She gave me some water and propped me up long enough for the photographer to finish his job.

July 24

The doctor couldn't find anything wrong with me. Of course not. I will never tell them what really happened to me. I can't explain it. I keep Lizzie's doll hidden in my room. I can't explain that, either. And no one can help me.

July 26

I went to New York today. If Mama and Papa ever found out, well I don't want to think about that. I lied to them! But I found the store where Aunt Ruth bought the locket. The address was on the box it came in. There was an old woman there with so many wrinkles, I could barely see her face. She looked at me like she was planning to be mean to me. But I had to talk to her.

I showed her the locket and asked her where it came from. She told me a story about bringing it with her from the South years ago. She did sound like she was from the South. But sometimes she sounded like she was raised right across the street! I didn't believe her.

Anitra's fingers tightened around the diary. This was the same woman from Grandpa Jeff's story. From 1927. Anitra shuddered and kept reading.

The old woman asked me if I had worn the locket yet. I told her I had. She smiled the most frightening smile I have ever seen on a face and told me that now I knew its secrets. I dropped the locket on the counter in front of her. I told her it was an evil thing and I could not keep it! I even insisted she give Aunt Ruth's money back! But this terrible woman just laughed at me and said that Aunt Ruth didn't want her money back. That she knew the locket's secrets. That she knew what would happen! Wanted it to happen!

The old woman kept talking and talking. Saying the locket was supposed to be with me. A special locket for a special girl. I started to cry and told her I didn't want it. She said I could try to get rid of it, but it would come back, she warned me. It would always come back.

I threw the locket on the floor and ran away. I cried all the way home. How can such a beautiful thing be so evil? That woman said it would come back. I never should have gone there!

How could Aunt Ruth do this to me? She wants to hurt Mama by hurting me. Does she hate us that much? I'm so frightened!

The remaining pages were blank. Anitra wondered if Lydia had managed to forget just like she had. Maybe this diary was here because she had hidden it from herself just like Anitra had hidden her letter to Carrie. Maybe Lydia had forgotten until she'd begun to meet the people from her locket-induced "dreams." Maybe that was when she had begun to slip.

Anitra wiped tears from her eyes. The locket had claimed a fifth victim in the Cole family.

ᏚᎧᏟᎡ

"Hard to believe, isn't it?" Grandpa Jeff asked as he came back to the living room. His voice had a strange, tinny quality that she'd last heard that 1974 night when she tried to tell him and her grandmother what had happened to her.

"No harder than the rest of this whole thing," Anitra said.

"You see how it happened to her...to Lizzie...to you?"

"Yes," Anitra whispered.

"Just like the woman in the store said. It stayed in the family. Got passed along."

"And like she told Lydia, it always came back."

He nodded and sat next to her.

"Grandpa, what about all those things Lydia said about Aunt Ruth? Was that true?"

"Seems it was. Well, everyone in the family had their own version of the whole thing. But they said Papa's mother and aunt had a terrible falling out over his father not long before the marriage. Ruth ended up marrying some fellow from New York instead. They had a baby, poor thing died, then the husband died not long after that."

"Oh, that's terrible," Anitra whispered.

"Broke her heart in two. She never married again. Guess she figured it was all my grandmother's fault, you know, taking away the man she should've had, having the children she should've had."

"So she found a way to get back at her. The locket. But how did she find it? Who was that woman?"

"I don't know. No one in the family ever knew what the locket did. They had no reason to talk about it. And that woman...I...I don't..."

Fear gripped his face as the memory tormented him.

Anitra jumped in to protect him. "So Aunt Ruth used the locket to hurt the family, starting with Lydia."

He nodded and sighed. "That's right. We never knew what to expect from Aunt Lydia. Fine one minute, going off the deep end the next. And Lizzie, oh, Aunt Ruth was absolutely terrified of Lizzie. Now I understand why, but at the time it hurt Lizzie's feelings so. Oh, Lizzie...Lizzie..."

"It's okay, Grandpa," Anitra whispered, wishing she could believe her own words.

"That poor girl. No one knew. No one ever knew..." He was already off in a trance again, talking to someone other than Anitra.

Anitra grabbed another tissue and started in on its slow demise. The picture of Elizabeth on the table owned her full attention.

"They didn't know...they never knew..." he said.

"What is it, Grandpa?" Anitra dropped the tissue pieces on the table and took his hands.

"So terrible not to know…" His hands trembled inside hers like a lost bird.

"Grandpa…are you all right?" He was scaring her now. "We don't have to talk about this anymore. We can…"

But he wasn't listening. "Adam had come home a few days before Thanksgiving. One day, he and I went to see his old high school football team practice for the Thanksgiving Day game. Later that night, when we came home, there was a commotion in the house."

He stared into the past. "Lizzie was missing. And back then, children didn't just turn up missing like that. Not in Louiston."

Anitra held his shaky hands and felt her stomach twist into multiple knots.

"She was supposed to be with Charlotte at her house. Papa took Adam and Uncle Marcus out to look for her, all the men in the neighborhood helped, Mama called the police…" He stared into the air watching a scene from the past.

Anitra picked up the tissue pieces and crumpled them together.

"They couldn't find her…they thought someone took her…couldn't imagine who or why… Poor Mama, just about sick with worry… Then two policemen came to our door and said…" He stopped. His eyes closed as the rest of the horrible scene played out in his memory.

Anitra dabbed her eyes with a fresh tissue.

He opened his eyes and continued, still in his trance. "They said they had found her…in the park…no coat…didn't know what happened to her…"

She trembled as she recalled the newspaper articles. Her tears fell freely.

Grandpa Jeff put his hands on his knees and stared at the table. "The police…they kept asking questions…all sorts of questions." His jaw tightened. "I couldn't tell them…I couldn't tell them…" he whispered.

She put her arm around him and rested her head on his shoulder.

"They never knew. My father and mother…they buried their baby daughter and never knew why."

Rare tears rolled down his cheeks and burned Anitra's heart. She sat up as the pressure inside her head quickly grew to unbearable.

"I know what happened!" she blurted out. Finally.

Startled, Grandpa Jeff looked up and stared. "Peanut, what are you talking about?" he whispered through his tears.

Anitra stumbled through her words. "I…" Oh, this was hard. "I was there. I went back one more time. And…and I know what happened to her."

"You saw?" Grandpa Jeff whispered.

"Yes." Anitra nodded and took his hand again. "I was there."

Grandpa Jeff stared at nothing for what seemed like hours. Taking in her words. Tossing them around to keep them from burning him.

"It's okay, Peanut," he finally said, his voice remarkably clear. "Tell me what you saw."

"Well…" Anitra swallowed hard to clear a huge lump in her throat. There wasn't enough air to breathe anymore. What happened to all the air?

"It's okay, Peanut," Grandpa Jeff whispered.

"That time, when I woke up, it was November 1927 again. But this time it was the twenty-second. I knew because I saw the newspaper." She felt her grandfather's eyes fix on hers.

Anitra began her story of that last trip to the past: deciding to save Elizabeth, running to the school, hearing their conversation at lunch, running back to the house to search for she didn't know what. She told him she had found the box in Elizabeth's dresser.

"The locket," Grandpa Jeff whispered.

Anitra nodded as she shredded more tissue. "But I didn't know that's what it was. I didn't get a chance to open it. See...I started to, but..." She closed her eyes.

Now it was time to tell him. Everything.

ఖ25ఞ

Anitra felt cold. Even though she couldn't really feel the November freeze that sat outside, a deep shudder seized her and the red dress she wore. She felt the small, tattered box drop from her hand and felt her neck snap her head up. She felt the scream burst from her throat. Because suddenly, there were loud footsteps at the top of the stairs, and Elizabeth bounced into the room.

Elizabeth's smile immediately disappeared, and she gasped as the air suddenly vacuumed out of her. She stood in the middle of the floor staring directly at Anitra. Instinctively, Anitra crawled back away from Elizabeth. What was she doing here? When did she come in? Elizabeth looked too terrified to move, and the skirt of her green plaid dress shook violently.

As Anitra gradually pushed herself to her feet, she spoke barely above a whisper. "Elizabeth, it's okay. Don't be scared." She held her hands out to Elizabeth. "It's okay. I'm here to help you."

Elizabeth slowly backed away shaking her head and

mouthing the words "No...no...no..." as tears filled her eyes and she began wringing her hands.

She looked at the unopened box on the floor. Quickly, she grabbed it and jumped back to a safe distance. For a moment, she stared with enough intensity to burn a hole in Anitra's forehead. Looking back down at the box, Elizabeth slowly lifted the lid and peered in. Terror spread across her face. She looked back at Anitra and shook uncontrollably.

Anitra tried to calm her. "It's okay, Elizabeth, it's okay, it's okay," she repeated, taking a step toward Elizabeth.

Panicked at Anitra's step, Elizabeth finally opened her mouth and shrieked "NO!" in a horrible, foreign voice. She turned and bolted out of the room and down the stairs.

"Elizabeth! Elizabeth!" Anitra ran down the stairs after her. But she was too late to follow her out the front door. Elizabeth had already slammed it shut behind her. Anitra was stuck! She had found "it," but now Elizabeth was slipping away. Panic squeezed Anitra's neck harder every second. If she didn't find a way out, the panic would choke her to death.

Some way out...some... Turning in nervous circles by the door, Anitra tripped and fell over something on the floor. A coat. She sat up and felt the heavy brown wool in her hands. Elizabeth's coat. She picked it up and held it close, grateful to be able to feel something other than a painful need to scream.

Somebody would come home soon. Adam would come home in the next minute and open the door and let her out. Anitra looked up at the door, and it seemed to grow bigger and heavier as she watched. She clutched the coat tighter, pulling the collar to her face, and ran her right hand across the coat's softness. Her hand stopped on a warm, red mitten sticking halfway out of a pocket.

Somebody please come home somebody please open this door somebody please help... Anitra rocked in her little spot on the floor, hugging the coat, fidgeting with the mitten she had pulled onto her right hand. She stopped. There was a noise outside. Was it...no, just some car. Anitra leaned back and put her hands on the floor, sighing.

Her hand...the one with the mitten on it...touched the floor!

She touched the floor! Really touched it, not just hovered over it! Anitra popped up and slammed her mittened hand against the wall. She touched it! Felt it hurt! She dropped the coat, reached for the knob, and opened the door.

&)C&

Betting on the newspaper article, Anitra had sprinted to Grant Park as fast as she knew how. A few yards back, she swore she saw the blur of Elizabeth fade into the park. But now Anitra stood at the entrance and looked across the park, rubbing her bare hands together to calm her overworked nerves. That mitten had fallen off somewhere, and she hadn't even noticed.

There was no one in the park.

No! No, that couldn't be! How could someone get to Elizabeth so fast? Had they been waiting for her in there? In a small patch of snow, Anitra found a tiny footprint pointing toward the woods. *Where was she?*

"Elizabeth!" Anitra ran into the woods, ignoring the panic, ran back and forth, trying to breathe, ran between knotty trees, yelling Elizabeth's name. Nothing. Not a whisper, not a crunch of dead leaves, not a button popped from the green plaid school dress. How could Elizabeth be so gone so soon? Tears stung Anitra's eyes, partly from the tight, burning pinch in her heart. Mostly from imagining what could have been happening to Elizabeth right now.

Anitra shot out of the woods and stood in the clearing. "Where are you! Elizabeth, please answer me! I can help you! Please! Tell me where you are!"

She turned back to face the woods, put her hands on her head, and looked up into the bare, spiky treetops. "Where are you?" Anitra whispered, wiping her tears.

Then it caught her eye, caught her ear. A movement so small, so tiny, it was barely more than a breeze nudging the limbs of the big tree to her left. The brittle brush of something against bark. Tiny fingertips gripping the base of a branch. And a small, brown eye staring down. From halfway up the tree, Elizabeth watched.

"There you are!" Anitra said. All her yelling in the woods must have scared away whoever was there to hurt Elizabeth! "You're okay! You're okay!"

Elizabeth kept watching.

"Elizabeth?" Anitra said gently. "It's okay now. You can come down. They're gone. See?" She slowly waved her arm around her. "There's nobody here but me."

Elizabeth didn't move.

Anitra stepped closer to the base of the tree.

"You stay where you are! Don't you come near me!" Elizabeth screeched. Then in a small, pleading voice, she said, "How?! How did you get it?! Why..." Her words trailed off as sobs overcame her.

"Elizabeth..."

"Stay away from me!" Elizabeth screamed. "I told you! Get away!" She shifted her position, keeping the trunk between herself and Anitra.

"But it's okay..." What was wrong with her?

"Get away!" Elizabeth cried harder.

The words dug into Anitra's ears. "Please, Elizabeth. I'll help you. I promise. Please, please come down." Why was she still afraid?

Elizabeth shifted once more. "NO!..." Her one visible eye gaped upward and her hand flew into the air. Her foot scraped the tree. She fell backwards. All Anitra could see was Elizabeth's hand falling, falling, falling, her sharpened scream cut short by a dull, sickening thud as she hit the ground.

"ELIZABETH!"

No answer.

"Elizabeth?"

Silence.

No, no, no! No, she couldn't be...she had to be okay...a little hurt, maybe...maybe... maybe broke something and couldn't move...maybe...

Anitra forced her legs to move, one leaden step at a time, to the other side of the tree. First she saw the badly scuffed brown shoe, then one leg bent at the knee and pointing away from the tree, the other pointing in the opposite direction, the thigh scraped and bleeding under the long, ragged tear in the plaid dress. Anitra shook her head. She wasn't seeing this.

Elizabeth was sprawled on the ground like a discarded rag doll. Anitra dropped to her knees and gently shook her.

"Elizabeth?!" she pleaded, desperate for Elizabeth to answer. "Elizabeth, please wake up! Please, please wake up!"

Elizabeth didn't move. Thick, sticky breaths forced their way in and out of Anitra's lungs as she stared at the large rock resting like a cold, unyielding pillow under Elizabeth's head. With a badly shaking hand, Anitra reached down and gingerly placed two fingers on Elizabeth's neck. It felt warm, and despite the cold air, small beads of sweat, unsettled by her touch, gravitated toward Anitra's two fingers. There was no pulse.

She shook Elizabeth in one last, desperate attempt to try to wake her. Elizabeth's head slipped off the rock and onto the ground. Anitra jumped. A large, red stain traveled down the back of Elizabeth's neck and onto the white collar of her dress. And in the waning light of dusk, a hideous red smear stood out brilliantly from the dull gray of the rock's jagged surface.

Anitra looked up at the tree and saw a small, dark patch of ice near the branch that had held Elizabeth. Then the full weight of the truth slammed into Anitra. Nothing had reached out and grabbed Elizabeth. No one had been out to get her. Anitra hadn't prevented Elizabeth's death. She'd caused it.

⊱⊰

It was amazing how still and quiet it was. How the one and only sound was her heartbeat crashing in her ears as she rocked herself back and forth, back and forth, back and forth. How flat-gray everything looked through the dark, shadowy blur pooled in eyes that couldn't blink. How icy-numb her hands seemed even though she couldn't really feel the sharp cold in the air. And how Elizabeth's hand could be so warm.

As the last few days, few minutes, few seconds invaded her mind and pierced her soul, a furious shudder claimed Anitra and shook her whole being. Kneeling over the body, she clutched a lifeless hand and pressed it to her cheek, feeling the warmth. She thought she felt herself trying to scream, but nothing came out. It was stuck somewhere deep inside her. Gradually, a small trickle of sound emerged from her throat and woke her from her trance. The sound grew and strengthened, and deep sobs finally gushed out, stinging her throat. As she squeezed her eyes shut, her large, heavy tears plunged and dripped slowly, so slowly, down Elizabeth's arm.

Anitra leaned forward, gently rested her head on Elizabeth's motionless chest, and cried.

❧26❧

Anitra found herself running down Fisher Street faster than she knew she could run. She didn't remember deciding what to do, getting up, or leaving the park. But there she was, running furiously back to the house. She had to find Jeff. She had to find him and let him see her so he could help. Maybe...maybe Elizabeth wasn't really dead. No. Not yet, not yet. And maybe there was still time. Yes, that had to be it. There was still time. And somebody could help her. Somebody could help her. It was already getting dark, and Anitra knew it was very cold outside. Elizabeth had no coat on. If she wasn't already dead, she would certainly freeze to death.

Anitra reached the house and flew to the back porch. She looked through the window in the back door. The girls moved about the kitchen preparing the evening's meal, happily chatting and laughing and finishing each other's sentences. Anitra was faced once again with closed doors. But this time she wasn't worried about being seen; this time she wanted, no, *had* to be seen. But her fists made no sound when she pummeled the door.

"Help! Please, can you hear me! Please help!" she screamed.

No response.

"Somebody help!" She turned from the door and jumped down the stairs into the yard. Fighting back tears, Anitra looked at the door that kept her from the help she so desperately needed. She scanned the house from bottom to top and stopped at the attic window. Jeff! Maybe he had come home. Maybe he'd be able to hear her. He had to be there.

"Jeff!" she shrieked.

No answer.

"Jeff! Jeff, help!"

Still no answer.

As she ran back to the house to bang on the door again, the black Chevrolet truck pulled into the driveway, and Papa Russell, Mama Sarah, and Jordan got out. Anitra bolted to the back porch, and as they entered the house, she followed them in.

"Help!" she screamed in a futile attempt to get their attention. With tears stinging in her eyes, she punched and kicked at everything in the kitchen.

They heard nothing.

"Listen! You have to listen to me!"

Anitra turned to Irene. She was the one who tried to tell everyone that something was wrong with Jeff, who seemed to pay attention, and who noticed Elizabeth's book out of place on the bookshelf.

"Irene!" Anitra put herself directly in front of her. "Irene, can you hear me! Irene!"

Anitra put her hands on Irene's shoulders and tried to shake her. But she couldn't. She couldn't touch her. *She couldn't touch her!* Irene continued to laugh with her family about their Thanksgiving plans.

Anitra backed away as a new round of sobs grabbed her around the waist and twisted. She stumbled out of the kitchen and fled to the attic demanding that Jeff be there.

"Jeff! Jeff!" she shouted as she flew up the two flights of stairs.

Jeff's room was empty, his school clothes strewn across a not-quite-made bed. Only Jordan's quiet laughter bounced around the room as he played with his wooden horse. Where were Jeff and Adam? Why weren't they here when she needed them most? Anitra rushed over to Jordan and landed on her knees in front of him.

"Jordan! Jordan, can you hear me?" She waved her hand in front of the boy's face.

Nothing.

"Jordan!" She punched the floor with her fists. "*Jordan!*"

He dragged the horse across the floor.

She stood slowly and felt the incessant, thick pounding in her head as her hope died. What else could she possibly do? She couldn't touch anything in this room to...

Wait! Elizabeth's room! She would go downstairs to Elizabeth's room and make some noise with some of her things! Get someone's attention. Then she could lead them to Elizabeth, if she didn't scare the hell out of them first. Maybe she could write a note. It had to work. It had to. It... had to...

But before she could reach the stairs, that awful, sharp pain invaded her neck and doubled her over. And for the first time, she tried to fight it. She felt herself drowning. She was drowning in a cold, dark, dread-infested pool, flailing, trying to claw her way out. But in the water there was nothing to grab on to but the slimy, rotting leaves that had fallen from surrounding trees months ago. The sides of the pool were miles away, and the surface only appeared in a smoky dream.

"Nooo!" she screamed through the excruciating pain. "Not now, no!" The pain dug in. She couldn't fight it any longer. She took two labored steps forward, gasped, and collapsed.

⁎⁎⁎

Grandpa Jeff sat back on the sofa, stunned. Anitra sat with her head in her hands and let the last of her sobs pass through her as she gently rocked herself. The phone rang, and neither heard the message being left on the answering machine.

"We didn't believe her," Grandpa Jeff said to the air. He squinted at his thoughts. "We should have believed her, helped her. Wearing no coat...all her sweaters on the floor. Her coat on the floor by the front door. She was supposed to be with Charlotte. Charlotte told us Lizzie went home to get a doll, but she never made it back to the Thomases' house. We never knew what happened." His eyes seemed to be following the torment in his mind.

"I never should have gone back," Anitra said to a totally different patch of air. The picture of Elizabeth burned her eyes. "No wonder she was so scared. She'd seen me before, in the seventies. Then she saw me in her own world. She was so terrified! I saw the date in the newspaper back in 1927. I thought it meant I could save her." She shook her head, trying to shake the guilt away.

For an uncomfortably long time, the two sat in tortured silence, letting the shock run its course. The distant sound of the refrigerator occasionally snuck in and gave Anitra something meaningless to concentrate on.

Grandpa Jeff sighed. "That poor girl," he whispered.

Anitra squeezed her eyes shut.

"I've tried to figure it out so many times," he continued. "I gave her the locket one day…it scared her…we threw it in the park. All in the same day."

Anitra squeezed her eyes tighter.

"Weeks later," he said, "she took Jordan to the park…he found it in the woods…she brought it home and hid it somewhere…you found it…she saw you and ran to the park."

"She saw me wearing the locket, Grandpa," Anitra said, opening her eyes. "And she saw the locket in the box, too. It was in two places at once. Just like I saw the red dress in her closet while I was wearing the same dress."

"No wonder she was so scared," he said. "She was taking the locket back to the woods. Trying to get rid of it again so it would stop hurting her."

Anitra nodded.

"Back then Charlotte and I knew she must've gone to the park because of the locket. We thought something happened, and she couldn't hide the locket anymore, and she had to get it back to the park, back to where we threw it. We had that part right. But then we started seeing her ghost…you. Thought she needed help. And we had to help. Least we could do. We thought it was our fault she died 'cause we didn't help her. We decided she needed the locket. Everything always came back to that locket…"

"Grandpa, you don't have to do this…"

Grandpa Jeff didn't hear her. "…but no one ever mentioned the locket when they found her body. So we thought she hadn't taken it there after all. And we couldn't figure out why she'd go there without it. We looked all over the house. Tried to figure out where she would have hidden it. But it wasn't anywhere in the house."

"Grandpa…"

"So we knew for sure she'd taken it back to the park the day she died. That was why she was there. We went there to get it back the day after her funeral. Thought we could give the locket to her ghost and help her somehow. When we found it, it had little tooth marks in it. Some animal probably took it away and dropped it deep in the woods. Maybe it flew out of her hands when she fell. In any case, the police never saw it."

Anitra, tangled in her own torture, hugged her grandfather. "I thought I could find the locket and save her so she could live and grow up and have a family of her own. I should have listened to Grandma, should have gone back to the pool, but I didn't listen. Instead I watched Elizabeth die. I made it happen. I tried…tried to go back one more time, but it wouldn't work. I thought I could still save her…I wanted to save her…but the dress wouldn't work."

"…wanted to give her the locket," Grandpa Jeff said, "but she didn't come back. Not until Easter…"

"…the dress just wouldn't…Oh no! The locket!" Anitra dropped her hands from her face and sat up straight.

"Peanut?" Her outburst pulled him back to the present.

She put her head in her hands. "I tried to go back that last time, after I saw her die. I had to try! So I put the dress back on. But nothing happened, and I couldn't get back. I thought something was wrong with the dress. But…"

She shook her head and lightly pounded her head with her palm. "But I didn't put the locket on! I was so panicked, I couldn't think straight. I was in such a hurry to get back, *I never put the locket back on*! I could've gone back!" Anitra said, hiding her face in her hands. "I still could have saved her! I could have saved her!"

As he listened to Anitra, Grandpa Jeff eased out of the

place in his mind that had held him together. Slowly he reached for his granddaughter and pulled her into a tight, secure embrace. Anitra melted.

"I'm so sorry, Grandpa...so sorry. I thought I could help her. I was trying to save her, but...but...it was all my fault." Anitra let out a long, cleansing sigh and turned to look him in the eye for the first time since she began her story.

"It was my fault, Grandpa. I did it." Her voice hadn't been this clear all day.

"Don't you talk like that, Peanut." His voice shook terribly. "It wasn't your fault. It was an accident. You couldn't have known what was coming."

"But if I hadn't gone there in the first place..."

"And if I hadn't given her the locket, and if Jordan hadn't found it in the woods, and if I had helped her more... We could go on for days with ifs."

"I know, but..."

"Do you know what your grandma and I went through because of feeling guilty? We thought if we had helped her more, believed her, it wouldn't have happened. We couldn't talk to anyone about it, and we swore we'd never tell. Who'd believe us, anyway? We kept that secret and lived with it. Tried to forget it, even."

"Grandpa, you were just children. You couldn't have known. *I'm* the one who killed her. It was my fault! I killed her!" The sobs grabbed her again.

"Peanut! Please don't do this!" Grandpa Jeff insisted. "It was an accident. That's all. There was nothing more you could've done. You didn't even know that the locket would have worked that last time."

"Yes, but..."

"Honey, some things are just meant to be." He stopped to pat her hand. "You have to let this go."

"I don't know that I can. I'm not sure I know how."

He turned her face to look into her eyes. "I want you to understand something. For sixty-some years your Grandma and I carried around all kinds of guilt and fear over what happened to my sister. All those years! And we did our best to forget. Honey, that's a long, long time to be feeling so bad about somebody, and I don't want that to happen to you. As it is, you've already spent over twenty years living with your own guilt. You need to let it go, now."

Anitra squeezed her grandfather's hand. "You're right, Grandpa. I know you're right." But making it happen was a different issue altogether.

"At least...at least now I know." He hugged Anitra once more. "That's right, Peanut. All that time, we never knew. We thought someone grabbed her and killed her. And the police just gave up. Now I know that didn't happen. Nobody killed Lizzie. It wasn't your fault, and it wasn't my fault. It was an accident. A terrible, terrible accident."

He wiped tears from her cheeks and smiled. "Thank you, Peanut," he said softly. "Thank you for telling me what happened to my sister."

Anitra managed a tepid smile.

Grandpa Jeff pushed the locket aside and handed her the box with the note paper, the picture of Elizabeth, and the diary. "I want you to have these," he said.

"You do? Why?"

He sighed and sat back a little. "Before your grandma died, she and I agreed that we wanted you to have them. But not right away. You see, when you tried to tell us about all this back then, well, it was such a shock to us. We didn't understand..."

He frowned away the jumble in his thoughts. "Anyway, I suppose we weren't ready for what you had to say. We had done such a good job of forgetting for so many years."

Anitra thought back to that night. It gave her chills.

Grandpa Jeff held her hand. "It took us a long, long time to bring it up again and even to begin to think, really think, about the little bit you told us. Not until I found the diary. After your grandma got sick. When we found out it had happened to Lydia, too, we realized what we had done, not letting you tell us. So, we decided to keep these things for you for when you were ready to talk about it again. When they wouldn't be so painful to you."

Anitra stared at the box.

"So now I want you to take these."

"I will," she whispered. She thought for a minute. "Grandpa?"

"Mm hmm?"

"If you don't mind, I'd like to take the locket, too."

"Peanut, no! It's nothing but trouble! I only kept it long enough for us to have this talk. Now I'm going to destroy it. I promised your grandma!"

"I just...I want to hold on to it for a while."

She cringed at her own morbid curiosity. The locket had changed three lives and destroyed two, but she wasn't ready to let it go. After years of assuming the dress had been the cause, she needed to absorb this new truth. She didn't want to cause him any more hurt, but she needed this.

"Just let it go!" he insisted. Now it was his turn to pace. "It was nobody's fault. It's time to move on."

It was clear that this was as far as he was willing to go with it all. He had heard her story. He knew the truth about Elizabeth's death. Now he needed to believe it was all just meant to be, and she needed to let him.

With some effort, she convinced him that she only wanted to find out how old the locket was and maybe where it came from. He finally agreed to give it to her after securing promises to be very, very careful. Above all, she was not to put the locket on. An easy promise.

So the locket was hers. Despite what she told Grandpa Jeff, she really didn't know what she would do with it. She just couldn't let it go.

❧27❧

It looked almost the same. Standing at the top of the
stairs, Anitra tried to figure out what was different
about the attic. It still had that stale, antique smell of
air that hadn't moved in a long, long time, and all the boxes
and old furniture sat pretty much where they had always
been. It didn't look any different. But it wasn't *The Attic* anymore. It was just...the attic.

Anitra pulled the locket box from her pocket and removed the thick rubber band she had wrapped around it. She
took out the locket, held it up and watched it dangle from its
chain. The damned thing kept coming back into her family
like a choking clot of weeds.

She thought about pulling it apart and throwing away the
pieces but was afraid it would reconstitute and track her
down. So she put the locket back in its box, wrapped the
rubber band around it several times, and put it back in her
pocket. She'd take it home and find a place to safely keep it
until she could figure out what to do with it.

Anitra walked into Grandpa Jeff's childhood bedroom

and opened the window to let in the early evening air. The faint *whirr* of a neighbor's lawn mower wafted in as she propped the window open with a stick. Looking over the boxes and trunks, Anitra smiled as she remembered the countless times she had stood in that very spot deciding what box to dig into first. This time, she opened a garment bag and reached in. She wanted to see it. Touch it. She pulled out the red dress.

"Yes, it's still there, Peanut."

Anitra jumped and turned to see Grandpa Jeff at the top of the stairs. He walked over to her and put his hand on her shoulder.

"Grandpa, you scared me." Anitra put her hand on her chest to see if her heart was still there.

"I'm sorry, Peanut," he said with an poorly masked chuckle in his voice. "I thought you'd be up here."

"I guess I had to see it again. It looks so small now," she said, examining the dress. She traced the lace pattern on the collar.

"Mm hmm, Lizzie was a tiny little thing." He smiled.

"Yeah," she whispered, thinking of the terrified little girl in the park.

"So were you." He tugged her hair and made her smile.

Anitra gingerly placed the dress back in the garment bag. Then something came to mind. She went to the dresser on the other side of the room, opened the top drawer, and found the family photo album in the same place it had been years before. She turned to the portrait and looked at Elizabeth.

"Well, I'll be...I can't believe I never noticed..."

"What's that, Peanut?" Grandpa Jeff stood next to Anitra and tried to see what she saw.

"All the times I looked at this picture. For years I looked

at this picture. And I never noticed."

"What? I don't see anything different."

"Elizabeth." Anitra pointed. "She's not wearing the locket. Just like you said. It was off because it had already scared her that first time."

"Mm hmm."

"Funny how I put it on in the first place so I could look just like she did in the portrait. It was packed with the dress. I assumed she wore it." Anitra shook her head.

"Well, Peanut, it was just meant to be."

Anitra nodded and bit her tongue.

"Let it go," he said, squeezing her hands. It was what he needed.

Her first thought was to change the subject, like she knew he wanted. But no, this pattern was going to be broken once and for all. Secrets had scarred the family for too long.

"Grandpa, I understand what you mean about letting go." She sighed. "But it won't be easy. I almost wish I could talk to Elizabeth one more time. Just once, you know?"

He nodded again and sighed. He seemed to know what she needed, too. "You can, Peanut."

Anitra looked at him; she wasn't following. What, was there another red dress her size in here somewhere? If so, she was leaving. Right away!

"You think it over." He said, tugging her hair. "You'll find a way. You know you always do. You just remember, Peanut, there's always an answer."

He had reached his limits; she couldn't push him anymore. But he still gave the best advice. He was right. There was an answer.

ഇറ്റ

"I can't believe it!" Carrie said. It was all she could manage to repeat while Anitra told her everything.

"Well, believe it, girl!" Anitra said, giving Carrie's arm a friendly shake. "And snap out of it!"

Carrie's living room was quiet as her brain churned through Anitra's story.

"Carrie! Say something!" Anitra laughed. "Look at me, I'm smiling. I'm laughing. I'm okay!"

Carrie finally smiled back and shook her head. "I know I told you to talk to the man, but all this!" Carrie said. She studied Anitra's face. "Are you sure you're okay? I mean this is a lot to take in in just one day."

"Carrie! I'm fine!"

"For now, yeah, but it might not really hit you until later, and...and that locket..."

Anitra put her arm around her friend. "Will you stop it? I'm safe, I'm happy, I'm okay." Sometimes Carrie worried too much.

Carrie sighed and gave in. "All right. Well, you must be so relieved."

"Oh, girl, you just don't know," Anitra said. She thought for a moment. "Then again, I guess you do."

"So what'll you do now?" Carrie asked. "You going back to your parents' house?"

"No, not yet. I'm having dinner with Grandpa." Anitra smiled proudly. "And, Carrie, you won't believe this, but I'm staying the night."

"Whaaat?" Carrie had a mock heart attack, and the two burst into a fit of laughter.

"Yeah, that's right," Anitra said after composing herself.

"Same room?" Carrie cringed a little.

"Absolutely!" Anitra grinned. "First time since… Well, it's been a while. I'm sure Grandpa's got some new stories to tell. We're both just happy to be able to spend time together again."

"No more secrets, huh?"

"No."

"Not even Lydia. That's something else! See, now aren't you glad…"

"Yes, Carrie, you were right! You told me so."

"Hey, what can I say?" Carrie laughed.

"Well, I can say thanks again. For being there for me." A tiny tear sat in the corner of her eye, and they hugged.

"Any time, girl. You know that."

"I know," Anitra said, preparing to leave.

"So where ya headed now?"

"Well, like Grandpa said, there's always an answer." Anitra winked. "That's where I'm going."

Carrie grinned. She knew. That's what Anitra loved about her best friend. She always knew.

ℬ28ℭ

The aroma of fresh coffee and Sunday breakfast lingered in the house and inspired Anitra's memories of Grandma Charlotte. It made Anitra smile and pause from gathering the things she had bought last night for her unplanned overnight stay. She sat on the bed and reflected on the Grandma Charlotte stories she and Grandpa Jeff had told each other for hours last night.

Along with Grandpa Jeff's old shoe box, Anitra tossed her things into a plastic bag and set them aside on the bed. She looked at the three thornless red roses she had also bought last night. As she left the room, she plucked them from the small vase on the dresser and indulged herself in her favorite scent all the way down the stairs.

ℬℭ

Immersed in her thoughts, Anitra drove the four miles to her destination. She kept the roses in her hand as she drove and slowly breathed in her favorite scent. She barely noticed the stores, houses, and train tracks gradually shrinking in the rearview mirror. Instead she split her focus between the road and one of the roses with a funny curl in one petal.

Slowing, she turned left onto a long dirt road announced by an open iron gate. Carefully manicured grounds replaced concrete sidewalks and winter-cracked pavement. Quiet gray stones replaced the churchgoing traffic. She passed rows of sleek, new headstones and stopped when the scenery gave way to a noticeably older section. As she stepped out of the car, a soft spring breeze gently brushed her face. Small puffs of dust, stirred by the car's tires, settled around her feet.

Leaning against her car, Anitra lifted her face and took in the sun's warmth while still enjoying the scent of her roses. She walked to the family plot to the sound of birds in a nearby willow tree.

"Hi, Grandma," she whispered as she read the name of Charlotte Thomas Cole on one headstone. She brushed dirt off the top of the stone and crouched to place a rose in a small flower vase attached to the side.

"I sure do miss you," she said, remembering last night's stories.

She ran her fingers across her grandmother's name and replayed the raw, newly-released memories that still sought a comfortable place in her heart.

"I want to thank you for leaving those things for me. For understanding what I wanted to tell you back then. I know it must've been hard to open it up all over again."

She tried imaging her grandparents discussing it for the first time in decades. She couldn't even begin to guess what that must've been like.

"You know I'll take good care of these things."

She looked at the dates on the headstone, and suddenly it hit her. How this all started. The date of Grandma Charlotte's death was close to the date of the first haunting nightmare that had begun to shake her orderly life out of sync seven months ago. The nightmares had invaded her head more and more frequently until she could no longer ignore them or explain them away, and the last one had nagged her every night since John proposed. Funny, but there had been no nightmare last night. Just a plain old dream she couldn't and didn't need to remember. Normal.

"I love you, Grandma," she said, kissing her fingertips and touching the cool top of the headstone.

She stood, stretched, and looked around to locate the older family graves. She found Lydia Cole's headstone and placed a rose on her grave, too.

"I wish someone could have helped you back then," she said. "It must've been terrible to go though so much all by yourself. How could Aunt Ruth do that to you? To all of us? But you did help me. Your diary explained things I never would have known. Thank you. Thank you so much." She touched the headstone and smiled.

She walked a little further, preparing herself for one last stop. She found the weathered headstone only a few yards away:

ELIZABETH SARAH COLE
BELOVED DAUGHTER AND SISTER
JANUARY 7, 1915 - NOVEMBER 22, 1927

Reading those words made Anitra's eyes glassy. She gave herself a quick hug.

"I'm so sorry, Sweetie," she said, kneeling and placing the third rose at the base of the stone. She took a minute to place it just right. "I wish you could've known I was trying to help you. I wanted so badly to save your life. But I couldn't. I wanted to give you a chance to grow up and be whatever you might've wanted to be. To get married and have kids of your own. Even grandchildren."

She laughed a little. "Grandchildren! Can you believe that? For the longest time I felt like I'd taken all that away from you."

Contemplating her own words, something became remarkably clear. "That must be why I kept running from having all that myself. Didn't deserve to have what I took away from you." She rested her hand on her forehead. "I can't believe it. An eye for an eye, I guess."

Anitra sat on the ground and let the sun warm her face as her revelation rapidly churned through the fog and cobwebs that had owned her for so many years. She felt lighter than she had since she didn't know when. She even started to feel that restful sensation she always got after a good, solid workout and a hot bath with one of her many scented bath gels. She wiped away a tear.

"I wish I could sit down with you and explain it all," she said to Elizabeth. "I wish you could've understood what really happened so you wouldn't have been so afraid." She touched Elizabeth's name. "Maybe even forgive me."

Anitra paused and closed her eyes to listen to the birds and let the breeze massage her face. Distant voices pulled at her attention, and she watched as two old women arranged flowers on a grave that seemed ages away.

She gently touched the name again. "Maybe someday, Sweetie. Someday we'll meet, and we'll have that talk. I promise." Anitra pulled her hand away from the stone and began the short walk to her car. Wait a minute...

She turned and walked back to the grave. "You know," she said to Elizabeth, "with all that time travel, maybe we already have."

She winked at the stone, smiled, and walked back to her car.

80C3

"Grandpa?" she called. She was ready to get on the road, and she returned to the old house to pick up her things and say her goodbyes. Aunt Maryanne would still be in church, but Grandpa Jeff should have been home somewhere. Despite her serious arm twisting, Aunt Maryanne could never haul him off to church with her. Anitra found him upstairs just waking from a quick nap.

"I'll be going soon, Grandpa. I'm just getting my things."

"Okay, Peanut. I'll be there in a minute."

Anitra went to her room to pick up her bag. As she turned toward the bed, she suddenly gasped.

"Grandpa?! Uh, Grandpa, can you come in here… please?" She tried to control her tone of voice to keep from alarming him, but it came out wobbly nonetheless. Wasn't this over yet?! This was supposed to be over!

"What's wrong, Peanut?" Grandpa Jeff asked, sounding worried.

"Look," Anitra said dryly, pointing to the bed.

Resting on the pillow were a small doll in a blue dress, identical to the seven in the attic, and the thornless red rose with the funny petal she had placed on Elizabeth's grave. The doll's blue dress looked brilliant and new, not faded and worn like the others were now.

The all-too-familiar veil of fear worked it's way across Anitra's face, and her stomach turned back into painful knots. Not again! This couldn't be happening again! Not after all this time. She looked up at her grandfather expecting to see his fear, too. But to her surprise, he smiled.

"What...? Grandpa, I don't understand," she said.

Grandpa Jeff gave Anitra a hug. "She heard you, Peanut. Whatever you said, however you did it, she heard you."

Anitra tried to blink away the confusion. "What?"

"That's right, Peanut," said. "That doll sitting there, well, that's the eighth doll."

"Eighth doll? You mean..." Anitra began.

"Mm hmm," Grandpa Jeff said. "Those seven dolls used to be eight. Two dolls with each color dress. There was a second doll with a blue dress, and it's sitting right there on the bed."

"But..."

"It's the one she was buried with."

Anitra felt her throat parch. "Oh, Grandpa..."

"Mm hmm. The eighth doll. Irene put it in Lizzie's coffin so she wouldn't be lonely. Look how pretty and new it is. Lizzie just wants to tell you she's all right. She understands, Peanut. She understands."

"Oh, Sweetie," she whispered to Elizabeth, wherever she was. "You *do* understand, don't you? Is that what you're trying to tell me?"

"I believe she is," Grandpa Jeff said. He squeezed Anitra's shoulder.

Anitra nodded, and an uncontrollable smile took over her face and caught the single tear that slid down her cheek.

"Yes," Anitra said, "she does! She understands!" Anitra almost laughed as she stared at the doll and the rose on the pillow. Elizabeth was free to rest. And so was she.

සාශ්

Anitra opened the sunroof and savored the breezy drive back to her parents' home. For the first time since that summer twenty-two years ago, she knew she had been forgiven. And more important, she had found a way to forgive herself. It would take a while, but she would once again find her strength and direction.

Reaching into the shoe box on the passenger seat, Anitra set aside the doll with the blue dress then nudged away the locket box. It slid back, bumped her hand, and made her jump and snatch her hand away. She sighed and shook her head.

Daring to reach back in, she carefully avoided the locket and let her fingers relax around the stem of the rose with the funny petal. She would have it preserved. Dried or pressed or whatever they did to flowers these days. But for now, she would enjoy its deep, delicious scent.

She would find a way to apologize to John. Explain as much as she could. Maybe if she truly opened herself to him, he'd eventually understand, and she would finally take that walk down the aisle he had asked her to take.

Smiling, Anitra allowed herself the possibility of a new name: Anitra Cole Morgan. Mrs. John "Zip" Morgan. Carrie's sister-in-law. And her smile grew as she thought of the hours of stories she would tell her own children. Especially the one they'd never believe.